Where the Wildflowers Bloom

Where the Wildflowers Bloom
A 19th Century American Odyssey
Copyright © 2025 by Terence T. Brown

Additional copies may be ordered from the publisher for educational, business, promotional or premium use.
For information, contact ALIVE Book Publishing at:
alivebookpublishing.com

Book design by Alex P. Johnson

ISBN 13
978-1-63132-256-3
Library of Congress Control Number: 2025907014

Library of Congress Cataloging-in-Publication Data
is available upon request.

First Edition

Published in the United States of America by ALIVE Book Publishing
an imprint of Advanced Publishing LLC
3200 A Danville Blvd., Suite 204, Alamo, California 94507
alivebookpublishing.com

PRINTED IN THE UNITED STATES OF AMERICA

10 9 8 7 6 5 4 3 2 1

Where the Wildflowers Bloom

A 19th-Century American Odyssey

Terence T. Brown

ABOOKS

Alive Book Publishing

Contents

Poem	*All That Came To Pass*	6
Dedication	*A Brief Note*	7
Summary	*A Story With History*	9
Introduction	*Territorial Expansion*	11
Part One	*Mid-West Roots*	21
Two	*Bound for Utah*	67
Three	*The Trail West*	79
Four	*Provo*	165
Five	*The Telegram*	215
Six	*Prospecting*	239
Seven	*Survival*	261
Eight	*A Rude Awakening*	271
Nine	*Homeward Bound*	295

A time of deep reflection
On all that came to pass
Concerning insurrection
Of it's heavy toll en masse
A Union Lieutenant lies in a ditch
Mouth agape and stare fixed wide
As if to have given a final pitch
To advance before he died

- T. T. Brown

To my late centenarian mother, Dolly, who encouraged me in earlier years to write and tell about the world around me, while also expressing my inner visions and dedication to that which is historic, for others to hopefully take note of and appreciate.

Summary

A Story with History

Author Terence, AKA Terry T. Brown, makes his entry into the fictional side of writing with this unusual presentation after his two previous non-fiction offerings: 'Clearing Vietnam' and 'Tales from the Cut.' However, the writings recorded here were not entirely fictional, as the period's history was extensively researched before using much of it to surround the fictional story and make it more plausible in a greater sense.

All historical references were in keeping with the given period of the story, along with other researched data that pertained to material items and other general info of the time. However, as it all unfolded and took form, the period's history helped with shaping the story to give readers a broader perspective on where this elaborate tale would ultimately take them.

Introduction

Territorial Expansion

After the early 1800s, when Meriwether Lewis and William Clark traveled out to the Oregon country and reached the Pacific Ocean with the Corps of Discovery, it became clear to Thomas Jefferson and all other U.S. Presidents of that century that the acquisition of western territories would eventually help to expand the size and influence of the United States of America.

As the country's early pioneers ventured into untested terrain to fulfill America's dream, their new sense of entitlement drove a determined effort to convert the rough landscape into productive farmland and eventually build townships and cities within the various territories. However, there were obstacles involved with the settlement of U.S. emigrant families from the East, who were determined to start their lives anew in a raw yet promising environment. One of the main obstacles involved the various Indigenous tribes of native Indians who were already entrenched and occupying the lands where the settlers had ventured, having been living there for several centuries as long-time residents on the sacred land of their ancestors. While ultra-protective of their tribal homeland, most were entirely unwelcoming toward the Americans, as they became overly hostile while posing a dangerous threat to all migrants journeying westward.

Additionally, for these emigrating pioneers, the overland trip was not without its natural perils, as there were significant hardships and risks associated with traveling by covered wagon over seemingly endless stretches of the rugged western landscape. These migrants wearily plotted their way across the open prairie lands and over the mountain passes where the established trails had taken them while braving the changing weather conditions and occasional lack of water. The trip alone tested their overall stamina and heartiness while strengthening the determination of some and weakening it in others. At the same time, some of these travelers had succumbed to sickness and disease in the form of cholera and dysentery, primarily attributed to the somewhat unsanitary conditions associated with water and hygiene along the trail. Over time, those trails westward had been marked with numerous grave markers as a sign of the trials they all experienced, serving as a grim reminder and a testament to the courage and determination of those who had braved the journey.

But once they arrived at their destinations, life would be filled with hard work, such as building a home, digging a well, living off the land while raising a family, and making things work, to effectively prove up the land and make it their own. This was a new and risky endeavor for those who didn't know much about resettling in a strange new land, given that it was essentially a back-to-basics approach to life in a completely new environment. Yet most were eager to learn while being more than willing to apply themselves, as it meant free land ownership for them, according to the U.S. government. However, for some, their newly established ownership of workable land was also fraught with resentment and violence from the Red Man, who did not want them there, as they saw the settlers as a direct threat to their well-being and traditional tribal ways. Because of this, many outnumbered homesteaders were faced with having to fight off attacking braves who were often successful with their raids, taking all they could from these settlers, including their scalps.

While some of these settlers were entirely bent on taking advantage of the available workable land, others were more focused on searching for gold and silver in the western territories. In time, as these migrants developed their homesteads and farmlands, towns would emerge to further establish the landowners' placement. As these towns eventually emerged, merchants would lead the way by establishing businesses to provide supplies and services for those in need.

This book tells a fictional but historically accurate story about these American settlers of the mid-19th century who moved westward in search of a new beginning. It showcases their hope for a better life and their tremendous resiliency in the face of danger and unexpected hardship. But it also directly addresses the involvement associated with 'Manifest Destiny' and its impact on all parties, including the indigenous tribal populations who lived off the land while traditionally respecting the Earth's evolving cycle of life. For the former European settlers and their leaders in Washington, this concept, spread as a mantra, had blended ideals involving American exceptionalism and romantic nationalism to effectively drive the successful efforts of Western expansion.

This historically enhanced but personalized story of westward migration originated within a thriving farming community in southern Illinois. It centers and focuses further within the western territory of Utah, where the tale's noted family had ventured, in which to re-settle and start fresh. Despite all the risks and hardships, they eventually arrived to take up a new life on the western frontier, beside the rocky slopes of the Wasatch mountain range, southeast of Salt Lake City.

These were troubling times for most who traveled through or had already resided somewhere west of the Missouri River. It was where Lewis & Clark and the Corps of Discovery at the beginning of the 19th century had previously started from when traveling west to the mouth of the Columbia River in the Oregon country. In those days, the various native tribes they encountered did not see them as a significant threat, for the most part, as much as they regarded them as a curiosity, given that they had not seen but very few white men before.

But the story here takes place over 60 years later, as America was on the move after purchasing or laying claim to several territories of land in the western portion of North America. These territories were acquired legally from other prominent countries that previously held title to them. However, at the time, little attention was given to the titles or claims in those same noted areas by the existing indigenous tribes, as they knew nothing of such things, only that the area where they lived was their homeland. Moreover, these various tribes had resided throughout most, if not all of the continent's regions for many generations while naturally considering it as their homeland and sacred tribal domain.

After acquiring these territories west of the Mississippi River and elsewhere, the U.S. government believed it had the right to encourage settlement by pioneering individuals, hoping to eventually turn the territories into new productive states of the union. Supported by Congress in Washington, along with past presidents and even the current one for the time, the movement west was given a title that prospective pioneers could rally around, called 'Manifest Destiny.' It signified that they had a God-given right to be part of this westward movement, which would effectively expand the boundaries of the United States while offering new opportunities to potential settlers. In that regard, it would represent a massive land grab in territorial areas where primitive indigenous tribes were already present. These various tribes had made their previous claims on the lands while having protested incessantly that these were the inherited sacred grounds of their forefathers.

However, the government and their pioneering settlers were not of a mind to respect and recognize such unauthorized and unsupported claims on land where the suggested sacred areas had not been fully defined nor outlined territorially. The natives had stated that all the lands were theirs, leaving little room for compromise or settlement with these determined American pioneers. Yet, not much of it was populated by the natives, while in many cases, these tribes were nomadic and did not farm the lands extensively as the white man did. This was especially true with the roving tribes living on the Great Plains.

It should be noted that all historical facts woven into this story were thoroughly researched to be accurate and relevant to the book's subject matter. All other descriptions that were not historic but were otherwise commonplace for the time frame were also researched and given to the story as part of the overall observation of that period.

Focusing further on this human time capsule involving mass Western migration, it was found that a great deal of recorded history had helped to bring this story more to light. It allows the reader to learn more about the different mindsets and hard truths involved with all that went on during those formative years of America's migrational campaigns within its various western frontier territories. As a result of all that transpired, this actively aggressive 19th-century period of expansion would eventually serve to complete the overall geographic configuration of the contiguous United States.

Essentially, the former Europeans who had become American pioneers had developed a firm mindset concerning this matter while feeling entitled to what they were told was theirs. They knew the United States had obtained official title to those declared territorial lands, which was honored and respected by all on the world's stage. At the same time, racial and cultural differences had also played a role in empowering them to surge forward and take the lands for settlement. However, it would come down to having to go to war against many of the offending tribes to eventually get a handle on the situation and drive them out. In this case, Manifest Destiny was used to justify the United States' rightful claim to the land while eventually replacing what was seen as an underdeveloped or primitive culture with a more advanced and determined one. During this unfortunate, dark process of legalized land acquisition and Indian relocation, the pioneers and settlers felt utterly justified in their actions, with the eventual removal of the land's original occupants.

Many of these migrating individuals had their various stories involving harrowing experiences regarding their overland journeys, occasionally encountering unexpected situations. Some had even seen a little more than their fair share of armed conflicts that came with their fully supported conquest of the territory.

The territory of concern, in this case, was one such

southwesterly one, located out beyond the Rocky Mountains that was called Utah. For about ten years since gold was discovered in 1848 at Sutter's Mill in northern California, prospective miners had been steadily migrating over the western trails to get there. Quite notably, that ongoing flow of migrating humanity traveling down through the Salt Lake basin and on toward the goldfields of California and the San Francisco Bay was the largest by far among all who traveled westward in the 1800s.

But some travelers who didn't have the gold fever alternately decided to settle and farm in other places along the way, working to prove up the land they had chosen in which to make it their own. As a result, new towns sprang up around them in the territory. At the same time, commerce and trade later began to build some of these towns into cities, where they would eventually become business hubs for the surrounding areas. One such city was Salt Lake City, which lies within the Great Salt Lake basin, where there was farmland aplenty, with a goodly amount of enthusiastic and determined farmers to go along with it. With these rich potential farmlands becoming available, some of the streams of settlers passing through Salt Lake on their way west had decided to stay and partake while giving themselves to the available land within this sprawling Utah basin.

In Salt Lake City's case, most who had settled there and built up the area were of a particular religious Christian order called Latter-Day Saints, otherwise generally recognized and referred to as 'Mormons.' When initially taking to the territory, these Mormons had to repel and sometimes even decimate the indigenous tribes of Indians that would attack them unmercifully as outsiders when settling on U.S.-owned territorial land. In protest, the various tribes were quite adamant that it was *their* sacred soil that was being disrespected and unduly populated without their consent. However, these Mormons were quite tenacious in their own right, having been able to defeat the tribes and eventually drive them almost entirely out of the territory.

As their population grew, the religious sect spread to other noted areas of the territory, while the Mormons had hoped to create a land almost entirely influenced and controlled by their church's involved hierarchy. At some point, they even petitioned the U.S. Congress to accept the territory as a new state of the union, under the guiding influence of the church of Jesus Christ of Latter-Day Saints, while insisting that the new state should be named 'Deseret,' which is French for Honey Bee. However, since Utah was still a territorial possession of the federal government, the Mormons lacked the power and authority to declare it as their exclusive sovereign domain to be governed and influenced by the existing religious order. So, it allowed many others of different religious influence, or even of no particular influence, to come west and settle into the Territory. In that regard, Mormons had generally referred to these interloping migrants coming into their perceived territory as 'Non-Believers' or 'Heathens.'

In some cases, these 'non-believers' came to help themselves to the geologic treasures to be found there, which existed at that time in the form of silver and gold deposits, mainly excavated and panned from various areas in and around the Wasatch mountain range, located east and south of Salt Lake City and Provo. However, the Mormon-influenced government and its tolerance of polygamy had made it next to impossible for the territory to be accepted by Congress as a new state. Because of this, it wasn't until many years later that Utah was finally accepted and recognized as a state for all people and religions after its legislature had finally outlawed polygamy. The U.S. Congress then granted statehood while retaining its original territorial name of Utah.

Part One

Mid-West Roots

Wandering bleary-eyed from his bedroom to the breakfast table after being awakened from a dream state, 10-year-old William Forrest Glover, known as 'Will,' had been presented with a hot breakfast of eggs, flapjacks, and a glass of milk. The meal would kick-start his day before having to walk the 20-minute distance southeast, down the old Murphysboro road to the schoolhouse in Carbondale, Illinois. His mother, Margaret, prodded him to finish up while giving him his sack lunch to take with him, as his father, John Glover, scolded him for slouching with his elbows resting on the table. It seemed like a typical morning at the Glover's farmhouse as the family of three were readying themselves for another day within their rural southern Illinois community.

Two years had passed since Will started school there in Carbondale, having acclimated himself to walking the distance to and from school each weekday while also getting used to the routine of attending class in a one-room schoolhouse with the other children from town. As he was making his way to the schoolhouse on a clear, cool morning after a rainy spell had thoroughly drenched the area for four days straight, he came across a situation where he spotted a couple of distressed sheep. They had gotten bogged down and stuck in saturated and softened ground within a creekbed that was about 100 yards away from the road and down in a gully. It was located in low rolling pasture land where a few horses and dairy cows had been actively grazing upon the area's abundant green grasses. Taking notice that there wasn't anyone around who could help, without a farmhouse in sight to alert the responsible farmer, he thought he might see if he could help free the sheep from their boggy situation. Driven by instinct and empathy, he wandered down the creekbed to see if he could somehow assist these helpless, wooly animals. However, when involving himself with this, it became necessary to get a bit muddy as he eventually managed to pull both of the sheep back up to freedom before finding himself well muddied, up to the middle of his thighs on the denim overalls he was wearing, while also accumulating a goodly amount of it up to about his elbows on the freshly laundered white dress shirt his mother had pressed for him on the previous night.

When he arrived late at the schoolhouse, the teacher took one surprised look at him and sternly sent him back home, as his classmates shared a good giggle at his unsightly and unclean state of attire. Arriving back at the farm, a much-surprised Margaret had him strip down to his altogether and hop right into the washtub while boiling up batch after batch of water for him. When protesting his exposure with a new-found modesty at his much-advanced age of 10, Margaret smiled and said, "Look, son, I am your mother, who birthed and brought you into this world. You were just as unclothed then as you are now. So, be the son I know and get yourself cleaned up." When he finally explained what had happened, she told him that the next time anything like that might occur, just "let the dumb animals perish and get on to school."

When Will entered the world in early July of 1836, the town's doctor was late attending the delivery. However, Margaret had already assigned and prepaid her neighbor,

Ella Rhodes, to assist in the birth. She was a local friend, seamstress, and occasional midwife who had prior experience with such things. While John was highly concerned with the situation, he could not bring himself to be with his wife during the birthing process, leaving Ella to coach Margaret through labor and delivery by herself. By the time Ella took delivery of a crying baby boy with the umbilical cord having been cut and tied, the Doctor finally came onto the scene to note that everything was done quite well, with baby and mother both doing fine.

He was raised as an only child to a chicken and pig farmer on a 4-acre home enterprise, northwest of town, called Glover's Farm. During his early formative years, the farm and its activities were what he encountered most every day once he found his legs, as he would learn all about the farm's animals, becoming quite fascinated from a child's view of things.

His mother, the former Margaret Forrest of nearby Carterville, served as a pleasant source of calm for him during his early years, as she had helped to give him proper direction while teaching him manners and showing him his place in the world. Conversely, his father was strict and overbearing when correcting his demeanor and teaching him the ropes about the care and upkeep of the family's farm, as it was meant to be passed on to him someday when John could no longer work it.

Glover's Farm was a working, profitable enterprise for the family, although detailed involvement was needed in maintaining their animals' upkeep and general welfare. On that note, they had monthly overhead expenses to pay for sacks of chicken feed, bales of hay and straw, etc. As a passed-on type of home business that John had inherited from his father some twenty-five years earlier, it had always proven to be sustainable for a family if attended to with the right sort of diligence and dedication that would keep it operational and productive. It was mainly an egg farm, which supplied the local grocery markets in and around town and the nearby outlying areas where chicken eggs were always in high demand. Occasionally, pigs of various sizes were raised at the farm for marketable meat to help supplement their income, although they weren't a regular feature.

Their modest single-story, white-painted farmhouse stood out between the large oak trees at the front of the property, situated just west of town on the south side of Murphysboro Road. The road meandered northwesterly from there to the nearby farming community of Murphysboro, roughly about a little over an hour away by buggy, wagon, or horseback. Trailing in the opposite easterly direction from the farm, one's venture along that route afforded just a 10-minute ride, where it snaked down and into the central part of Carbondale. From there, the same roadway meandered farther east to the town of Carterville and beyond to the fair city of Marion. The farm's barn, henhouses, and pig pens had all been laid out at the rear of the house, just beyond where their all-important outhouse was standing in service to all.

As to the farm's henhouses, there were a series of six wire-enclosed pens, all of which contained large wooden nesting houses for the hens, each with a barren yard to roam around in during daylight hours. It was where they would receive their feed and table scraps daily, as the hens always scurried to it in a frenzy whenever anything was put down for them. The large-scale henhouses were built to easily accommodate 15 hens, with the accessible nesting boxes at one end of the structure having lift-type leather-hinged doors for easy harvesting of the eggs. On any given day, most of those nests would each contain at least one or two fresh eggs to be harvested, while on average, it could be safe to say that each of the six henhouses might typically produce 30 apiece over two days, more or less. If up to pace with the average, the Glovers could expect an overall yield of around 170 to 180 fresh eggs every couple of days from all of the henhouses. It was generally a notable enough haul to peddle to the surrounding community while they could still retain some for themselves. However, it should be noted that there were times when a few of the hens would hit a dry spell and maybe lay one egg every third day or so, which would affect the overall count to moderately limit their supply. However, that didn't occur often, as they usually provided the town of Carbondale and its surrounding area with all they could handle while making regular deliveries every Monday and Friday using their horse-drawn buckboard to complete the process.

But when a hen suddenly stopped laying eggs, it was time to pull her from the pen and use her alternately as a meat source. While noting that some of the hens regularly outproduced others, they all tended to slow down a bit as they aged. However, to continue the production cycle with replacement hens, several were taken to a nearby farm where roosters were present, to mate, in which to fertilize the hen's eggs and produce chicks. It was about a two-week process to eventually see fertilized eggs developing within the eggshells through the use of candlelight, where newly formed blood vessels could be seen within. With the hens nesting over the eggs to effectively incubate them, they eventually hatched new broods of chicks to be raised until ready to join the others within their pens. After another two weeks, the hens would no longer produce fertilized eggs and could then be placed back within their henhouse for regular production of consumable eggs.

At about two years of age, Will curiously followed his father into one of the enclosed cages, which was left unattended for the moment, while John went to the barn to bring in some new straw for additional insulation. As the little tot curiously gravitated toward the henhouse, he somehow managed to fit his small body inside the small building's entryway after crawling up the hen's ramp, gaining access to the roosting and egg-laying area. When John returned after just a few minutes, he noticed Will was no longer there and figured he must have returned to the house. So, when finished, after locking the cage door, he decided to take a break and get a drink at the house, as he asked Margaret if she'd seen Will. She said, "No, I thought he was with you. He's missing?" John replied, "I'll go hunt for him. He couldn't have gone far." Then, as John exited the house, he heard his son crying out from the rear enclosure that housed all of the pens and proceeded to follow the sound of his screams. The reason for Will's distress, as it turned out after he managed to squeeze into the hen's entryway, was that he couldn't get back through it again, having gotten stuck in the process. Plus, the new addition of straw that John placed while unaware of Will's presence made the way out even less accessible.

Once John finally found which cage it was, he opened it and could see that Will was stuck within the opening. "I'm here, son. I'm here. So, relax...I'll get you out," he said reassuringly. He quickly returned to the barn, retrieving a sharp knife, which he applied to the wood between where Will's heavy wool jumper was stuck against it, by carving shavings of the wood away on both sides of the opening before finally being able to free him. However, as the two of them walked back to the house, John did not scold nor admonish him for that incident, as he recalled a similar incident when his father, Carl, had to rescue him from a rather dumb and embarrassing situation.

The farm's enlarged henhouses were all second-generational representations, with a few design improvements from their original configuration, as a young John Glover and his aging father had labored to tear down all the original ones some 30 years earlier. It was found that all of them had noticeably deteriorated over the years from the overall test of time, with the consistent hot, cold, and wet weather conditions affecting the wood over the years. After removing them, they reconstructed six new ones in their place. Since that earlier time, some additional minor repairs were called for to upgrade and help maintain them for the years to come.

On a day when Will was about six or seven years of age,

his father caught him talking to a few chickens while calling them by names that he'd given them. John admonished him for it, even though it seemed innocent enough. But he said, "If you give the animals names, it'll only be disappointing and upsetting for you when the time comes for them to go into the cookpot. These farm animals are an important part of what makes this operation a business, and they just can't be regarded or treated as pets."

While John enjoyed having his young son there to learn about and participate in the farm's upkeep, Margaret realized that he should also be enrolled at the elementary school in town, which was about a 20-minute walk from there. So, at some point, as the new session began in the early Fall of 1844, she gathered him up and took him into town early one morning in their horse-drawn buggy and introduced him to the teacher, or 'School Marm,' Mrs. Edith Johnson. Just two years prior, Mrs. Johnson, who was 29 then, had taken over the schoolhouse when moving to Carbondale from St. Louis. She was rather plain in appearance, tall and slender, with long brown hair neatly piled atop her head in a bun. In addition to her almost floor-length but somewhat plain, early Victorian-era dress, she wore brown button-down leather high-top shoes with heels that noticeably clicked when walking around on her classroom's hardwood planked floor.

At her age, most of the townspeople considered her a spinster, while she otherwise seemed quite happily married to her academic profession. Concerning her demeanor, she was always pleasant; however, she was very much to the point with visiting parents when explaining the curriculum and her particular style of presenting it to her students.

Initially, when taking over the schoolhouse, some of the

townspeople thought she was too forthright, stuffy, and full of herself to teach anything of lasting value to their children, while she was paid a paltry amount for all her efforts. However, that soon turned out to be a mistaken notion, as they had judged her like a book's cover without considering its actual content. But much to their chagrin, they would soon find her to be 'just what the doctor ordered' when it came to instilling their children with all that they could not even begin to offer them in the way of education, knowledge, and culture.

It would serve as Will's first day of schooling, as his mother placed him directly into this woman's hands to teach him what he needed to know within this one-room building designed to serve as a schoolhouse. However, for the boy, there was still the prospect of walking back to the farm when class would eventually let out in mid-afternoon.

He was eight years old, and it was his first time being on his own. However, Margaret felt it was high time for him to get used to the short walk to school and back every weekday. She knew that it was vital for him to adjust to a different routine where he could pay full attention to what the teacher had to offer in the way of learning. Plus, while it was a new experience for him, it also allowed him to associate and interact with others closer to his age while exposing him to a world outside of his father's farm, where he only had his folks and the chickens to talk to. She would commonly pack him a sandwich and a hardboiled egg for his lunch and send him off to walk the road to town in the early morning. Otherwise, when weather conditions were wet or snowy, Margaret would take him there in their covered buggy while making sure to arrive by the 8 O'clock morning bell and then pick him back up when class would let out at 3 O'clock. But in clear weather, Will had about 40 minutes each day of round-trip walking to get in, except for Saturdays and Sundays. However, at the time, Margaret deemed this to be a good, healthy means of exercise for a young growing lad of only eight.

Carbondale's stately schoolhouse featured only one rather large room that served exclusively as a classroom. The building's interior had a relatively sizeable black chalkboard affixed to the back wall, with the teacher's desk positioned just to its left. The students' oakwood desktop seats took up two rows of space on both sides of the room to accommodate 16 students, filling the classroom. However, that number generally fell by one or two per yearly session. In the center aisle of the room was a somewhat large potbelly stove standing between the rows of student desks for better heat distribution in the colder Fall and Winter months when it was called on to properly warm the room. Also in the center of the room was an overhead oil lamp chandelier hanging from a rope on a pulley that was lowered each day to light the six lamps upon it before raising it back up to cast an abundance of light upon the room. In warmer weather, the windows and curtains on both sides of the building were opened for ventilation, allowing for adequate sunlight to penetrate and brighten the room further. Mrs. Johnson tended to assign one of the older boys to handle those tasks for her, as she prepared to begin each new day by addressing her mixed assembly of students. To the right of the back wall, aside from the chalkboard, another doorway led out and down a few steps to where the building's accommodating 'one-seater' type outhouse could be accessed over about 25 paces along an embedded trail of stepping stones.

The school Marm, despite her critics at the time, had proven herself to be the right choice for the job, in being retained as Carbondale's adopted school teacher back in 1852 when the locality had officially become a township. At that time, a formal contract between her and the town had been agreed upon, with an increase in her salary being noted. However, while the township had become more officially organized at that time, she first came to the more informal town of Carbondale ten years earlier in the Spring of 1842, with the schoolhouse already standing and available, but without the missing element of a credentialed instructor like herself, to make it operational and bring basic knowledge and functional academic skills to this developing farm community.

Upon hearing of the school Marm's position being available in Carbondale, she decided to pursue it, even though it made for a somewhat lengthy journey of 120 miles to relocate southeast from the Saint Louis, Missouri suburb of Cheltenham. She had previously graduated from nearby Lindenwood University in 1837, earning her bachelor's degree in education. At that time, Lindenwood, in the suburban city of St. Charles, was one of the few undergraduate universities within the established states that welcomed women to the pathway of higher learning. In contrast, most other Universities of that era and before it had only accepted white males as a rule.

When she took the job, she made it her mission to instruct and educate her students while helping to guide them toward greater awareness of the world around them. She believed this approach would help set them up for a better future. Plus, it was part of her teaching style to instill in them the concept of not just going through the motions of learning their daily lessons but, more importantly, coming to fully understand the knowledge and meaning of what she was opening their minds to. When teaching them to read and write, she didn't want to merely present them with words and the construction of sentences, preferring instead to delve more into the various meanings of each word as applied in forming sentences. This would enable these children in their later years to write more thoughtful and meaningful letters to friends and relatives, and perhaps even to businesses and public officials.

Quite remarkably, as her students had absorbed and realized more about what she was instilling into their heads, their parents had marveled and were most appreciative that their children were quickly coming to grasp and understand so much more than *they* had ever been taught. However, it was probably a little unsettling for some of them to occasionally be corrected by their offspring on their own misuse of grammar and the occasional misapplication of words.

In short, what Mrs. Johnson was providing to these children of Carbondale was a personalized 'old school' type gift of public tutoring that enabled her students to understand more fully what was being taught. Edith Johnson had a driving passion for her craft, unlike many other teachers of that era. She believed that, with the right application, her students could become more enlightened and thoughtful citizens within their growing mid-western community. She had always felt that learning didn't come from simply absorbing the curriculum as much as from truly understanding it as a result of how it was presented. In her own unique approach to teaching, she was hands-on and personal with all of her students without being overbearing in any way. She would effectively let them know that each of them shared a trusted one-on-one working relationship with her and that she would be there for them if they ever struggled with anything.

When dealing with misconduct, she would calmly remind the student in question that unless he or she straightens up, they would be dismissed from class until eventually returning with one of their parents to apologize to the class while acknowledging their wrongdoing. With that standing rule in place, it tended to cut way down on any misconduct, especially in cases where one or more of the attending boys might be implicated, as they knew they would also likely have to stand for a sound thrashing from their disappointed and angry fathers.

In addition to the primary curriculum of reading, writing, and arithmetic, Mrs. Johnson had also given some attention to worldly subjects like history or even out-of-this-world sorts of things, like the illuminated celestial bodies in the dark evening sky. She taught them about Copernicus and his correcting observation during the 1500s that the Earth and all the other planets in the solar system revolved around the Sun, instead of the earlier adopted theory, which had erroneously suggested that the Earth was at the center of the solar system. She also enlightened her students regarding Galileo and his telescopic observations about the universe. Additionally, she pointed out the position of Polaris, 'the North Star,' to her students, along with the big and little dipper and the other various identifiable constellations in the night sky, drawing each of their dot-connected illustrations on her chalkboard.

With the ringing of the bell at 8 A.M. when the schoolhouse opened, the teacher would ask her students on cold wintery days to help maintain the necessary heat by fetching one or two pieces of firewood from the stack outside to keep the potbelly stove in the center of the room well stoked throughout the day. There wasn't a thermometer on the wall to monitor the room temperature. But she managed to get a good feel for just how many split pieces of firewood she would have to periodically push into the cast iron stove while adjusting the damper to control the airflow to the flames. It simply came down to her acquired touch to maintain a warm enough classroom that wouldn't become overly warm or stuffy to put her pupils to sleep.

Occasionally, she would welcome one or two students to her class who were slow to grasp things while showing signs of learning difficulties. For these children, she would work with them after class to give them the further confidence they needed to understand what she was trying to teach them while referring to all of her pupils as young men and young ladies instead of children. She also had to deal with a stutterer now and then, finding that if she could calm the child and teach them how to take some of the pressure off with a simple breathing exercise, they would see that their condition would not become so entirely detrimental to their learning abilities.

From within the schoolhouse, the children of Carbondale had learned the various important aspects of the curriculum from their teacher. But also, over time, they gained a better understanding of themselves as developing individuals growing up in a small and somewhat insignificant farming community near the southern tip of Illinois.

Among the children attending the Carbondale schoolhouse for their primary education involving reading, writing, and arithmetic were two little girls, sisters Evelyn and Lucy Proctor. They lived with their wealthy parents in a large Victorian house in town, within close walking distance of the schoolhouse. Being so young, they would have to start fresh with the curriculum, beginning with the most basic lessons, while others in the classroom were older and more advanced in their studies. Due to the varying ages of the students in townships with one-room schoolhouses, teachers of that era had to create daily lessons and assignments for multiple grade levels. They had to switch their focus and assignments between students each day to accommodate and stay on course with their different levels of learning. To make things a bit easier, Mrs. Johnson would divide her classroom, placing the younger students on one side of the center aisle, with the older ones occupying the other.

In addition to the two Proctor girls, it was known that a young dark-haired boy named William Glover had also attended the Carbondale School back then while alternately working for his father on the family farm. Having already attended grade school for several years in the one-room schoolhouse with about 14 other children at the time, he only knew of Evelyn Proctor and her younger sister Lucy as being a couple of the little girls that regularly attended class there, as he was a good five years older than Evelyn anyway, and had mainly associated in the school yard with the few boys that were nearer to his age. Little had he known or even suspected that there might have been any future connection involving himself and these two Proctor girls. Although, as a few years went by, Will began to notice Evelyn, the taller of the two, catching glimpses of her in the schoolyard while admiring her silky strawberry-blonde hair. He would look at her on the sly, hoping no one would notice, until on one occasion, she quickly turned her head and caught him staring at her. But much to his surprise, he soon found the shoe on the other foot, as she would occasionally get caught staring at him across the aisle in the schoolhouse, as they seemingly shared a mutual school boy/girl crush.

Growing up within a mid-west Christian family during the mid-1800s, Evelyn Proctor was raised with the sort of biblically influenced family values she and her younger sister Lucy were instilled with. It came directly from their spiritually steadfast parents and through the bible teachings of the local Presbyterian church in Carbondale. In addition to attending the Carbondale School, she and her sister were homeschooled by their mother to learn about the important domestic aspects of maintaining a household for their future families. They were taught to focus on keeping things tidy, washing and mending clothing, planting and tending a vegetable garden, and mastering the art of cooking. It was believed that being actively skilled in cooking was essential for attracting a suitable, God-fearing man when the time came.

When attending class, Will had found that the dozen or so students gathered within that one-room schoolhouse with him were of various ages, from about 7 through 14. Once a student had reached 16 years of age, Mrs. Johnson would announce at the end of the school year that he or she had completed the entire curriculum, which included reading, writing, arithmetic, and some additional subjects involving science and biology.

When finally finishing with their curriculum, upon reaching the end of their final grade level, there wasn't a diploma or anything ceremonial involved to mark their graduation from the Carbondale school. Instead, they would receive a congratulatory handshake from the teacher with a sincere wish of "good luck." At the same time, the younger classmates would enthusiastically show their approval by offering up a rousing round of applause along with the melodic acapella song, "For he's a jolly good fellow," followed up with a few celebratory adjoins of "Hip, hip, hurray!" Other than that, graduates from the Carbondale schoolhouse were then free to go out into the world and find a purpose for which to apply much of what they had learned. With that pronouncement, the student could seek employment if someone was willing to hire them at the age of 16. But jobs, especially for ones so young, were not so plentiful in Carbondale, to say the least, except for a few farm labor positions that involved muscle and stamina. Otherwise, they would more likely be inclined to return to their family's farms and apply themselves to whatever may be needed to help their parents while serving the better interests of their future inheritance.

But while the schoolhouse regularly cycled its students through their elevating grade levels, a farmer in the area would occasionally become frustrated, taking issue with his son attending school each day, as some of the farmers in the area had often come to depend on their young sons, in tending to the essential chores while helping with the needed affairs of the farm. In that regard, it had been noted on one particular occasion that a farmer rode into town and burst into the schoolhouse to call upon his son to "stop this foolishness" and come back with him to resume the crucial duties on the family's farm where he was needed. While frustrated and dismayed by the sudden disturbance, the teacher knew from previous involvements where education sometimes interfered with farm life, or vice-versa, that she should wisely avoid these matters where she realized she would have no authority when objecting to it. Instead, she would tell her pupil to "go and help your father with his burden and perhaps come back another day when it may be possible to resume your studies."

When 12-year-old Will had taken his father's 20-gauge shotgun, with John's approval, and headed out to the back adjoining property of the farm, he then proceeded to wander on up a rolling hill while hiking a short distance beyond it, to where a grove of oak and maple trees had grown tall and wide with the nearby creek having fed their root systems over the years. But when traipsing through the grove, he moved about very slowly, anticipating the movement of a squirrel or rabbit he might bring back for his mother's cookpot. As he continued to creep forward with John's shotgun at the ready, without making much of a sound, suddenly, his gaze was drawn upwards to see a man in a brown suit hanging from a branch on the big maple tree.

Without hesitation, he raced back to the farm and, while nearly breathless, reported the sighting to his father, who then saddled his horse and rode into town to report it directly to the sheriff. As the sheriff and one of his deputies cut the man down from the tree and secured the body to take it back to town, John told them that he had never seen the man before and didn't think that he was even from anywhere around the area. But it was later learned that he was the brother of another farmer from 2 miles up the road, who had come to visit him and his wife, although the brothers had some hard words with each other and a serious fight had broken out. As it turned out, this man wound up stabbing his brother with a knife and running off, apparently believing that he killed him. They speculated that, in his grief, he committed suicide by affixing his leather belt to a tree branch while tying his necktie to it and hanging himself. Meanwhile, the other brother came into town and had the doctor treat his wound.

This was totally out of the ordinary for the small-town farming community to encounter in a place that rarely had much of anything involving the sheriff. But it was news, and it gave the biddies in town something to chew on and gossip about, including the idle regulars down at the saloon, as there generally wasn't all that much for folks, young and old, to jaw about when the majority of the townspeople were just simple hard-working farmers.

As an established, slow-growing community at the time, the town's population was still insufficient to support higher education beyond what was taught in their local schoolhouse. So, for further studies and higher education, the city of Carbondale had to wait several more years before a high school could finally be erected, as they hadn't been properly platted as an actual township until 1852.

During the 1840s and 50s, the children in southern Illinois received what was considered a sufficient education, given the town's limitations and the times. Many of these children were expected to continue with their parents' work on the family farm anyway, with their primary education at the one-room schoolhouse becoming quite useful to them. Their education had equipped them with language and math skills and a general understanding of society while it prepared them to engage with the world beyond their small town. Plus, their newfound levels of awareness, attributed to the trusted teachings from Mrs. Johnson, had also opened their eyes to give them further confidence in applying much of what they had learned.

In addition to the regular curriculum, Mrs. Johnson, in harkening back to the time of Cotillion, wanted to introduce her class to the organized cultural form of dance. So, while pushing all the desks back against the walls to provide more floor space, she lined the girls up on one side and the boys on the other, instructing them to choose their dance partners. Immediately, Will found himself on the other side of the room, standing directly before Evie, nervously trying not to appear awkward. She smiled shyly and took his hand to become a dance pair while the others also paired themselves up. Mrs. Johnson then isolated one of the couples while instructing them on basic two-step type movements, turnarounds, and the like as the others looked on. She then told them all to practice those steps while developing a flow to their movements until, after a while, she could see that they were getting it and beginning to enjoy it. She then pulled out a violin and drew a bow against it, playing a slow-style waltz tune that suddenly livened things up. Will and Evie immediately took to this dance concept rather well, smiling and looking into each others' eyes with all their shyness removed. For all the students, it was one of the more unusual and surprising classroom lessons from Edith Johnson, as it introduced them to a cultural aspect they may not have otherwise been exposed to. Little did they even know she was an accomplished violinist, as she would occasionally draw her bow again to a classical tune for the class.

By 1852, Will had spent eight years at that schoolhouse. At 16 years of age, having learned all of the available curriculum, he was congratulated and set free to walk the short distance back to Glover's Farm. Mrs. Johnson shook his hand firmly, telling him he was an exceptional student while wishing him well with his future endeavors, as he half-blushed for all to see. She then applied the metaphoric idiom, "Now that you've learned to fly, it is time to leave the nest." Receiving the usual fanfare and good cheer from his fellow students, he then walked the length of the schoolhouse to exit the building, while brashly winking at Evelyn Proctor. She smiled while showing some embarrassment before he turned and shouted, "God bless Mrs. Johnson!," as the children all cheered. At that, she waited for her students to quiet themselves before finally dismissing the class. It marked the end of the school year and the end of Will's academic association with the schoolhouse and his teacher.

As he made his way back up the old Murphysboro road, he felt somewhat empty, as if he had lost something, instead of feeling fulfilled and carefree when gaining his freedom from the Carbondale School. He previously thought he would be overjoyed with not having to go to school anymore.

But with his newfound freedom from having to go to school every day seeming strange at first, oddly even bittersweet, he found that he had already missed the friendships he had with some of his classmates, and even Mrs. Johnson, for that matter. However, when settling back into the work at the farm, he found that while his father now paid him a fair wage for the time he put in, he was free to go to town and socialize with some of those he had previously attended school with. For that, John allowed him the use of their horse, Spitfire.

For Will and his father, John Glover, the farm had consumed much of their time and energy each day, save for Sundays, which was a day of rest according to the teachings of the bible and the Christian beliefs of the nearby Presbyterian church. Egg collection was nearly a daily involvement for the Glovers, while deliveries were done twice weekly. Both John and Margaret tended to alternate with each other on the delivery days for their supply of fresh eggs around their locale in Jackson County, using their horse-drawn buckboard. They had a regularly established route when making their delivery rounds to the few markets, hotels, and restaurants that had come to depend on their continuous egg production. Along the route, a few residents would regularly stand out beside the road to purchase one or two dozen from them as the wagon made its rounds. But because of the fragile cargo, they had to slow the horse's pace as they steadily rolled over the earthen roadway to complete the delivery circuit, given the existence of potholes and ruts that developed in different spots along the way. On occasion, because that nagging condition had come to annoy John to no end, he would pack a shovel along with the cushion-lined boxes of eggs while stopping to fill in the potholes and ruts as he went. It made for a much smoother delivery route, with little or no further egg breakage occurring along the way.

For eggs to stay fresh back then without refrigeration, which hadn't been developed yet - along with electricity, consumers had to find a cool, dark place where they could be safely stored to reasonably last up to 10 or 12 days at room temperature or cooler, unless they might be consumed before then. With root cellars being somewhat common in the mid-west for storing vegetables and other food stores, they had also become ideal places for egg storage, as the lower ground was commonly even cooler than room temperature.

In addition to the egg business, John made his pigs readily available to the market while occasionally transporting the fully grown ones in his enclosed wagon to the nearby slaughterhouse. They would be butchered and sliced into roasts for brining and smoking to create marketable hams while rendering other vital parts of the animals into bacon from the animal's belly, along with shoulder roasts that made for good barbecue pulled pork, etc. The other less significant parts of the animal, like the snout and ears, along with its meaty foot knuckles, were generally retained for pickling. All of the marketable meat, along with these lesser pig parts, would be salvaged and marketed by the slaughterhouse's owner, who also owned the meat market in town. For John's part, they would weigh the slaughtered and gutted animals and pay him the per-pound going rate for the meat, making the process much easier for him. Also, in the interest of having other meat choices available for his table, he would occasionally trade one or more of his animals for value toward future purchases of beef, chicken, or catfish (*caught from the nearby Big Muddy River*), at this local meat market in Carbondale.

Over the years, Will had learned all of the necessary daily duties that went along with maintaining his father's farm from an early age, having grown up with it as it became a relatively common thing in his young life. He would diligently feed and water the chickens and pigs early each morning before heading off on his walk to school.

On a bright sunny day in Spring, when Will had finished his early morning feedings before going into town for supplies, he was unaware that he hadn't quite latched the gate to one of the pig pens, which he had always latched religiously every morning. So, when John exited the house after finishing his coffee, he alarmingly found the gate to that one pen wide open and noticed that it had spilled its contents. Frantically, he ran around to the rear yard, where the henhouses and pigpens were contained by a surrounding outer fence, to see if all four in that pen had at least remained inside the main farmyard enclosure. Luckily, he did find one of them down at the corner of the fence line, still within the enclosed compound, while spotting the other three outside of the fenced-off enclosure, way out within the grassy rolling countryside of the back property. It appeared that the other escapees had found a low spot at the base of the fence and dug it out further to effectively make their break. So, he grabbed up a short string of rope after quickly going back into the house for a supply of Margaret's carrots while descending through the tall grass to finally get the attention of one of them where he could entice him with the bait. When dropping a carrot on the ground in front of the escaped porker, it immediately allowed him to get a rope loop around his neck and draw it tight before giving it a good pull to persuade him to follow while showing him the other carrots he still had. One by one, he had to go through the same procedure with all the others until he finally got them all back inside their pen without any further issues. But it became such an incident that his son Will would never hear the end of it.

When John stepped back into the house to take a deserved break after rounding them all up, Margaret asked, "Did you happen to see my carrots that were here? I was going to use them in tonight's beef stew." With that, he could only roll his eyes, leaving her wondering what that might have meant.

Most inhabitants who lived in and around Carbondale were farmers, much like the Glovers, in the form of livestock ranchers and growers with various products to plant, nurture, and harvest for the market. Whether it was wheat or corn, chickens and eggs, pork and beef, or multiple varieties of fruits, vegetables, and nuts, the locality of Carbondale in the southern region of Illinois was somewhat of a thriving agricultural area at the time, which had served as a relative 'breadbasket' for that lower mid-western part of the country.

Quite notably, the southern Illinois town of Carbondale was situated in an area commonly known as 'Little Egypt,' as the name arose in the 1830s when cold weather had brought about a very poor harvest in the northern part of the state. The Winter between 1830 and 1831 was known as "The Winter of Deep Snow," with the arrival of Spring being late that season. Then, later that September, an early hard frost had ruined most of the season's crops. As a result, it turned out to be a terrible year for the folks in northern Illinois, as they fell on lean times due to the severe lack of food and feed for their animals. Because of this, and the fact that the distant areas lying farther south of them had not suffered the same fate, droves of people from the north headed down to the more bountiful southern part of the state to buy grain, feed corn, flour, vegetables, and other needed supplies to transport back north to their communities.

John Glover remembered that winter well, as he and Margaret did their part in helping their northern neighbors by selling a few of their older hens along with one of the pigs, and providing them with a certain amount of eggs while retaining enough for their regular distribution around town.

During the return trek north with their wagons filled, these Christian northerners had compared themselves historically and biblically with the children of Jacob, who, in a time of famine, were forced to head south to Egypt in search of food for their families during those unusual lean times. So, in fleeing to the Carbondale region as they did, it was well noted that the trip south had essentially saved the lives and livelihood of the Illinois northerners and their animals, much in the same manner as in those early biblical times. As a result, the extreme southern part of the state was referred to by its adopted and forever revered nickname, "Little Egypt."

In 1854, the Illinois Central Railroad established a new rail line extending through the southland, as the tracks came right down through Carbondale. With a station built near the middle of town, the railroad ceremonially ran the first steam train through the southland on Independence Day of that year. On that well-noted occasion, the townsfolk turned out in good numbers to welcome a new beginning for their locality. For the farming community, this marked a major progressive stage in the further development of the southern Illinois area while providing a broader means of distribution for some of the exported materials and goods produced within Jackson County. Plus, while it brought passenger service to southern Illinois for the first time, with direct access to Chicago and all other rail hubs, it also offered quicker delivery and better handling of mail-ordered goods to the local citizens. As a result, this new addition to the town's placement on the map also helped to raise the living standards of many of its citizens to a growing extent.

With this new start-up rail service taking shape, it was found that business supplies and local goods were no longer shipped to and from Chicago by freight wagons. They could all be sent along with the daily mail via railcars instead. In this newly established mode, everything could be delivered much sooner, with less chance of any breakage or damage involved. Suddenly, it was as if the modern world had come to Carbondale to transform it and move its citizens into a new age. But that was precisely what the emergence of the railroad had done for numerous other localities as well, where the tracks ran through and created new profitable possibilities for local commerce.

Carbondale, Illinois Station

At that time, the townsfolk of the area were also quite overjoyed to know they could board the northbound train and arrive several hours later that same day in downtown Chicago. It was astounding, to say the least, for most who had never experienced train travel in the past, as it was still a relatively new development within the midwestern states at the time. However, rail travel heading farther westward was not established quite yet, as it slowly ventured out into other areas of the mid-west and south first, until the Trans-Continental Railway, which was slated to run east and west, spanning the entire 2,900-mile-long U.S. portion of the continent from ocean to ocean, would eventually become a reality in 1869.

When laying out the tracks for where the trains would travel, strict attention was always paid to keeping them close to a water source, given that the early locomotives were driven by wood-fired steam engines dependent on sufficient water for their boilers. So, the rail company designers tended to purposely lay out the course of their tracks alongside where rivers and abundantly fed creeks had commonly flowed, and where overhead water storage silos could be strategically positioned and accessed at scheduled water stops to effectively refill a train's boiler as needed. Also, in some places, windmills were constructed and placed nearby, which would reliably pump water from the flowing streams up into the overhead water silos in which to fully facilitate the system. Most of those same track lines, as they were laid out back then, are still in place today while the diesel-powered trains running now are no longer in need of a water source, although the rivers and streams still tend to provide a degree of charm and beauty out along the old scenic train routes.

With several years having passed in Carbondale, Will had become a more responsible and focused young man. He continued to help keep up the productive animal farm for his family while often using his evening hours to socialize in town with his friends. Even with the railroad having made its presence known in Carbondale, the old town hadn't changed much over the years, from when Will had to walk home each day after class from the old schoolhouse. It was an old-world locality that was slow to change from its earlier ways and keep pace with the other growing communities in Illinois. But, with the railroad having established itself as a portal to the outside world, there had been a marked change in the overall economy within Jackson County, as it tended to remove some of the town's negative reputation of being slow to change.

It wasn't but only a short while later when Will had unexpectedly encountered Evelyn Proctor once again, on an occasion when riding to town in the family's buckboard to pick up several sacks of grain and chicken feed for his father's farm. Upon seeing her near the dry goods store, he suddenly recognized his former schoolmate and reached out to talk with her before finishing his task. When chatting and reminiscing about past school days, he visually appreciated how she had transformed from a plain Jane little girl into a beautiful young woman, five years his junior. While enjoying their friendly interaction as they stood and leaned against the wooden railing on the steps of the dry goods store, he was surprised by how different and mature she was in freely exhibiting an outwardly friendly and cheerful demeanor, which seemed to perfectly rhyme with her outward beauty. It intrigued him when she said she missed him after all the time since he left the schoolhouse, while one of the things she always remembered was the time they shared at Mrs. Johnson's version of Cotillion. He then echoed the same sentiment as they locked eyes and saw something they both desired. Even in those moments while getting reacquainted, one could easily tell they were naturally attracted to each other, with other personal liaisons bound to occur in the future from that chance encounter. As things progressed, the two continued to see each other regularly, with their deepening friendship eventually manifesting into a serious courtship.

On fair weather days, they sometimes went on buggy rides, taking picnic lunches together out and away from town to enjoy the serenity, peace, and quiet of the nearby prairie country of southern Illinois. They would playfully chase each other on the open prairie land while gleefully rolling in the tall green grass like young, carefree children. Additionally, They found themselves reviving their unforgotten Cotillion dance with each other, with Evie humming a tune in the absence of music. The two smiled broadly while merrily waltzing around the grassy prairie country, with a few puzzled prairie dogs looking on curiously.

They would often be seen around town together, with their growing love for each other becoming quite evident to all who knew them and even those who didn't. Oddly, they often agreed as like-minded individuals in their conversations and observations involving the world around them. However, Will soon learned that Evie was a somewhat strong-willed person as an outspoken free thinker overall, which was uncommon for women of that time during the mid-19th century. While she wasn't what could be called a 'Suffragette,' she abhorred the misuse of alcohol from what she had seen displayed in public on certain occasions, along with the disgusting habit of tobacco chewing. In her view, the human condition could use some cleaning up in certain areas of society's cultural underbelly. For most men of the day, this was viewed as insulting while not being taken as acceptable criticism. Yet, with the proper respect, she would occasionally offer her advice to Will when she thought it to be appropriate. With regard to this, Will had developed a different mindset than his generation of traditional contemporaries. He believed that women should be able to speak their minds freely while expressing themselves respectfully, without others treating them like second-class citizens or less.

Nevertheless, he found himself head over heels in love with this fair-haired, beautiful young lady whose natural charm and cheery disposition exuded positivity while giving him a kind of joy and confidence that he had never known before. So, at some point, after courting for about eight months, he found the right moment and asked if she would consider marriage, which she excitedly accepted.

After nearly a year's engagement, it was during the Spring of 1860 that then 24-year-old William Glover married the former Evelyn Proctor, who was called 'Evie,' as they were both solidly compatible and nearly as inseparable as turtle doves. Since they were both Presbyterians, they were wed in front of family and friends at the nearby Presbyterian church. She was just 19 years old at the time.

But when the war between the states suddenly broke out in April of the following year, Will felt compelled to enlist with the Army to train in field artillery as a cannon gunner. He immediately announced his decision to Evie, and also to his parents. Evie hated the thought of Will going away to war, where he may never come back to her. But she painfully offered harbored support anyway, despite her fears. John was more concerned that it would put more work on him if his boy were to leave, while Margaret was heartbroken but supportive, much like Evie. He was to be stationed for training in an area north of Springfield, Illinois, at the Union Army post, Camp Butler. As an Illinoisan and a believer in the federal government's bill of rights within its constitution, he felt a strong need to help defend against its possible overthrow, which he believed would drastically change everyone's way of life.

Throughout Will's training with the other men at the Union camp, he and Evie would write to each other twice a week to describe what he was assigned to do with the Army while relating some odd or funny encounters with a few of his company's characters there. From her end, he would learn what Evie and her parents and sister were doing while he was away. Of course, their letters would also express their undying love and affection for each other, with both hoping he might secure leave at some point and come home, even if only for a few days. In one of her letters, she reported that her sister Lucy had recently married a Blacksmith's helper named Ben Lockhardt, a big, strong, but kindly man who is planning to get on as a regular iron-working Black-smith somewhere. In closing her letter, she told him she would go over to Glover's Farm now and again to look in on John and Margaret and see if they might need anything.

Will had also corresponded with his mother Margaret now and then, as she would keep him up to date with what was going on with the egg business and the farm, along with the yearly social gatherings in town for the 4th of July and other noteworthy events. She would mention a few unusual or humorous interactions with one or two townspeople, hoping to keep his spirits up. At the bottom of one of her letters, she noted that she had recently run into Edith Johnson and said, "She wanted me to give you her regards and to wish you a safe passage in whatever you may be assigned to do during these uncertain times."

But for the longest time, all that Will was doing at Camp Butler each day had involved intensely detailed training with his cannon at the range while also training others in the functional operation of various other field artillery pieces, like the smooth-bore 'Napoleon' cannon. Plus, much of their time was also consumed with the daily cleaning of their weaponry after each firing session at the range. With his continuous training running for more than two years there, he often wondered if the Army had ever meant for him to apply that training outside of Camp Butler, within the theater of the ongoing Civil War. But there was no call from his battalion for him to do anything except to continue with the training.

After Will had been garrisoned there for nearly three years, his mother Margaret had suddenly fallen ill and subsequently died from an inner ear infection in early July of 1863 while he was out on maneuvers. The Doctor had determined that there wasn't much that could be done to help with her condition, as infections were difficult to treat at the time, and the inner ear was an area of the human anatomy doctors still knew little about. Although, he had persisted with the ancient and still not outdated practice of blood-letting to no avail. Will received the sad news of his mother's passing from his Company Commander, Captain Knox, through a letter from Evie. She wanted someone to gently break the news to him vocally and not in letter form. He managed to secure sufficient leave time from his Commander to return home for her burial before returning directly to his post. Wearing his Union blue uniform, he stood by as Margaret was laid to rest, with his father, John, and a number of townspeople who also knew her well, being in attendance to solemnly honor her sudden passing. In his tearful grief, Evie had never left his side, as she devotedly gave him all of her empathy and support while knowing that Margaret was Will's guiding light during his earlier years. He spent at least two nights with Evie in the Proctor's guesthouse before saddling his Army-issued horse and returning to the camp.

As he mustered himself back to Camp Butler in the wake of Margaret's death, an overwhelming degree of sadness continued to stay with him, which served to separate him for a time from his fellow battery mates. When en route, he had stopped by a stream and sat under a tree for nearly two hours, mourning the loss of his mother while recalling some of the various moments in his life with her. It made him smile when remembering her laughter and lively conversations from earlier years. Plus, he remembered her telling him on one occasion when, as a tot, he had cried much more than she was willing to tolerate. So, she reacted to it by tying him onto the clothesline to quiet him down, leaving him hanging there, suspended helplessly, while she took in the laundry.

Upon his return to Camp Butler, his usual cheerful nature had surrendered for the most part to the dark specter of gloom as he went through his daily routine without his usual self, feeling dead inside, for the most part. At some point, as his battery mates became concerned when realizing he was missing meals, a few of them came by his bunk to check on him and ask if he was alright. It helped to bring him out of his funk and back to his senses again, with his depression then beginning to dissipate as he eventually re-focused on his routine and connection with the other men at the camp.

When growing up, Margaret had always been his primary source of refuge from the emotional storms in his life, as someone who could understand his feelings and help him get beyond them while seeing his problems differently. From her enduring patience and wise understanding of the world, she helped to make him the man he had become. Whenever things seemed to matter the most, he could always count on his mother to help him, through her insight, which only the two of them could appreciate, as he knew that his father had little or no understanding of such things, let alone the patience for them. To Will, before Evie came into his life, Margaret was his spiritual connection to his faith and belief in God, along with his trust in the world around him, and he came to fully realize it during his formative years when growing up at Glover's Farm. So, for a time, it was more than difficult for Will to accept and come to terms with his mother's sudden passing, as she had been his guiding light for much of his early life.

About ten days after Will returned from Carbondale, he had been given orders to report to the 3rd Illinois Cavalry Regiment in St. Louis, where he would then take up with that unit to actively participate in the nation's unprecedented involvement with the Civil War. He had long awaited those orders to come. But now that he finally had them in hand, he didn't know whether to be disappointed or jubilant in getting an opportunity to apply his field training skills as a Union Army cannon gunner.

Back in Carbondale, with Margaret now gone and Will off to fight against the Confederates, John felt abandoned at the farm while resenting his new situation, as if his family had intentionally betrayed him and left him to manage things on his own. He had sulked over it for a time, knowing that he couldn't do it all to keep the operation flowing as it was, in maintaining both essential aspects of the farm. So, he reluctantly decided to sell off about ten of his pigs at different early stages of their development. At the same time, he opted to hang onto his four remaining mature pigs, to be slaughtered and rendered out in only a few months. But in that regard, while having to choose, he much preferred to keep the egg operation going instead while realizing that he could manage its upkeep independently, given that it wasn't as overly detailed and time-consuming with its daily maintenance as the pig-raising business was. It was also found to be more lucrative while notably generating a constant flow of income.

At that time, John was 56 years old and suddenly without anyone to share his concerns and observations about maintaining the farm and keeping the operation going. The sudden loss of his wife and close confidante, as well as Will's activity with the Army, had completely changed things for him. Although, oddly, when they had previously resided there with him, he often tended to treat them more like employees than loving members of his own family. His developed obsession with the farm and its daily upkeep had become more about his particular interests and the all-important maintenance of what was once a shared family operation previously run by his father, Carl Glover, and Carl's father, Jacob, before him.

Never being a man to express much in the way of laughter in sharing a lighter moment in conversation, or ever to exhibit sheer joy about much of anything, except perhaps with a slightly wry, cynical grin showing on occasion, John's darkened personality had become more one-dimensional after Margaret had passed. Without her, he became all the more self-absorbed in his lonely existence at the farm. The absence of his wife and son had represented an entirely new situation for him to come to terms with and make sense of it all for the sake of the farm and for his own sake, moving forward. However, in his deteriorating relationship with his son, it became more evident to others that a certain amount of shared resentment had created an impasse between them.

After the Civil War ended at Appomattox, VA, in April of 1865, and after being honorably discharged from the Union Army a little over a year later, in June of 1866, Will returned and tried to make a fresh start with his father on the family's 4-acre ranch and farming homestead within the 'Little Egypt' area of Carbondale. He didn't have any other immediate job opportunities at the time. But upon his return, after having given the Union Army a full five years of his life, Will could see that his help would no longer be needed to manage things with the chickens and the distribution of eggs around town. John was able to take care of that entire operation. So, he found some work in the carpentry trade to save some of what he might earn for his still uncertain future. However, with only a few jobs available for carpenters in the area and a somewhat depressed post-war economy not helping matters, he became increasingly frustrated and disenchanted with what he felt had amounted to much less than what might qualify as a decent living, to properly support a new family.

But upon returning to Carbondale, Will was quite over-joyed to be reunited with Evie. Plus, he had come home as a father, while having met his daughter for the first time. He moved into the Proctor's small cottage on their estate in town, where Evie and Maggie had been living as guests and welcome neighbors to Evie's loving parents, who resided in their big two-story Victorian home at the front of the property. Lush manicured grounds and leafy trees added charm and beauty to the surrounding area, setting off the house from a distance to be viewed as that of notably prominent residents.

But when he visited the farm, his interactions with his father had become quite strained after all that he had experienced serving as a battlefield soldier in the foreign territories of the former southern Confederate states. He now found his father to be more like a distant stranger to him than the man he had come to know since he was a tiny tot, as he knew that there was something wrong with him at this point.

To Will's disappointment, John did not express jubilation that his son had come home safely from combat action in the country's Civil War; there was only indifference. He simply acknowledged that Will was back in town while casually resuming his duties with the chickens. This behavior was not what Will had expected. It pained him, as he wondered if his father might be mentally ill, feeling that his relationship with him had, at that point, deteriorated further to become unsalvageable as it was. He also knew it was not his place to freely dictate the direction of things at the farm, as it was his father's house and land and not his in which to decide much of anything. Because of that, along with some particular personal friction he and his father had developed between themselves in the past, he felt that he needed to find his own place....his own piece of land to work and live on, where new opportunities might come available to him while also bringing further meaning and purpose into the lives of his newer family members.

After Margaret's passing, it became clearer to Evie, who had occasionally visited the farm while Will was involved with the Army, that John was no longer the same man he had been when Margaret was there by his side. Also, she later came to see that even with the return of his son from the war, John and Will Glover did not see eye to eye anymore with each other, and Will couldn't lend himself toward acquiescing in possibly reconciling their differences. At that point, they both knew he would have to let go of his father and leave him unto himself, as there was no further prospect of salvaging things between them. When she and Will came to realize this, it brought tears to his eyes, as he broke down and cried while Evie held onto him.

But despite all of that, Will no longer wanted to involve himself with animal farming anymore, anyway, as he was more interested in striking out for himself somewhere, to experience a more independent sort of existence for himself and his family, so long as he could make a decent living at it. So, while life there for him since returning from the war had become entirely disenchanting, if not downright disappointing, he soon realized that it no longer mattered and that it was neither his fault nor his father's fault as it was.

It was just unfortunate that their preferred differences, with fits of anger having influenced things, had served to darken their relationship and separate them as father and son.

However, if there was a bright spot to be found for Will at that time, it was with his wife, Evie. Now, at 25 years of age, Evie had adored her husband. She tended to follow his cue and support him in most cases while agreeing with his notions of redirecting their family's prospective future to wherever it might lead them. However, this is not to suggest that she didn't have a mind of her own, with her own independent thoughts and ideas about their future, as she was quite outspoken about many things for a young woman of the time. She even told Will on one occasion, "The day would come when all women could vote alongside their male counterparts." Standing at 5 foot seven and a half, with long, curly strawberry blonde hair and a slender, attractive body, all who met her had come away feeling quite charmed by her light-hearted, well-mannered, outgoing nature. She was just the spark that Will needed in his life, and he knew it. Having been raised by pleasant, supportive, and religious parents, she brought an air of positivity into their marriage, which helped to fill Will with a brighter and broader sense of himself.

So, with both of them coming together to share in their prospectus, he and Evie began to lean toward moving away from Carbondale to see where they might find a potential placement to serve their family's destiny, where it may also be more affordable and hold promising possibilities for their future.

At some point, after serving out his 5-year enlistment with the Army, Will had read an article in a copy of the Carbondale Illinoisan daily newspaper, which contained an intriguing quote from a notable newspaper editor in New York, and it piqued his interest, as it said:

"Washington [D.C.] is not a place to live in. The rents are high, the food is bad, the dust is disgusting, and the morals are deplorable. Go West, young man; go west and grow up with the country."
– attributed to Horace Greeley, New-York Daily Tribune, July 13, 1865

One of those prospective yet hopeful possibilities he and Evie had entertained by way of information gleaned from other friends and acquaintances, would involve a far-off trek out to the distant and remote U.S. territory of Utah. It was where new settlements were growing within that still somewhat virgin part of the country, after becoming a U.S. territory in 1850. Land values at the time were down significantly within that newly established region of the United States to attract more homesteaders who would take advantage of it and move west now that the Indian problem there had effectively been quelled for the most part.

In some of the territory's areas, the land was freely open to homesteaders for settlement and new construction, provided they could work it and 'prove it up' accordingly. In some other places where existing structures and water wells had already been established by previous owners willing to sell, it made for an easier transition to a new life there, provided one could afford the asking price of an established homestead.

However, with the most influential of possibilities, in helping to drive their thoughts of heading west into Utah territory, it was known that Evie's younger sister, Lucy, and her husband, Ben Lockhardt, had already taken up residency two years prior in the small territorial town of Provo. They had beckoned her and Will in letters written to Evie to come out and join them there, where there was more opportunity to grow and flourish as young families yearned to do. In one of her letters, Lucy stressed that the area was where they could freely farm the more affordable land and raise animals while becoming part of the new, rapidly developing community.

The more Will and Evie looked at the prospects of resettling there, the more they considered it, as Lucy's letters had greatly influenced their decision to join them in Provo.

So, with that mutually agreed-upon plan now firmly in mind for this newly made family's seemingly promising future, Will and Evie then set about to make arrangements for their imminent journey westward, in which to take up a new life for themselves, out in the new territory of Utah. With that new prospect settled between them, they fully intended to pick up and leave the only place they had ever known for sights almost entirely unknown and unseen. When breaking the news of their life-changing decision to Evie's parents, the Proctors were disheartened to learn they were losing another of their daughters to Western expansion. However, they supported Evie's desire to branch out to new areas with her newly formed family, just as they had with Lucy. For John Glover, he acknowledged the news, while in his mind, he felt he had already lost his son anyway.

Many early pioneers had flocked to the open territory of Utah beginning in 1848 when the U.S. had won the war against Mexico. In a signed treaty, after American troops had seized Mexico City, President Santa Ana was forced to cede to the U.S. all of its declared lands north of the Rio

Grande River, which the Mexicans had previously inherited by default from the earlier Spanish occupation. At that time, while a few established pioneer settlements had existed around Provo, the area was still mainly recognized for its Army outpost, Fort Utah, having been placed there to protect against hostile Indian tribes and the earlier warring Mexicans. The surrounding area of Provo, along with the town itself, as it formed in later years, was named after a man who would never come to fully appreciate the use of his namesake.

Fort Utah, in the late 1840s (Provo area)

Étienne Provost was a noted French Canadian fur trader who first arrived in the area, later designated to become the town of Provo in 1825, a good 25 years before it was incorporated as a city. *(The town was founded in 1849 and incorporated in 1850.)* Unfortunately, Provost died on July 3, 1850, only months after the town was named for him.

Somewhat notably, as settlers began to flow into the territory, it had come to be known that some of the non-Mormons emigrating from southern slave states had brought a few enslaved Africans along with them. At the same time, some other settlers had alternately purchased certain enslaved Indians from an Indian slave trade market, in which to work their farmsteads and to build their homes and barns up while also moving large rocks and tree roots from the land before tilling its soil for the eventual planting of crops. However, things completely changed sometime later, concerning the use and ownership of enslaved people within the territory, after the practice had officially been outlawed by the Federal government in 1862.

Pocket discoveries of gold and silver had occurred somewhat regularly in some of the rocky regions of the territory, bringing more non-Mormon prospectors and merchants into the established areas to help offset some of the population's disparity while raising concerns among the Mormons, who had viewed the territory as their exclusive enclave and sanctuary. However, as people migrated to this new land, some non-Mormon settlements were established in other parts of the territory.

The official seat of government was initially located in the Millard County town of Fillmore in 1851 before it was eventually moved to Salt Lake City in 1856. *(Both noted jurisdictions had been named after Millard Fillmore, 13th President of the U.S.)* Located way south of the Salt Lake basin and even a far distance southwest of Provo, Fillmore was a two-and-a-half-day ride from Salt Lake City. It was found to be entirely unsuitable for its remote location, away from population centers, before relocating back to Salt Lake City.

In 1850, the U.S. Congress established the boundaries for the various new territories in the West, along with the broad rectangular-shaped territory of Utah. The initial boundary included present-day Utah and Nevada and small parts of what would later become Wyoming, Colorado, New Mexico, and Arizona. However, those parts were later excluded to reduce the territory's size when the surrounding areas had become part of the aforementioned states established by Congress. Utah's final geographic configuration and territorial bounderies were later determined by default before finally becoming the Union's 45th state in 1896.

The United States in 1850

Congress would have approved their statehood nearly 50 years earlier if the overwhelmingly Mormon inhabitants had outlawed polygamy sooner, as it was an unlawful practice throughout the rest of the country that quite simply would not be tolerated by that collective body of governing federal legislators. If the abolition of polygamy had occurred many years earlier, the geographic configuration of the state would likely have been closer to the territory's original size compared with what they were left with in 1896.

The territory's predominantly Mormon population wanted to call their new state Deseret, with their signature beehive icon serving as a state symbol of industrialization. However, the U.S. Congress, in not wanting to give partisan favor to the Mormons' insistent proposals, had instead decided to retain the name of Utah, in direct reference to the indigenous tribe of 'Ute' Indians that were an offshoot of the Shoshone nation, having been well noted and historic caretakers of that land. Other nearby tribes, like the Pueblos in Colorado and northern New Mexico, along with the Apaches in western New Mexico and Arizona territories, had referred to the Utes as "Yutas," which meant 'Mountain People.'

Part Two

Bound for Utah

Lucy's husband, Ben Lockhardt, with all 6'3 and 240 lbs of him confirmed as a stout and muscular individual, had prior experience with fashioning and fabricating steel and other metals as a journeyman Blacksmith after serving an apprenticeship back in Carbondale. So when coming west, he had somehow known that Provo or areas nearby likely needed such skills to help outfit horses and mules with new shoes, along with other needs in a growing community where different fixed or functioning configurations of steel were called for. He made door hinges, handles, and uncommon farm implements like large steel leverage bars to remove sizeable stones and small boulders.

He previously honed his skills in Illinois by fashioning different replacement parts for wheel hubs on wagons while occasionally straightening a bent wagon axle or creating a new one. With confidence showing, it was clear that this man, at age 28, had come to know his way around a forge. While he was perfectly able to perform the simple tasks that tend to come up almost daily, he also had well-tested skills that were more on the level of thoughtful and creative artisans, as he could even take on some of the more challenging and somewhat artistic projects as well.

After he and Lucy had arrived in Provo, Utah, in the Summer of 1865, Ben immediately attempted to offer his skills to the local townfolk, with all of his prior experience noted. However, when inquiring with them, he found that while they already had a Blacksmith, it was also revealed that the man had taken ill just a few weeks prior, with the shop now closed indefinitely. So, realizing that his services were in even greater need, he decided to inquire about the shop to see if he might at least fill in for the regular blacksmith, as he met and spoke with the Blacksmith's wife, Julia McBain. After hearing about Ben's abilities and experience, she decided to bring him on to reopen and run the forge for her husband, Tom, temporarily, at least until he could sufficiently recover.

However, when Tom McBain passed away a few months later due to his serious illness, Ben and Lucy saw an opportunity and made a fair and reasonable offer to purchase the Blacksmith's shop in town. The shop included the forge, all associated tools, anvils, and the property it sat upon. They were somewhat skeptical as to whether Mrs. McBain might accept it or perhaps even raise the ante. But she answered their offer by saying ' yes,' confirming the sale of the shop and the land where it sat by signing it over to Mr. & Mrs. Ben Lockhardt at the nearby mercantile store owned by Mr. H. W. Lawrence.

In continuing to run the forge while familiarizing himself

more and more with the townspeople, he soon fashioned a metal sign to advertise his presence there. He hung it, much like a doctor hanging his own professionally recognized 'shingle,' with the simple announcement of 'Ben Lockhardt, BLACKSMITH' boldly written upon it.

The quick sale of the shop, coming just after Tom's burial, allowed Julia to pick up and return to Ohio, where she and her husband were originally from, as she still had relatives living near Cincinnati. Along with the payment received from Lucy's caring parents in Carbondale, the purchase allowed Ben to apply his proven skills, hard work, and expertise in fashioning various metals on a regular basis. For the Lockhardts, it provided a golden opportunity for them to start a ready-made business. Needless to say, they were fully prepared and ready for this opportunity.

While Ben was a man with little or no supportive means by way of his father, who remained alone back in Carbondale after Ben's mother had died from a stroke six years earlier, Lucy, on the other hand, still had concerned parents back there who continued to help support her and Ben with money sent to them from time to time. Their further support had represented sufficient funds toward getting them situated well enough to where they could then stand on their own feet and be productive citizens. Evie and Will were also looked after in the same way, as the wealthy elder Proctors had sent Evie a significant amount of money in the form of a bank draft addressed to Lucy. This was intended to help support them once they got there, as they would start a new life in a sparsely civilized area of the country known as Utah. But quite the contrary to Ben, Will tended to resent the extra money that Evie obtained from her parents, by which he felt they doubted his ability to provide well enough for their daughter and granddaughter's welfare.

In addition to regularly repairing wheels and crafting horseshoes and harness rings, Ben also spent some of his time making more artistic creations from steel. He crafted several types of full-tanged knives, using Elk and Deer antlers for the handles while making leather sheaths during his free time at home. He took pride in his new craft of fashioning functional hunting knives that were nothing short of beautiful, much like pieces of art. Plus, because some of the town's folk had inquired if he might also make kitchen cutlery, he took on the challenge and made several kitchen knives, using local oakwood for the handles, which he managed to glean from the surrounding countryside. He kept all of these knives, along with a few hatchets and axes that he made, on full display in his shop for customers to view and purchase if they might be so inclined.

That thoughtful aspect of creating sharp and durable cutlery for the townspeople and others passing through had given his business an additional boost. It also established his notoriety throughout Utah's central and southern parts as perhaps one of the best metal craftsmen of the territory in presenting quality cutlery and other types of utilitarian sharp-edged implements. However, sourcing the steel and other needed metals to stay in business and provide such offerings had proved challenging at times while he relied on small amounts of scrap metal that could be found in the immediate area, which would be melted down and re-purposed into the form of other saleable items. At other times, Ben would travel north to the Salt Lake City area in search of more significant amounts of scrap metal to stockpile, whether it was in the form of broken axels or rusty old plow blades, damaged iron woodstoves, or anything else that offered a significant amount of iron or steel to be melted down and re-formed into something else. Another source in Salt Lake City was The Silver Brothers Iron Works & Foundry, where Ben was able to obtain sizeable amounts of quality steel in the form of scrap from the foundry process. However, in this case, it wasn't free, although still reasonably priced. So, because of a lack of availability, many territorial Blacksmiths had to make due as best as possible until the future arrival of the trans-continental railroad would allow their trains to haul a limited amount of metals to rail hubs beginning in late 1869.

In their second year of residency in Provo, Ben and Lucy had come to consider the prospect of starting up a second business there by renting a small shop just across the street and up a few buildings from the Blacksmith's shop. So, when deciding to take on another family involvement, Ben offered some of his monthly earnings to help Lucy with the first month's rent, hoping her business would soon catch up and independently pay its way. She had already ordered about twenty rolls of colorful fabrics, along with some sewing supplies to start Lucy's Fabric Shop. The shop would offer women in town a variety of up-to-date woolen and cotton fabrics for the making of clothes for their families, curtains for their windows, and more. While Lucy had noticed many women in town who were shopping for groceries and dry goods each day, the thought of appealing to them more personally with a shop they could relate to might hold some merit in Provo.

At that time, it was known that two ambitious inventors, Walter Hunt and Elias Howe, had developed and patented the first sewing machines only a few years earlier. They were two tinkering mechanics in New York City and Connecticut, respectively, who had each come up with their own versions of the 'Lockstitch' working sewing machine. In creating their designs, they were inspired by an earlier machine from 1830 invented by a Frenchman named Barthelemy Thimonnier. However, Thimonnier's machine was made specifically for embroidering. Many of the machines Mr. Hunt and Mr. Howe made were later introduced to the American public. Mr. Hunt's machines, in particular, had notably formed the beginning of the renowned Singer Sewing Machine Company, owned by Isaac Singer.

Since electricity would still have to wait several more decades before its presence could power numerous items, including sewing machines, these basic forerunner-type machines of the earlier era were manually powered by way of a mechanical treadle or foot pedal, which rhythmically moved with the constant pressing of one's foot to create sufficient movement in getting the fixed threaded needle to move up and down fairly rapidly, in which to effectively mend and create items of clothing in just a fraction of the time, compared with having to do it by hand.

The first U.S.-patented mechanized sewing machine,
invented by Elias Howe Jr. in 1846

However, because of reported design flaws involving the
feed mechanisms with both of those early-developed machines, Lucy decided to advertise and recommend a more
improved version by Wheeler & Wilson in her shop. Overall,
it was less troublesome than the ones she had read about,
while a few locals were quite taken in, to the point of asking
Lucy if she could order them one.

But, given that many women could not afford to buy one
of these machines at the time, there were optionally a few
ladies of the town who were quite renowned for their dress-
making skills while stitching everything together to form
gorgeous dresses and gowns of the day - the old-fashioned
way, by hand. Along with the colorful fabrics offered to the
women in town, Lucy's shop had also accepted and offered
dresses on consignment that some of these skilled pioneer
seamstresses had made and agreed to sell, with a small per-
centage of the sales going to Lucy.

In time, she would also have various mail-order catalogs
available in her shop for customers to view items that were
not readily available in Provo but could be ordered from

Chicago or New York. From shoes to yarn, to trousers and hats, and most everything else that was featured in those catalogs, Lucy could order by sending out an order form for anyone who had a serious notion of making a purchase. Most of the orders came from either Chicago or Salt Lake City, with the more oversized items having to be transported by freight wagons at the time. The smaller packaged items tended to arrive intact after being stuffed inside the rear boot of an Overland Stagecoach. However, considering the overland route and mode of travel, it wasn't uncommon for a customer to wait at least six to eight weeks before receiving their ordered merchandise.

By early 1867, Lucy's Fabric Shop had become a notable business in its own right within Provo, with ladies of the day showing more interest in sewing and making their own visually stylish variations of women's clothing. The shop also had dresses and other articles of locally crafted women's wear hanging upon racks, readily available to the public if there might be something among the offerings to suit their size and fancy. Otherwise, customers could order through Lucy to have a dress handmade and fitted by one of the local accomplished seamstresses in their particular size, using the fabric of their choice.

On a slow day at the blacksmith's shop, Ben walked over to Lucy's shop around noontime while wearing the thick, dirty leatherwear that always protected him from the heat of the forge and the red-hot pieces of steel he commonly worked with. He sauntered in to show Lucy that he needed a small patch sewn on to cover a hole that developed in his pants at a spot just above his left knee. Seeing the triviality of his request, she playfully grinned and said, "Sure, honey, just remove your leathers, and I'll bring them over to you when I'm done."

Back in Carbondale, with funds provided by Evie's parents, who resigned themselves to the fact that another one of their daughters was fully bent on following her husband out to the new territory of Utah, Will had managed to locate and purchase a sturdy and well-built covered wagon for the overland trip. He also secured a fine pair of stout Missouri mules to pull it over the long haul across the open prairie lands and out to the unknown territorial landscape that awaited them.

The three kept their travel attire simple, only packing two or three sets of over-and undergarments, a heavy coat, and an extra pair of shoes. As for their head coverings, Will would wear a wide-brimmed black hat much of the time to protect him from the intense rays of the Sun. Evie and Maggie would don bonnets for the same purpose but also to help keep the trail dust out of their hair.

While intending to keep things simple by mostly packing only their essentials, they managed to keep the wagon's load relatively light, with just clothing and other crucial items for the trip, as Evie would need her basic pots and pans and silverware, plates, etc., along with certain spices in her collection to enhance the tasty dishes that she would prepare on the trail. Will packed the essential tools he would need when arriving in Provo to possibly establish a new homestead for his family. These tools included a shovel, an axe, a couple of saws, a hammer, draw knives, an awl, chisels, a collection of files, and other more specific tools and implements, a few of which were strapped to the outside of the wagon, like the shovel and axe. He managed to store the smaller hand tools within a long pull-out drawer beneath one of the bedframes. While her mother packed her clothes, including an extra pair of shoes and a heavy coat, Maggie was just content to have her rag doll, "Polly," traveling with her, tucked in and closely clutched under her arm.

But two other essential items they felt were called for when traveling out through Indian country had come in the form of a long gun, as a .44 caliber Spencer Repeating Rifle, and an 1860 Army Colt revolver, both of which Will had managed to purchase at a discount from the Army at the end of his enlistment. When the war ended, it was found that the Union Army had a surplus of these arms that had been stockpiled, while soldiers leaving their ranks could secure an excellent deal on them as the Union's way of thanking their men for their service during the war. Will had stowed these firearms in the wagon's jockey box, down beside his feet, where he could easily access them when driving the mule team.

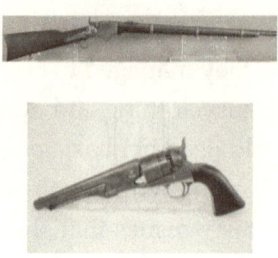

In view of the latest developments, with Will and Evie preparing to depart for the Utah Territory, Mary decided it would be most appropriate to at least throw them a farewell party, in giving them a show of support. They invited friends and nearby neighbors to their spacious home for a dinner party that would send Will, Evie, and Maggie more positively on their way. Among the guests was an aging Edith Johnson, who was in the final year of her commitment to the Carbondale school system after moving out of the old schoolhouse to take up her curriculum at the other end of town where a new building with three classrooms had been constructed. For the gathering's listening pleasure, she was asked to bring her violin to play a classical tune for everyone, which became the hit of the party.

So, when the time finally came, Will gave only so much as a 'fare-thee-well' to his father when moving his wife and 3-year-old child from the southern Illinois town of Carbondale where he had grown up and gotten entirely used to the ways and means of things there. The three of them had then pointed their wagon westward while intending to make their way across the country to Provo, Utah, in the Spring of 1867. Fully aware that they were leaving everything they had ever known behind, except for their essentials, they climbed aboard their covered wagon, pulled by their trustworthy mules, and traveled over a distance of 400 miles to St. Joseph, Missouri. Upon arrival, they would join a wagon train while paying a sizeable fee as the going rate for guided travel over the California - Oregon Trail. That well-noted and popular western migrational route of the era would take them farther west while skirting along the North Platte and Sweetwater Rivers before leading out over the open prairie, past the Wind River Range to South Pass, Wyoming.

Part Three

The Trail West

Before leaving St. Joseph to join a long line of wagons heading west, Will was informed, along with all of the other men, that the wagon master wanted to gather them together to provide further details about the upcoming journey. In alerting the men from all 120 of the train's wagons, he began to brief them on the particulars involving this lengthy trip across the country while warning the entire party that sickness and disease were possible to contract along the way. In that regard, he warned the group further about the possibility of contracting illnesses such as scurvy and smallpox. Plus, it was somewhat common to become ill on the trail with dysentery and cholera, generally caused by drinking water contaminated with animal fecal matter or undetected organisms from lakes and slower-moving streams.

So he brought their attention to the fact that any water taken from these standing streams and creekbeds was highly suspect, with the folks having been instructed to simply boil all of it to stay safer when using it in cooking or as drinking water. Otherwise, it's best to avoid water from these slow-moving creekbeds, if possible. River water or that taken from fast-moving streams is generally less suspect, as disease-causing impurities tend to be mostly diluted or absent from water moving in a more progressive flow. He also reminded the group that everyone needed to keep a vigilant watch on their well-being throughout the entire trip while pointing out that the practice of walking beside their wagons for much of the journey would tend to sap them of their energy. So, he advised them to limit that activity to the cooler morning hours each day to serve as their proper daily exercise periods. In making that work, husbands and wives would have to split their time driving the teams, as one would walk beside the wagon while the other handled the animal's reins. Because these wagons tended to kick up a fair amount of choking dust, he recommended that everyone wrap scarves around their necks, whereby they could pull them up to cover their mouths and noses while walking. On the more oppressively hotter days, some further relief can be found by wetting those scarves before tying them around your neck.

However, there was little or nothing to protect their eyes from the dust except to wipe them periodically with a saturated rag.

In addition, he announced that it was not uncommon for his collective train of wagons to encounter small bands of Indigenous 'American Indians' at different places along the way, "some of which are friendly like many of the Pawnee, who are just looking to trade their goods with like-minded white people, although they would still need to be watched." But, he also warned of a few roving tribal bands of hostile Indians that roamed the plains in areas where their migrational route went through, who were willing to kill to get some of the supplies and animals that were contained within the wagon train, as this was well noted from previous encounters.

These remaining volatile tribal bands, mainly representing the Kiowa, the Northern Cheyenne, the Shoshone, Arapahoe, and the Piute, among others, were still determined to protect their migrational hunting grounds in the western great plains, as they resented the settler's persistence in coming through their land. In the southwest, settlers had to contend with a few fiercer and more determined tribes: the Comanche, the Chiracahua Apache, and other offshoot variations of the Apaches. However, the Pueblo tribes in the New Mexico territory and the Havasupai in the Grand Canyon areas of northern Arizona were generally peaceful people who wanted to be left alone.

"So, keep your rifles nearby and ready in case we may run into this sort of trouble," the wagon master concluded. But, as to both of the trains that the Glovers were to travel with, they were fortunate in that regard to have made it through the Indian country without any warrior-perpetrated injury or loss of life despite the real possibility of these occasional predatory attacks occurring. Of course, the fortuitous Army escort they received from Fort Laramie to Fort Bridger had at least promised to keep the wagon train mostly secure and free from attack over that stretch of the trail.

The only particular incident involving the aforementioned indigenous peoples along their route had occurred late one night while on the initial Oregon-bound train from St. Joseph. Six horses that were part of the train's remuda were silently stolen and weren't found around the area the following day.

In closing, the wagon master said that this overland trip, which is generally fraught with hardships, given its lengthy journey over the rough terrain, with terrorizing natives included, "will test the best of us at some point. It will also take a few of you from our midst to be given over to our heavenly father, as this has been somewhat common with all wagon trains. So, with all of these risks laid out on the table for all of you to digest, let it be known that you can still abort your plans and pull out while being fully reimbursed for your payments if you have a change of heart. Otherwise, this train will depart Saint Joseph tomorrow at sunrise."

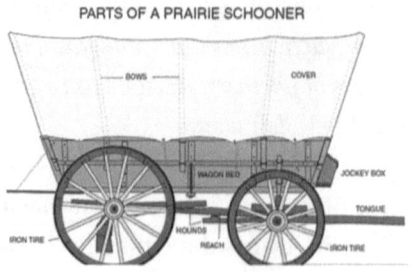

PARTS OF A PRAIRIE SCHOONER

The wagons approved by the wagon master for the long journey west were mainly steel-reinforced and hardwood-constructed. They were built for long-range travel, with vertically hooped steel ribs serving as a sturdy basis for the large stretched-over white canvas-covered bonnets. These bonnets comfortably sheltered the travelers with their belongings, protecting them from the rain, wind, snow, and the never-ending kicked-up dust from the rolling movement of the train of migrating 'Prairie Schooners.' The cotton canvas material was commonly treated with linseed oil or tallow, making it waterproof to fully protect the wagon's interior from snow and rainstorms.

Many of these wood-framed covered wagons were quite similar in design to others on the trail, as they all looked pretty much the same from a distance. However, some were quite different in their design makeup, given that they were constructed by other artisans who had their own ideas about how an overland wagon should generally perform and hold up over the long haul. Probably the most ideal design had to do with wagons that were sturdy enough but still relatively lightweight to keep from overstressing the animals that pulled all of what was carried within.

While nearly all of them were much the same as to their form and essential function, in serving as a rolling house on the prairie, they were comfortable enough, with wood-constructed bedframes that were rather narrow to only accommodate the width of one person, with an appropriately sized mattress to sleep on. The two wood-framed beds were mounted on both sides of the wagon's interior walls, each designed for one occupant. With three travelers riding in the wagon, where there were usually only sleeping accommodations for two, it tended to leave the husband or driver with the prospect of making his bed down on the ground beneath the wagon bed in warmer and dryer weather. Otherwise, an unfixed bedframe and mattress could be temporarily mounted perpendicularly at the front section of the wagon bed. But most travelers would tend to get used to these little inconveniences over time, short of having to endure periods of rain when sleeping outside. These covered wagons also housed various needed food supplies for their overland journey. It additionally carried a water storage barrel mounted on a small platform outside the wagon's wooden framework and canvas bonnet.

The strong oakwood spoked wheels and hubs, which generally absorbed most of the wear and tear when traveling over the challenging prairie lands and mountainous rocky areas, were smartly constructed to provide greater stability and lastability. The outer surface of these wheels, which would roll over uneven earth and rock, had been tightly banded with a thick layer of steel to help protect the wood and give further strength to each wheel. This formed a much more solid shoe-like surface for traveling over the rugged terrain while helping to support the wagon's heavier loads.

Some in the train's long line of wagons looked identical, given that the same manufacturer made them. In Will's case, he was fortunate to have found a rather well-built and highly regarded wagon back in Illinois, made by the Studebaker Brothers of South Bend, Indiana. They had constructed reliable canvas-covered wagons for the Union Army during the Civil War, while later, similar ones were built for overland travel by American migrants.

Interestingly, the Studebaker Brother's Company had continued to build horse-drawn wagons and carriages for many years during the 19th century, including stagecoaches, many of which were purchased by the Wells Fargo Company and other stage lines. When advancing into the 20th century, the company converted its operations to manufacture 'horseless carriage' motorcars. It continued with more modern vehicles until their final automobile rolled off the assembly line in late 1963.

Mules and oxen were typically hearty animals that the wagon masters had recommended and preferred for pulling these sturdily constructed, canvas-covered farm wagons. Common horses didn't have the same sure-footed stamina and muscular build to hold up over the long term in handling the load over the ever-changing rough and challenging terrain where there were occasional treacherous trails to follow, some of which were poorly defined. Solid teams of Oxen and Mules pulling the weight of these loaded wagons, especially over steep grades, made the way less problematic, with the train's steady progress more reliably maintained each day over the ever-changing landscape.

As all of the respective settlers had been assigned their positions in the train's travel line, the Glovers were given number 108, while knowing that they were to trail right behind the number 107 wagon of Garvin Hicks and his wife Thelma, an older couple in their late forties who were traveling out to the Oregon country from Madison, Wisconsin. Gavin, when conversing with Will, said they just couldn't stand another harsh winter in Wisconsin. So they elected to go west, as Horace Greeley had suggested. Directly behind Will & Evie in the line at number 109 was another young couple named John and Virginia Bertram of Evansville, Indiana, with a one-year-old baby boy named Teddy. Notably, Teddy never cried much while seeming more agreeably set on smiling whenever seeing other faces from the train. They, too, were heading toward the Oregon country, where the trail would eventually terminate just immediately southeast of Portland in the locality of Oregon City.

Today, there is an 'End of Trail' Museum in Oregon City, commemorating and paying tribute to all those who braved the hardships and elements while making it all the way there.

Will had also learned that another couple in the train were from Carbondale, along with the man's brother, as they were traveling in another wagon headed down to Salt Lake City. But neither Will nor Evie had known these folks, as they were from the northeastern side of town. Several other families intending to take the southern route at South Pass, Wyoming, were more bent on heading through and beyond the Salt Lake basin. Their intentions and interests were more focused on traveling to the gold country in the Sierra foothills of northern California, or to Sacramento, or beyond to San Francisco.

At this point, Will and Evie felt settled and ready for what they thought would become an exciting adventure to be long remembered as they began their journey to Provo, Utah, in the Spring of 1867. The two hugged briefly while the train was beginning to get underway, as Maggie was still asleep in the wagon bed. They were partly right by seeing it as an adventure. However, they soon learned to what lengths adventuring across the rugged, unforgiving landscape would test their physical and spiritual stamina.

Among the problems experienced by the native tribes, in areas near where the wagon trains ventured, had mostly to do with the aggressive and disrespectful nature of the white immigrants, concerning their established placement in areas where their hunting grounds and way of life were thought to be threatened. They feared how the disrespectful encroachment could lead to further aggression and even war between the whites, as their own protective tribal hatred was coming to a boil. It all came about from the propaganda-driven ideals of Manifest Destiny that encouraged the widespread and determined movement of these settlers, who often traveled into areas where various tribes of indigenous peoples had taken up arms against them. From the tribe's point of view, they had claimed those areas long ago as their ancestral lands, and they intended to protect their right to them from whom they termed as invading opportunistic interlopers.

However, prior to that time, the U.S. Government had purchased the Louisianna Territory from the French while also obtaining the rights to the Oregon Territory from Britain. Then, after defeating Mexico in war and forcing President Santa Ana to cede all of the former Spanish territories north of the Rio Grande river in a treaty, the U.S. believed they now had a right to occupy and settle all of the territorial lands west of the Mississippi River, extending out to the Pacific Ocean.

Unfortunately for the indigenous tribes, through the settler's urging motto of 'Manifest Destiny,' the steady flow of enthusiastic migrants had grown into an even greater proportion of occupiers, which continued to encroach upon them while creating a constant threat to their way of life. For them, they had no desire to change their ways and live alongside the white man, who now was in direct conflict with their seasonal migrational hunting habits. In that regard, as it pertained to certain tribes, it was found that the white settlers were killing a good number of Buffalo out on the rolling plains, which they felt they already had exclusive title to. Because of the number of animals that white men took, the tribe's meat and clothing supply source was directly threatened. This in itself was life-changing for these tribes, as they had traditionally depended upon the Buffalo for many hundreds of years. While becoming enraged by this, they knew they had to do something in response to the constant disrespect that the white man was showing them.

However, this business was nothing new to the prospective settlers, as the Indian conflicts they experienced had been ongoing for many years and decades, with the former English colonies and fledgling United States citizens having been constantly involved in conflicts with native tribes since 1775. Similarly, flows of settlers had advanced and populated areas within the eastern states where the same resentments and uprisings had previously been brought to bear against the perceived invaders for their encroachment and disrespect of the Indian's land and surrounding hunting grounds. But with each reprisal, the armed settlers had responded, having killed off many members of the opposing tribes to lessen their influence while eventually driving them out. As a result, the various tribes in the east were then pushed into the lands of the mid-west and, eventually, the west, where they might recover and salvage what was left of their people and their culture. However, all too often, these escaping tribes would be seen by other occupying tribes as invaders or unwanted indigenous migrants trespassing within their territories, and armed conflicts would tend to develop between them, making matters even worse.

"Where today are the Pequot? Where are the Narragansett, the Mohican, the Pokanoket, and many other once-powerful tribes of our people? They have vanished before the avarice and the oppression of the White Man, as snow before a summer sun."
– Chief Tecumseh, Shawnee

However, these Indigenous people who regarded yesterday to be just the same as today and tomorrow and who marked time not in minutes, hours, or days but in moons, were not progress-minded like the Whites were. Their seemingly primitive tribal culture had knowingly kept them standing still in time, without desiring a way forward to evolve and improve their society and way of life, just as their ancestors had practiced the same unchanging form of steadfast traditional culture hundreds of years before. However, that was just the natural way of their tribal culture. Their intentions were more about living simply for each given day while preserving their cultural heritage and practices. They did not concern themselves with technological advancements, like that of the white man's railroad and the making of various firearms and ammunition, along with the development of the telegraph and other new wonders of the age. However, in being mindful people of the land, the vast majority of Indigenous American tribes had always regarded the Earth as their all-providing 'Mother,' representing a sacred spiritual connection with the motherland and its natural habitat.

Interestingly, concerning these traditionally unchanging primitive tribal peoples, aside from their racial and cultural makeup, they appeared to be not unlike the tribal natives living in the dark wilds of Africa. In both cases, the tribes existed without regard to what others might project as progress, according to their long-held traditional ways.

But, with direct regard to this land, because of the noticeable racial and cultural differences existing between the Indian and White man at the time, there didn't seem to be any recognizable right or wrong position to take with the dual claim of rightful ownership. The so-called Indian Nations had not been duly recognized by the world as separate respective countries or sovereign nations in their own right, like the United States, Mexico, or Canada were. At the same time, the Indigenous tribes did not honor nor recognize the authority of the United States as having any rightful jurisdiction within the areas of their declared tribal territories.

In response, the leaders in Washington encouraged their settlers to go forth and migrate into the purchased and acquired lands to which they had official title, according to the present ways of the world. In effect, they encouraged them to occupy the land and spread their white American culture while helping themselves to the resources that the Native tribes had always depended on for their survival. This included the roving migratory herds of buffalo and other game animals the tribes had relied upon for food and for the buffalo robes that kept them warm in the Winter.

In effect, these Indigenous American tribes, while unorganized and unrecognized as sovereign nations, had set the premise for the United States to run roughshod over them and occupy the land by simply taking it. While their chiefs were often sources of great wisdom to their people, most had remained ignorant or naïve in their dealings with the aggressively opportunistic white man.

"The ground on which we stand is sacred ground. It is the blood of our ancestors."
    – Chief Plenty Coups, Crow

However, from early on, many of the traveling pioneers and their followers, in their dogged determination to impose themselves on the landscape while being led to believe they had a legal right to be there, had subsequently been attacked and killed by various tribesmen. In most cases, it was just for their crime of what these warriors had determined to be 'trespassing' while not respecting the Indian's land and its resources. Alarmingly, they not only brutally killed these seemingly innocent travelers but also, in following their long-standing tribal warfare practices from past Indian wars, they had scalped most of them as well. The accrued

cherished scalps would serve as trophies displayed in tribal
ceremonies to celebrate their successful defense of their
homeland and way of life against the white settlers. This traditional savage act, while helping to satisfy the building hatred and frustrations against the whites, symbolized their
cause as being a just one, which would help to preserve the
lands and cultures of their forefathers. It was also meant to
send a strong message to the settlers and their leaders in
such a vengeful way as to serve notice that they were not
entitled to settle on any of their lands and were not welcome
even to pass through. In addition, some of these tribesmen
took personal possessions and items of clothing from their
victims, as they would wear their cloth vests, hats, and neckties, also being noted as prized trophies from successful encounters in battle or from warrior-involved ambushes. But
to the white settlers, these barbaric acts only confirmed their
previous judgments that these primitive tribal people were
ruthless, uncivilized humans who were much more predatory and animal-like in their ways.

But as a result of these constant savage attacks on settlers
traveling out on the prairie and moving across the plains,
the situation became what was known in Washington, DC,
as the ongoing 'Indian Problem,' where many western
colonists in their unprotected covered wagons were being
attacked unmercifully on a regular basis. These resentful
tribesmen believed that while their ancestors had resided
for centuries on their tribal land, their descendants had always been entrusted to care for and maintain the land for
the good of the tribe. In that regard and way of thinking, it
gave them rightful title to the land, for them to serve as
guardians of their sacred, yet mostly undefined, territorial
property. These violent tribal activities against the whites

continued for several more years along different parts of the settler's wagon trails, as some wagons managed to make it through intact while others did not. Settlers traveling alone or in small parties were especially vulnerable, as it was always inadvisable for anyone to travel through Indian territory in small numbers.

Occasionally, when killing the adult settlers in their covered wagons, the warriors also found children among them who had survived, and subsequently abducted them to raise among their own people while being forced to serve as white slaves. Tragically, when many of these 'stolen' children were rescued in later years, they no longer remembered much of their previous identity or language while having been thoroughly indoctrinated in the ways of the tribe. Surviving young women would also be taken to serve the tribe, while some of the braves would keep them as wives in the form of sex slaves who would also produce children for their indigenous husbands.

Quanah Parker was one such child whose white mother, Cynthia Ann Parker, was captured in central Texas by Comanches in 1836 at nine years of age, along with her younger brother John. When she was older, after assimilating into the tribe, the war chief, Peta Nocona, took her as one of his wives, and she bore three children from him. One of the three was a male child named Quanah, who later took his mother's last name. Tall and muscular, at age 15, he became a tribal warrior, engaging in raids with his Kwahadi band of Comanche braves. He later assumed the role of war chief after his aging father relinquished the title. Recognized as a tenacious and highly focused fighter, he became a war chief at a relatively young age.

Historically, the Comanche eventually developed into a sepa-

rate tribe many years earlier when they moved south into the
southern Great Plains after being part of the Wyoming Shoshone.

Comanche Chief Quanah Parker

In December of 1860, a large group of Texas Rangers attacked a Comanche encampment on the Pease River in
northern Texas while re-capturing Quanah's 35-year-old
mother, Cynthia Ann, and her daughter, Topsanah (*Prairie
Flower*), both of whom had no interest in returning or being
subjected to white American culture. However, while it was
unknown if her husband was around the area then, they
were escorted to her Uncle's farm in Birdwell, Texas, where
they reluctantly stayed after realizing her people were losing
their fight with the whites. In 1863, Prairie Flower suddenly
became ill and died of influenza, while her mother, suffering
from depression, eventually starved herself to death eight
years later in 1871.

After most of the Comanches had capitulated to the
Army in 1865, they were then forced to move to reservations
within the Oklahoma Territory. However, Quanah Parker
and his band of followers had previously broken away from
his tribe as they continued to raid white settlements, with U.S.
troops being unsuccessful in their efforts to round him up.

In 1874, the Quanah Parker-led band of some 500 Comanche and Kiowa warriors descended upon the settlement of Adobe Walls in the northern panhandle of Texas, which is now a ghost town, to attack white hunters who were decimating their herds of buffalo. However, they were only to be repelled by them, after being alerted by their bartender who had known about the impending attack. But the Army quickly followed up that attack, locating and killing a significant number of the band. A year after the Red River Indian War ended victoriously for the Army, Quanah and his small remaining band of warriors finally surrendered at Fort Sill in the Spring of 1875 to rejoin his tribe on designated land in northeastern Oklahoma.

However, in contrast to all of the fighting and bloodshed, not all of the tribes were violently opposed to the white settlers coming through their territories. A few were more interested in trading with the settlers, as animal furs were often exchanged for food and ammunition for hunting if they could get it. Plus, even whiskey was occasionally traded with them in some cases. However, it was a taboo item, as the Army had prohibited any exchange of alcohol with the Indians.

"A long time ago, this land belonged to our fathers, but when I go up to the river, I see camps of soldiers on its banks. These soldiers cut down my timber, they kill my buffalo, and when I see that, my heart feels like bursting."
– Satanta, Kiowa Chief

Kiowa Chief Satanta – 1868

On a smaller scale than the country's Civil War, the so-called 'Indian problem,' later to be noted as the Indian Wars, from 1850 to 1890, also resulted in a significant loss of life. In the eventual aftermath, over 6,500 white and black settlers and military personnel were left dead due to these armed uprisings over nearly 40 years of conflict. Some of the migrating families of former black slaves had also lost their lives in their quest to find a new life as free people in the West. Various tribesmen had angrily enforced their version of territorialism with acts of extreme vengeance toward all intruders, no matter the color. Some of their victims had also been mutilated, with more scalps being taken as celebratory trophies from their collective involvement. In retaliation, numerous indigenous Indian lives were also lost as a result of tribal village massacres when coming up against the Army and the government's legalized act of conquest in the name of Manifest Destiny. All told, over the same 40 years of constant indigenous conflict with the settlers and the Army, some 15,000 native people from various tribes throughout the country west of the Mississippi River had lost their lives.

In contrast, not all areas of the country within the different western territories had experienced conflict with Indian tribes, leaving many settlers with mostly peaceful conditions as they toiled to work their land and happily got on with their lives.

With various treaties having been brokered and established through the Army, it brought relative peace to many disputed areas for a time, even to the point where the Indians, in many cases, learned to live alongside the white man. Constructively, it created an active trade market between the two factions, with each side cooperating while tolerating the other's mistrust of one another, for the most part. This brought more peaceful settlement for migrants, as they continued to develop their farms and townships.

However, while treaties between the two were seen as an iron-clad agreement that was not to be broken, certain incidents would spark resentments on both sides to cause further violence to escalate into conflict, thereby breaking the treaty between them. In some cases, settlers would even overstep their bounds by attacking tribes without authorization from the Army, which would blatantly break the words and bindings of an established treaty.

Essentially, the unresolved conflict involving the various tribes vs. Manifest Destiny had been a mutually irrefutable dispute in which both sides felt justified and rightly appointed to their cause. But, the perceived rightful ownership of the territories was largely circumstantial for both sides, with little in the way of middle ground in which to forge a mutual agreement. However, no resolution could be agreed upon by the U.S. Congress until the Indian tribes eventually began to suffer more losses from battles against the Army than they could sustain. Plus, it became increasingly difficult for them to maintain their food supplies. So, at that point, they were forced to sign treaties in the form of ultimatums that finally ended the bloodshed. However, the treaties stipulated that the white leaders in Washington had then held indisputable titles over the land. At that point, the tribes were either asked to move away or were forcibly removed to reservations.

This is where some disagreeable and disgruntled break-away renegade tribesmen had taken it upon themselves to continue the bloodshed on a smaller scale, whereby some of their actions had broken the previous treaties. In other instances, the recklessness of some of the white settlers broke other treaties to further signify that there could not be a lasting peace between the two opposing factions.

When the Army became more involved in things while fully promoting and protecting Western expansion, it was the beginning of the end for the American Indians and their culture as they knew it. Many of the surviving tribes, with what remained of them within the various territories, were eventually forced at some point onto far-off reservation lands located mainly in northern Oklahoma. It would be where they could no longer threaten or hinder the Army and the American settlers, which allowed them to move farther westward to occupy and cultivate the available lands.

It would not be until sometime in the year 1924 that all of the occupation and subsequent Indian conflict would finally come to an end on the continent. Only deep-seated resentment remained within the hearts and minds of the various tribal factions that were removed from their former homelands to be placed on designated reservations in different remote parts of the mid-west and southwestern states. In some other areas of the country, many smaller tribes that were not warlike had acquiesced to the overwhelming white invasion, moving out of their homelands to forage for their sustenance elsewhere, in more mountainous environments where food was scarce and where most would slowly die out and fade into oblivion. As a result of all the positive and negative developments concerning Western expansion, the contrasting concept of 'Manifest Destiny' would soon become more fully realized by the United States and its determined pioneers.

Back within the wagon train's long line of wagons, Will suddenly felt an unusual wobble as he rolled along the beaten trail, noticing it coming from the wagon's left front wheel. Pulling out of the procession, he quickly halted the mules and got down to check it out, finding the wheel hub had lost its hold-down nut and had nearly drifted off the axle. Fortunately, he caught it just in time, although he hadn't a spare nut in which to lock the wheel hub back down to the axle again. Soon, the drag rider came trotting onto the scene to ask why Will had stopped, before hightailing it farther forward to see if anyone might have a hub nut to spare. In about 20 minutes, he came riding back while holding a lockdown nut high in the air for Will to see. After that, Will periodically checked to ensure the wheel hubs' hold-down nuts were tight and secure.

When stopping near the end of each day to establish their camps, the wagon train's scouts would select potential overnight locations where grass was plentiful nearby. The wagon drivers could then remove the yokes and harnesses from their draft teams to allow them to freely graze upon whatever natural grass and edible weeds may have been available to consume. When natural grasses weren't found for this purpose, the drivers would feed them portions of grain, generally kept in reserve within each traveler's wagon. For all the horses comprising the train's remuda, a separate grain storage wagon had been brought along to maintain their supply of life-sustaining grain. Close care and attention were paid daily to the draft animals and working horses, as they were the lifeblood of the journey west for these Pioneers, settlers, and wagon guides.

But in places where cases of anthrax had sickened some of the stock of oxen and mules, it forced the wagon master to then harness teams of horses to take the dead animals' place in pulling the affected wagons. But when shifting to horse-drawn for those wagons, he asked the owners to lighten their loads by discarding some of their heavier items that weren't of vital importance to them. This would make it possible for the few replacement horse teams to pull the lightened wagons without becoming exhausted to the point of collapsing and stopping the train. Plus, it still allowed them to carry a little more grain for these hard-working animals, which they could usually obtain from supply reserves available at Fort Kearny, Fort Laramie, or Fort Bridger, all serving as stopping points along the way.

In those cases where travelers had lost their oxen or mules to anthrax and had elected to continue with teams of horses instead, they were forced to part with some heavier items from within their wagons that they would have to reluctantly offload and discard right along the side of the trail. There were cherished items like family heirloom-type musical organs or small pianos and even fancy cast iron cooktop woodstoves that they had disassembled and so methodically placed within their wagons, and now so painfully had to leave behind if they wanted to continue their guided journey with the train.

Anthrax is a rare bacterial infection, picked up from the ground in the form of spores. It is also found in grasses ingested by animals, which makes them deathly sick.

When heading up inclines toward higher elevations, in making their way toward the mountain passes, these horse-drawn wagons needed to be as light as possible to make it through. So, except for the driver, the other occupants would shed further weight by stepping off and walking alongside it to scale the upward climb on foot while sometimes called on to help push the wagon from behind. If their horses were to give out from a heavier load to bear, they would likely have to abandon their wagon and most of their provisions, whereby the occupants would be split up and assigned to ride in other wagons with only their essential belongings being left to them. Otherwise, a team of oxen from atop the mountain pass could be uncoupled and sent back down the slope to pull the wagon up and salvage the situation, provided the exhausted horses might be able to continue to pull the wagon from there. Fortunately for the Glover family, they still had their trusty Missouri mule team, having been unaffected by the threat of anthrax, as they pulled the weight of their wagon without fault or failure in making their way over the more elevated mountain passes.

As successive wagon trains rolled over the same marked course westward, other travelers would encounter the perplexing scenes showing numerous discarded items alongside the trail, finding it a rather bizarre sight to behold. In some cases, travelers in the other wagon trains would salvage some of what was there for their benefit if they had the room and the animals to handle the extra load, despite some degree of rust build-up or other decay from sitting out in the elements for a time.

When rolling over the higher prairie country, Will encountered a young couple who were stopped beside the trail, with their weathered reins having snapped at a weakened spot on one of the long leather straps. So, when pulling out of the line and attempting to assist him, Will returned to the bed of his wagon, retrieving a fresh roll of leather strapping that he kept for emergencies while helping the man re-establish an extended length of it to restore control of his animals. While working with him, he learned that this man, Lyman Morrisey, who was coming west from Vicksburg, Mississippi, had served during the Civil War as a Confederate infantryman while now looking forward to a new life away from all of the post-war re-construction chaos that the south was going through. Lyman related to him that he had only served in one battle outside of Vicksburg, which resulted in catching shrapnel from cannon fire in both of his upper thighs. While still sporting a noticeable limp, he said the wounds kept him bedridden and incapacitated over a lengthy recovery period after surgery for much of 1863 and part of '64, afterwhich being medically discharged. Will also detailed some of the history regarding his own assignment in the war while wondering if his cannon battery may have been involved in the battle that Lyman described.

However, despite the differences in their involvement with the war, these two seemed to get along quite well during this part of their trek across the country despite having been enemies only a couple of years before. Evie and Maggie were also charmed and pleased to share company during the trip with Lyman's wife, Rhonda, a red-headed southern belle with a distinctly charming southern drawl accent and a smooth, gentle nature. As unlikely as it was, given their cultural and geographical backgrounds, along with the country's recent history, they all took a genuine liking to each other.

In the course of their travels on the California – Oregon trail, they exchanged courtesies while often inviting the

Morriseys to join them in camp for supper and vice-versa. From these informal gatherings, both families had established a warm friendship that helped to break up the monotony of the lengthy and mostly uncomfortable overland journey. For Will, it was also a way to help put the bitter memories of the Civil War behind him, at least for the most part, while reconciling his differences with a fellow American countryman from the South. Plus, when dining with the Morrisseys, the Glovers had a chance to discover the goodness of southern cuisine, as Rhonda was an excellent cook in her own right, often serving tasty southern dishes from her cookpot that Will and his family had never encountered.

On a partly cloudy day, as the train of wagons continued to move westward across the open prairie land near the Platte River, a lone Indian came riding up to the slow-moving line of wagons to look everyone and everything over while motioning to several of the travelers with a hand-to-mouth gesture, in which to say that he was hungry and needed some food. Initially, Evie was frightened at the sudden sight of him, although she soon realized that he didn't pose a threat and only wanted something to eat. So, she went into the wagon bed and brought forth several flapjacks left over from their breakfast, along with a few oatmeal cookies she and her mother Mary had baked before leaving Carbondale. She had previously packed dozens of them while sealing them into an old gallon clay pot, while finding a safe place for it within the wagon. Wrapped within a colorful cloth napkin, she reached out and handed her offering to this hungry Indian as he paused to admire her beauty and long reddish-golden hair before riding off to beg from another of the wagons just ahead. Seeing this, Will asked, "What did you give him?" When she related what it was, he yelled out, "Not the cookies! Once he gets a taste of those, he'll likely follow us to our next encampment". But as a compliment to her baking skills, he said with a wry grin, "I know I would."

Riding out abreast of the rear wagons while keeping this Indian in full view, the train's drag rider remained aloof, with his rifle lying deliberately across the front of his saddle at half-cock, in the event this Indian might pose a threat to any of the travelers.

When camping overnight, Evie occasionally had some time to sit down and write letters to her mother in Carbondale to keep her apprised of their progress on the trail while reassuring her that everything was all right and that they were in good hands with the wagon master leading them out over the prairie without incident thus far. However, she felt compelled to tell her about the lone Indian and Will's reaction.

Knowing they were scheduled to stop at a few Army forts and outposts along the way, she found it quite convenient to drop her letters off with the post's outgoing mail. She would also write to Lucy in Provo to tell her they were on their way and that all was well. The sisters were just a little over a year apart in age but quite close in personal regard for each other while considering themselves as sisters and very good friends.

For her part in the trip west, Evie would rise early each day to prepare breakfast for her family, as Will would start a campfire to cook on and boil water for coffee and tea. Once the fire was well established, he had a standing iron plate that he would assemble and put in place at a height just above the flames to establish a suitable cooking surface for pots and pans and such, which provided them with a more usable and practical method of cooking directly over a campfire. But when breakfast was over, and they had to break camp and hit the trail again, the iron plate was still much too hot to deal with after extinguishing the fire. So, they would have to waste a certain amount of water by dousing it each morning before being able to handle it safely enough to place it back into the wagon.

On the few nights when it rained, many families would put their buckets and available cooking pots out beside the wagons, collecting what they could to add to their water barrels. In most cases, it would only amount to a volume satisfying their animals' thirst. Still, this significant benefit helped them conserve their water supply over the more arid stretches where it became increasingly scarce.

On this arduous and tiring journey west, the train's travelers regularly took their water supply from the more notably voluminous and steadily flowing rivers and streams they encountered. However, on a few stretches of the trail in prairie country, slow-flowing creeks were the only remaining resource left to them, where occasional scummy-looking algae blooms were present in some spots that contained standing water. Because of this, the settlers were told to boil any water taken from them, which would tend to cook off any possible bacteria or other impurities while making it safer to drink.

THE OVERLAND TRAIL TO OREGON
AND CALIFORNIA

THE TRAIL ‑ ‑ ‑
OTHER PATHS ····

At some point, it was reported that Garvin and Thelma Hicks, who had started out in the wagon just in front of Will and Evie, had both taken ill while forced to pull out of their spot in the line as a result. The train's unofficial doctor and other personnel had recognized the sure signs and symptoms for them both as that of Cholera. The trail hands then placed them both back within their wagon while being tended to by a young woman who volunteered to help. One of the train's hands had then taken up the wagon's reins, serving as its driver to reposition it at the very end of the train so as not to slow the day's progress. But within two days, both Garvin and Thelma had weakened further and finally succumbed to this illness within only hours of each other.

Their passing had soon found the wagon master and many of the travelers assembling while standing over two freshly dug burial plots, poised to lay them both in and speak his words over them. Both Will and Evie attended, as they knew Garvin and Thelma as warm and friendly camp neighbors within their rear section of the wagon train. As a sad but consoling thought, Will realized that the two former Wisconsinites would never have to endure a harsh winter again. Just a few days after that, the same thing happened to a middle-aged man near the front of the train, although he lingered for over a week before finally giving up his ghost.

In another instance where contaminated water played a role, as the wagon master had warned his collective group of wagoneers about it at the start of the trip, an elderly woman in her mid-sixties had also died. Although considered old for her time, the formerly vibrant woman's kidneys had given out after suffering the draining effects of dysentery. With the mounting deaths and numerous graves being left on display alongside the trail by previous trains, and now by this one as well, it would appear as if they were passing through a cemetery instead of rolling over an immigrant trail that was to bring hope for all in the party. The sobering sight of this was a grim reminder to all who made their way over these trails that not everyone would reach their intended destinations, even with all of the wagon master's cautionary reminders being heeded.

Soon after, Evie had taken it upon herself to speak to an evening gathering of the rear section of the train's women, many of whom had fallen into a state of despair. She offered them her words of hope by explaining that they could all get through the hardship, discomfort, and tragedy on this long-distance land voyage over the unforgiving landscape, where so much of it lay barren and plain against their tired eyes, by simply helping and supporting each other. She told them to raise their hopes and strength again, as they would soon be seeing their destinations come before them. "Feelings of despair and hopelessness will only contribute to

depression and ill health, while we all need to keep our-
selves well and remain vigilant in fulfilling our original de-
sires of resettling in the West. Because these hardships also
affect the bodies and minds of our menfolk, we would all
do well in supporting them as much as possible to help get
through this and other ongoing situations."

With a few of these women's husbands having taken ill
while lying nearly helpless within their wagons, Evie and others would assist by cooking and bringing them hot food and
encouragement to help them recover. Over just a short period, most of them had recovered and returned to the driver's
seat of their wagons. Almost as a blessing, no one else died,
and no one was left behind, while the wagon train might have
only lost a couple of days at most in its westward travel.

While this was all unfolding out on the open plains and
prairie lands for the Glover family during the Spring and
early Summer of 1867, something entirely unannounced to
them, as a new type of cross-country transportation in the
form of the trans-continental railroad had been progressively moving from east to west and west to east, with separate rail lines being constructed from each direction. These
two rail lines would be set in place to eventually meet and
join together, forming one system of rails. At the same time,
certain tribal bands of Indians would make the project more
complicated by attacking the work crews and even the trains
before the two railroad tracks would come together. But the
eventual completion of this incredible undertaking would
mark a significant milestone in the westward migrational
movement of 'Manifest Destiny' by effectively linking the
entire North American continent, from the Atlantic Ocean
to the Pacific, with rail service running from New York to
San Francisco and vice versa.

When stopping to make camp overnight as they went, searches for dry firewood would generally yield a plentiful supply for the train's nightly campfires, as there always seemed to be an abundance of dead wood lying around to serve them. But on the rare occasions when sufficient firewood wasn't plentiful, available dried Bison dung would also serve as decent fuel for their fires. At that time, each wagon family or couple had commonly cooked their meals over their campfires, often with cast iron 'Dutch ovens' hanging above the flames, supported by a tripod, formed and fastened with long sturdy branches tied together at the top, helping to serve the intended purpose. When wandering about the encampment as folks cooked and prepared their evening meals, one would be overcome with the wondrous aromas emanating from each wagon's cookpots.

Many of these pioneering women, who did not always have direct access to fresh meats and vegetables for their cookpots, had portions of previously prepared cooked meats and stews, etc., submerged in a significant amount of animal fat while having been placed for storage in clay pots. To seal the food off in these pots, melted lard or candle wax was applied over the top, which would harden to complete the storage technique for later consumption, as they found that food sealed in fat would last longer when stored in ceramic pots. They also had cuts of meat that were heavily salted to preserve for longer periods without the need for cold temperatures to maintain freshness. However, when selecting some of this meat for cooking, it would usually have to soak in water for several hours to purge enough salt from it to make it more palatable. Also, among these travelers' food stores within their wagons was a sizeable supply of dried beef or venison jerky and hardtack biscuits, which would help sustain these settlers during the day as they continued on their overland trek. Additionally, without having the benefit of fresh fruit, some of these early pioneers had previously stored several jars within their wagons containing vinegar-based items like pickles, sauerkraut, and pig's feet, along with fruit preserves sealed with candle wax. All of these prepared items provided needed nutrients to help keep them from developing scurvy, which was a debilitating illness brought on by the lack of vitamin C.

For the wagon master, with his scouts and other working personnel under his care, he had his own hired trail cook and helper on hand, equipped with a fully stocked 'chuck wagon.' They would keep busy preparing hot meals twice daily for the train's workers, much like the dedicated trail cooks commonly employed on cattle drives. The train's scouts, who tended to be 'crack shots' with their rifles, would occasionally bring back a deer or even a grouse or two, otherwise known as 'prairie chickens.'

While often referred to as a type of grouse, prairie chickens were part of the family genus associated with pheasants and Ptarmigans.

Drifting off in his thoughts on the following day while handling the mule team's reins, Will had recalled that he hadn't traveled out to far-off places like this since he had served more recently as an artilleryman in the Union Army's 3rd Illinois Cavalry Regiment during the Civil War. After enlisting at the start of the war for the standard 5-year hitch, he immediately reported to Camp Butler, near Springfield, Illinois, which was a day and a half buggy or coach ride due north of Carbondale.

Keeping the dust-generating train of wagons ahead of him in view, he drifted back in his mind, recalling the year that he and Evie had gotten married, having declared their devoted commitment to each other in early April. It was during the following year when the country's rebellious southern states had seceded from the Union government in Washington. That collective secession of southern states quickly brought about the start of an unprecedented four-year period of bitter war on 12 April 1861 that would separate a nation and destroy hundreds of thousands of lives.

Ironically, earlier colonial migrations from England in the 1600s had already begun to set the stage for this war, as the northern colonies were primarily influenced by the arrival of the Puritans, a religious sect partially migrating from East Anglia in 1629. Additionally, Dutch immigrants from Holland, along with Germans and other eastern Europeans, had emigrated to the northern colonial states in the latter part of the 17th century. But more notably, a large contingent of another group from the south of England, called the 'Cavaliers,' having come from British nobility, had emigrated to Virginia and other southern colonies after being defeated by Oliver Cromwell and the Puritans in England's Civil War of 1642 - 1651. These colonial Cavaliers were some of the remaining loyalists from the reign of King Charles I after the former parliamentarian-led forces of Puritans had retaken the country by overthrowing the monarchy and beheading the King. In fleeing to America, many of these Cavaliers had hoped to reestablish their former agrarian upper-class ways in this more promising place where they could revive their nobility-influenced culture, as these former royalists brought their indentured servants along with them. These self-appointed upper-class colonial Cavalier citizens strongly believed in maintaining dominion over themselves and others, as it was to influence and shape their reestablished political society.

*Early official Seal of the State of Virginia, reflecting
on the restoration of Britain's King Charles II in 1660*

While the two respective regions of these newly defined British
colonial establishments had also attracted other persecuted groups
like the Quakers and Scotch and Irish Catholics from other parts
of the British Isles, it was the determined actions of the colonial
Cavaliers in the Southern region of America that opened the door
in 1619 toward the acquisition of numerous African slaves. These
kidnapped or purchased Africans were initially brought into the
English colony at Jamestown, Virginia, by English trade ships
from the Caribbean island of Barbados after being acquired at ports
along the African coast to provide free labor for these former royalists. They were to be used exclusively as indentured servants and
laborers. Through this adopted practice, these slaves, over time,
had formed the working nucleus toward operating profit-generat-
ing plantations, where various food crops, cotton, and tobacco were
grown and exported. The key beneficial factor involved with this
was forced labor that these kept human prisoners provided without
any payment. In effect, it realized a significantly greater profitability for plantation owners.

While this was primarily a cultural practice ingrained throughout the southern colonial states, some prominent northerners had

also owned slaves during the antebellum period to maintain their large estates in areas bordering Virginia. It came to be known that several of the wealthier, soon-to-be founding fathers of what would eventually become the United States had also ascribed to the adopted practice of keeping slaves. Plus, with the colonies being under British rule with several Kings and Queens having ruled their north American assets up to and including George III, slavery was held to be an acceptable practice that would further benefit the interests and coffers of the crown. But even as the colonies managed to shake free from the shackles of George III by defeating his armed forces in the American Revolution, the practice of slavery continued with the birth of a new nation. At the time, it became culturally acceptable to keep these black men and women to help with labor and domestic tasks for those who could afford to purchase them. It was also known that most of the early U.S. Presidents and other government figures had owned slaves, all the way up to Tennessee-born President Andrew Jackson, who held numerous slaves to keep up his Hermitage estate just north of Nashville.

With this new internal struggle and sudden mobilization of forces between the northern and southern states ongoing, Will had assumed that he would soon see action somewhere, although nothing was forthcoming. Instead, he was garrisoned at Camp Butler for three of his obligated service years before finally being sent out in a 100-man replacement column to St. Louis in late July 1863. With cannons in tow, he and his mates were to join Henshaw's Battery of Light Artillery to temporarily serve as a new artillery detachment while directly assigned to the 3rd Illinois Regiment.

However, prior to his deployment, while Will was still garrisoned, Evie had taken it upon herself to board a stage line in May of 1863, bringing her north to Greenville, Illinois. The coach and its occupants spent the night at an Inn before returning to the road the following day, driving their horses just beyond Springfield and directly to the post. Upon arrival at Camp Butler, temporary quarters were provided for her, typical for all visiting wives. While Will was quite surprised, he and Evie were more than overjoyed to be able to see each other again, at least for a short while anyway, as they suffered a little over three long years of being apart. After a week there, she was allowed to extend her short stay to ten days before bidding her husband goodbye and retracing her route back south to Carbondale.

Incidentally, this visit also brought about the conception and eventual birth of their daughter, Maggie.

However, only a few months later, she would see him again in Carbondale for just two days, at Margaret Glover's burial, before Will would receive his orders to report to the 3rd Illinois Regiment, posted at that time in Saint Louis.

Artilleryman's Kepi Hat

When finally reaching the encampment of Henshaw's Battery near St. Louis, Will fell in with the others there while getting acquainted with some new battery mates. His unit had been designated to replace a previously assigned company that suffered too many losses on the front lines to continue its war efforts effectively. As a newly promoted corporal, Will Glover had become an integral member of a Battery of men charged with maintaining and positioning their 10-pound 'Parrott Rifled' cannons onto the battle lines. At the same time, other larger traditional type cannons were also deployed. Each was pulled by a harnessed team of two horses, intended to be set up at designated battlefield encampments where regimental skirmishes with the Confederate "Johnny Rebs" tended to take place on occasion.

When traveling, the cannon's stock was commonly attached to a short two-wheeled wagon hitch called a 'limber.' The limber was hooked to a pair of harnessed horses and featured an attached driver's seat. This common cannon-connected vehicle then served as a functional four-wheeled wagon, with the cannon becoming a key aspect of the vehicle's full configuration.

For this new 'rifled' type of cannon, the artillerymen's job when they were in place on the battle line was to note the enemy's position while determining the distance to fire their ordinance onto those positions with consistent accuracy and effectiveness.

Interestingly, the artillery cannon that Will was assigned to as its Gunner was somewhat new to American warfare, or any warfare for that matter, as its barrel was grooved on the inside in a spiral pattern, which helped to actively place a more definitive spin on the conical projectiles used with this particular cannon when fired. This new 'rifled' technology for artillery, which was developed in 1860 at the West Point Foundry in Cold Spring, New York, by Union soldier and inventor of military ordinance Robert Parker Parrott, was found to have significantly improved the cannon's accuracy in getting very close to the intended target, if not right on top of it with each applied round. The degree of accuracy had commonly saved on the number of projectiles needed for these rifled cannons during battles, as they usually hit their marks with unrivaled consistency.

Civil War Cannon and Limber

As a muzzleloader, the 10 lb. Parrott gun that Will was charged with had a bore caliber of 2.9 inches and fired a pointed and elongated projectile that weighed 9.5 pounds. While effectively able to reach up to 1,850 yards, this gun was perfectly able to achieve those distances with even smaller charges of gunpowder. The gun mostly fired rounds with case shots (shrapnel), which could take out several enemy soldiers with the impact of each round. In addition, it fired a standard canister shell and a solid shot round for long-distance shelling. Most of the other cast-iron cannons in the Battery, which were of the earlier basic unrifled, smooth bore type style, had used the old conventional projectiles in the form of round iron cannonballs, which in comparison were hit or miss in determining their overall accuracy and range as compared with the new Parrott rifled variations. Even when using larger powder charges in the antiquated cannons, the old round cannonballs had only covered distances that fell far short of what the newer conical, spiral-influenced projectiles could achieve with even greater accuracy and less powder involved.

In early 1860, after R.P. Parrott had successfully developed this rifled cannon at the West Point Foundry to serve the U.S. Army's arsenal as a new and innovative artillery piece, it immediately proved its worthiness as a remarkably accurate cannon. In test firings, it consistently outperformed the Army's un-rifled, old-world versions to earn its rightful place among the military's existing artillery weapons. While not suspecting anything might be afoot, Parrott sold one of them to the interested state government of Virginia. While impressed with its overall range and accuracy, the Governor ordered a dozen more.

After the Civil War broke out the following year, with Virginia becoming part of the Confederacy, a handful of foundries were established in other southern states to replicate the design of the cannons acquired from the West Point Foundry. As expected, they made up a sizeable collection to build up and support the active arsenals of the Confederacy. At some point during the war, Mr. Parrott realized his folly in selling his new rifled cannons to a southern state.

On a side note, the breakthrough concept and design of rifling for the barrels of pistols and long guns had already been around for a few centuries before finally being applied to cannons, as rifling had first been invented during the 15th century by Austrian gunmaker Gaspard Kollner.

The men of Henshaw's Battery, along with elements of the 3rd Illinois Regiment, had hoped to apply their developed skills in operating their heavy cast iron artillery pieces in battle. They column-marched to far-off places, moving south from the area around St. Louis and considerably farther away from Illinois. Progressively pushing on while following their Regimental forces throughout Missouri by train, they marched down into parts of Arkansas and Tennessee with their gear and artillery pieces in tow. Soon, they would find themselves participating in notable clashes with tenacious contingents of Confederates who were spoiling for a fight. Occasionally, they would endure ambushes along some of the roads when moving to their intended battle fronts while suffering several casualties along the way. As they moved from battlefront to battlefront, they eventually joined other Union forces in eastern Tennessee, participating in battles in and around Knoxville to support Major General Ambrose Burnside in his series of notable clashes with Confederate General James Longstreet.

In late November of 1863, as supplies were brought in from the north, Will came across a copy of an Indiana newspaper in one of the wagons while camped in northern Arkansas. The headline and its following story had told about President Lincoln's recent address at the former battleground in Gettysburg, Pennsylvania, as his speech was transcribed there in its full yet relatively short-worded text:

> *Four score and seven years ago our fathers brought forth on this continent a new nation conceived in liberty, and dedicated to the proposition that all men are created equal.*
>
> *Now we are engaged in a great civil war, testing whether that nation, or any nation so conceived and so dedicated can long endure. We are met on a great battlefield of that war. We have come to dedicate a portion of that field as a final resting place for those who here gave their lives that that nation might live. It is altogether fitting and proper that we should do this. But in the larger sense, we cannot dedicate ourselves, we can-*

*not consecrate, and we cannot hallow this ground. The brave
men, living and dead, who struggled here, have consecrated it
far above our poor power to add or detract.*

*The world will little note, nor long remember, what we say
here, but it can never forget what they did here. It is for us,
the living, rather to be dedicated here to the unfinished work
which they who fought here have thus far so nobly advanced.
It is rather for us to be here dedicated to the great task remaining before us, that from these honored dead we take increased
devotion to that cause for which they gave the last full measure
of devotion; that we here highly resolve that these dead shall
not have died in vain: that this nation under God shall have a
new birth of freedom, and that the government of the people,
by the people, and for the people, shall not perish from the
Earth.*

- Abraham Lincoln, 19 November, 1863

The moving speech had given Will pause to reflect on his
plight in the war and that of his fellow Union soldiers. It
drove home the greater importance of why they should
carry on and push with more heightened determination despite the tremendous loss of manpower, as the President's
powerful words continued to haunt him for several days
thereafter.

Along with the newspaper that Will came across, he
noted several other wagons ladened with needed supplies
to feed this Army of hungry men. For this newly arrived
train of about eight wagons returning from a subsistence rail
depot at Paducah, Kentucky, there were bushels of potatoes,
onions, corn, and sizeable quantities of flour and sugar.
Other wagons were packed with large amounts of salted
pork, bacon, beans, rice, hominy, salt, pepper, and molasses,

some of which came in the form of individually prepared and packaged rations to be distributed to each soldier. Additionally, cans of condensed milk were included after being invented and packaged by Gail Borden, an inventor and manufacturing pioneer of the time. He had set up manufacturing plants in Connecticut, New York, and Chicago to produce this highly sought-after type of water-reduced milk that did not need refrigeration if consumed in one day once the cans were opened. It was an exclusive item for the Union troops in the field, which they greatly appreciated.

The other wagons there were loaded with produce, fruit, and cornmeal. Packaged hard bread, also commonly known as hardtack, was issued as an essential handy food item that could be pocketed and eaten during the day between skirmishes. These thick, dense crackers were readymade and provided as a thick, hard-baked biscuit made with flour, water, and salt, which consumers tended to gnaw on instead of eating normally as a common food item. Additionally, they tended to last for many days and weeks within a soldier's pocket. But, for men with dental issues, they were next to impossible to eat, as they were baked almost rock-hard as a mostly non-perishable food item. As a mid-day snack, they kept a fighting man's strength up for several hours. However, hunger was rarely much of concern when deeply involved in the fear-driven throws of battle.

Hardtack

At the back of the train, tied to the rear wagon, were several standing beef cattle that would be rendered and parted out as needed over the coming days and weeks. Whenever coffee was in short supply, the Union's Subsistence Department would substitute dried Dandelion root in its place, which had a mild, coffee-like flavor but without caffeine. However, when coffee *was* in good supply, some of the men on picket duty would commonly trade amounts of it with a Rebel sentry for fresh southern tobacco. It was deemed a fair trade all around, as the Confederates were entirely out of coffee to drink, having to resort to brewing up chickory instead. However, to them, real coffee was like gold. Nearly the same could be said by northerners for their newly acquired amounts of southern tobacco.

At that time, the Army did not employ cooks to prepare the essential rations for their men in the field. So, it was left up to each of these men to prepare their meals for themselves after some instruction was provided. For each soldier, one food item in the form of a pound of meat, one potato, one onion, and seasonings, etc., were proportionately distributed to them, along with other miscellaneous items like coffee and tea...and, of course, a can of Gail Borden's condensed milk. Commonly, groups of five or six men would bandy together with some of their food supplies, which served mainly as a social occasion, where one or two among them were designated as the cooks and preparers of their meals. These volunteering cooks usually escaped other camp duties, as it became an envious position within their group. The ones who demonstrated a greater level of skill when cooking and satisfying their unit mates usually remained as the group's camp cook while holding more recognized status among them. When fresh beef from a slaughtered animal was issued, many of the men would cook chunks of it over a campfire while skewering it with their bayonets. Alternately, these novice cooks would also make pots of beef stew, using salvaged metal containers they cut and formed into rudimentary cooking pots and pans that would serve them well enough until something else worked better.

While this tended to be the usual periodic shipment sent out by the Quartermaster's Department to keep the soldier's vitality and morale up, there were a few other occasions when the Confederates had intercepted the intended ration supply trains, causing the Union troops to fall on lean times. To deal with the situation, Company Commanders would send sharpshooting soldiers out into the surrounding countryside to hunt for game and forage while gleaning ripening fruit from tree orchards when and wherever available. They would also occasionally bring back a sizeable amount of dandelions, roots, and all, to be eaten as a salad, as the plant was tasty, safe to eat, and quite nutritious.

For the Confederates, food shipments were not entirely forthcoming after the second year of the war. While commonly in short supply, their troops were often left to subsist by living off the land for the most part. Gleaning and foraging had come more naturally to the gray coats, while they also resorted to hunting for game, small or large, when meat was scarce or unavailable. But meat and cornmeal were essential items when supplied, along with dried beans, and large sacks of peanuts, which were often included in their shipments as a nutritious food source with a good shelf life. Occasionally, when unable to acquire any game meat, they would be forced to kill and butcher one of their horses as a sacrificial act in providing needed protein for their men.

However, toward the end of the war, it was found that many Confederate soldiers had died from starvation and malnutrition as a result of not having enough, or the right kinds of foods available to keep their vitality and strength up. Their Quartermaster simply couldn't supply them because the Union Army was destroying shipping methods while demolishing many key railroads in the South. Also, because various fruits were unavailable in some areas, along with vinegar-based pickles and sauerkraut, some of their men contracted scurvy, which left them unable to fight or do much of anything. When left untreated without vitamin C, most of these men died as a result.

Organized medical teams for the Northern and Southern forces were kept equally busy day and night, with the constant influx of casualties from the battle lines. These were all notably trained and accomplished doctors, surgeons, and nurses. Their job was to keep the wounded alive and on the road to recovery while preventing infections from developing. Theirs was a never-ending, unenviable task that took a lot of inner strength to get through their grim and turbulent days and nights when deployed at the various battlefronts.

At one particular southern battlefield, when taking their positions against the opposing Rebel forces, the 3rd Illinois, with their artillery support elements, had engaged them and immediately found their adversaries quite resistant to their own aggressive ways. The opposing 'Johnnie Rebs' had pushed back the skirmishers on the battlefield before charging, managing to penetrate the Union's artillery line as they proceeded to over-run the 'Billy Yanks' within one weakened section of it. That section just happened to be right around where Will and his battery mates had set up their cannons, as many of the foot soldiers holding the line there had fallen.

On that sudden charge, they were left with having to fight them off by resorting to hand-to-hand combat with the close-quarters infighting that was going on immediately around them, using their rifle butts, single-shot pistols, and bayonets to fend them off. As the enemy's charge surged furiously through the breach in the Union's position, one of Will's battery mates had immediately fallen from a rifle shot, and another had been caught off balance and run through with a bayonet, much to Will's horror. When seeing them both drop right out in front of him, he desperately struggled to reload his rifle as blood flowed from his now wounded left arm. He had been shot and couldn't even recall it happening. However, he managed to evade the advancing Confederates by crouching low behind and close beside his cannon, where he couldn't be seen.

When field commanders saw this serious breach taking place in the line, where Confederate soldiers had penetrated to create havoc, reinforcements from the rear were immediately called on to rush forward and fill the gap. With that measure of support, the Union troops were then able to kill or drive the insurgents back to effectively quell the chaotic situation and restore order within the forward position of the line.

The gray-clad Rebels then halted their charge while re-treating to their previous positions across the battlefield, leaving scores of their fellow dead and wounded brethren scattered about, unregarded upon the grassy field as they withdrew. As the smoke finally cleared, it was found that the violent engagement at the Union line had left a large mix of dead and wounded soldiers from both sides. Sometime later, while only under the respected protection of a white flag, Confederate medical aid teams would be allowed to come up closer to the Union line to locate and recover their wounded while carrying them off on stretchers. But, re-garding their dead, they were left where they fell. From their close proximity, Union medics, when retrieving their wounded soldiers, had also occasionally taken a few of the fallen Confederate casualties on stretchers to the Union's medical tent.

In the battle's aftermath, it was found that Will's cannon placement had been compromised, although the cannon it-self remained undamaged, as two Privates and a 1st Lieu-tenant had been killed. Will had also taken a rifle ball to his left forearm while soon finding himself walking a fair dis-tance to the rear, with another soldier accompanying him to the medical tent, located farther back and well removed from the front line. He applied sufficient pressure to his

wound as he walked to control the bleeding until they eventually arrived at a large platoon-sized, white canvas field
medical tent situated within a grove of trees, where he was
brought in and deposited onto a chair. The bleeding from
the puncture wound was minimal at that point, although
the overall pain from it was still quite excruciating, with the
rifle ball still being well lodged within his forearm.

One of the attending doctors, who had other men's blood
artfully spattered all over the front of his protective gown,
along with his upper sleeves, in a somewhat ghastly or
macabre sort of appearance, had taken a close look at Will's
wound. Without hesitation, he motioned for him to lie down
on the examination table while giving him a short dose of
chloroform vapor to sedate him while still keeping him
halfway conscious but relaxed. He quickly worked to extract
the rifle ball that was lodged within the young man's inner
forearm, with a few brief outcries emitted from a partially
anesthetized Corporal Glover. The doctor then announced
that he had removed the projectile while splashing a stinging solution of iodine onto the hole that it left in the middle
of Will's forearm before closing it up with a few stitches.
The dose of iodine had forced Will to raise his upper body
momentarily as he briefly writhed in stinging pain, clench-
ing his teeth while lying there. The doctor then proceeded
to wrap it up with sufficient gauze, tying it off and supporting the arm by adding a sling. He then instructed Will to
"Keep it clean and covered so as not to invite infection."

"You were quite lucky that the ball hadn't hit any bone
or tendons, as it was only a rather deep flesh wound," was
the doctor's assessment as he handed the lead ball to Will
as a souvenir. But Will just glared at him and said, "No
thanks."

"Be sure to come back and see us in a few days for a new dressing to help it heal quicker. But try to stay on light duty for at least a few days, as you will still experience some degree of pain and general discomfort if you decide to use it in any way. Ok, you're now free to return to your unit, soldier!"

It was all that quick and straightforward, with wounds that were more workable and not life-threatening. However, while looking around the medical tent, Will could see just how lucky he was, given all of the suffering exhibited by men who had received much more severe wounds. Amid these bloody battles, field physicians and surgeons worked tirelessly to save lives, often having to resort to amputations, with nurses being left with having to medicate and console these men as best as possible. Anesthetics such as Chloroform or Ether were commonly used, with patients inhaling the fumes until they would become unconscious or, in some cases, nearly unconscious. Also, depending on the duration of the particular surgery involved, the anesthetic occasionally had to be reapplied, as the patient would unexpectedly awaken from their unconscious state to complicate matters.

Morphine, as an opiate-type pain-relieving drug, was commonly offered to those with issues involving more heightened levels of pain. In more involved cases, if a patient's condition after surgery was such that it was still painfully unbearable for them during recovery, this highly addictive drug was then usually given sparingly to control the pain.

Also, a pharmaceutically formulated liquid solution called Laudanum was often available in bottle tincture form at these field hospitals to help treat and control patients' more elevated pain levels during their recovery period. It was given out as a drinkable opiate-based medication, which was a concocted mixture of opium and alcohol. However, when taken daily over a week or more to control one's mostly unbearable discomforts, it was also found to be highly addictive.

Among the many soldiers who were brought into this sizeable medical tent during these open field skirmishes where surgeries and amputations were commonplace, some wounded Confederates had also been attended to and treated by the Union physicians before being released upon recovery. They would then be taken away as prisoners of war, while some of their other gray-clad comrades had died from their wounds on the operating table. But from within this medical tent, it wasn't at all uncommon to see an occasional Confederate soldier lying on a stretcher right next to other wounded or dead Union soldiers. Oddly, it was as if the war and its politically and culturally driven discords had been checked at the door, as the attending business at hand seemed far more important in comparison.

Even with his wounded arm painfully hanging within a sling, Will sauntered back to the line where his cannon was sitting idle, as he proceeded to set up the elevation and windage on it with his other able hand. He found that he could still roughly determine the distance out to where the middle of the Confederate ranks were standing while hoping to at least set the cannon to get it ready again. Although, with only one arm available to him, he found it too difficult to load the cannon's barrel with a powder charge and ten-pound projectile to ready it for firing. But while setting the cannon's directional coordinates, the other cannons left and right of him in his battery continued to fire on the enemy. With the immediate loss of two trained men from the cannon's artillery team, along with the 1st Lieutenant Battery Leader, Will noticed that another officer had been assigned to replace the former battery leader who had positionally stood out in front of his entire line of cannons to direct the volley of fire from each of them. Also, for Will's cannon placement, two raw cavalry foot soldiers had been reassigned to re-form the four-member team on the following day. They would help coordinate efforts associated with their artillery piece that stood within a line of five other cannons, hoping to keep it operational and in rhythm.

On that note, Will had his work cut out for him, with only one arm available in which to perform his tasks, as it was left to him as the cannon's gunner to instruct and train the new personnel on the necessary teamwork and timing involved with the loading and firing of the 'Parrott' gun with rapid efficiency. In application, one man would initially load the powder charge into the cannon's barrel, as another would use the ramrod to press the charge to the back of the cannon before another man would feed the conical projectile. In turn, the ramrodder would again use the rod's tamping end to push and compress everything firmly together, allowing the powder charge to provide the explosive energy that would propel the projectile to the target.

The cannon's ramrod featured a blunted wooden tamping piece on one end, with a bore cleaning swab on the other.

At that point, it was left to Will as the cannon's gunner after he pre-determined the distance and direction for the projectile to travel. He would then signal to the first Lieutenant Battery Leader out front that they were ready before receiving the command to pull the long trigger cord and fire the cannon. When this quickened repetitive teamwork was practiced and applied, it was much like a choreographed procedure, set in rapid motion, to create and maintain a constant barrage of artillery fire raining in on the Confederates' positions. However, with Will experiencing degrees of throbbing pain in his left forearm and frustration with this nervously uncoordinated duo of untrained replacements having been assigned as Will's new battery mates, he knew that any efficiency would be long in coming. When hitting their target, the projectile would cause enough damage and chaos to keep the enemy's foot soldiers and cavalrymen off balance, rendering a portion of their front line temporarily ineffective. However, much of the same could generally be said for artillery from the Confederate side, as they had employed the same tactic with their own rifled artillery pieces pointed at the Union's front line, unbeknownst to Will.

To the Confederates' credit, it was found that they, too, had some of these rifled Parrott cannons to compliment their mobile arsenals of field artillery. Having captured a small number of them from previous engagements, they also received shipments from their foundries that manufactured counterfeit replicas in various places within the southern Confederate states. These working foundries had kept busy reproducing the same rifled cannons that R.P. Parrott had regrettably sold to the state of Virginia.

They also learned the method of sighting it in, when targeting the standing lines of Union soldiers to inflict damage upon them while, in turn, rendering numerous casualties within their ranks. While Union forces thought they had a distinct advantage with these new rifled Parrott Cannons, they soon found it not to be the case, as the Confederates' covert acquisition of them led to a higher casualty count for both sides, which was not an advantage at all.

This was where Union Army ordinance inventor and designer R.P. Parrott erroneously envisioned that his rifled cannons, when produced and utilized in battle, would potentially help shorten the duration of the war for the North. However, it was his own blunder that effectively destroyed the potential advantage.

The only notable drawback with this particular cannon

was its recoil. As a mobile artillery piece, it was mounted on wagon wheels. With each firing, the recoil would consequently cause it to drift rearward about three or four feet, leaving the Gunner and other team members having to occasionally push it back into position by lifting the gun stock or carriage before reloading and firing it again. Having that occur each time, the Gunner would have to quickly re-sight the barrel to ensure the projectile would remain on target.

10 lb. Parrott Rifle conical projectile

The overall degree of accuracy with this gun was all on Will's shoulders, as he had been trained as a gunner on this tactical artillery piece when previously garrisoned at Camp Butler. To that effect, he was tasked with constantly adjusting the windage and elevation settings on the cannon before firing for effect. After the initial firing, he would be able to correlate where the projectile impacted with where he determined the rounds should land, again making the necessary adjustments to the elevation and windage to correct the positioning and get the projectile right on target. In simpler terms, the elevation setting was the means for determining the vertical height of the cannon to establish the distance to the target, while the windage setting was for adjusting the horizontal direction, left or right.

These openly situated battle skirmishes would generally

go on throughout the day and into the night until darkness made fighting impractical, leaving both sides with mostly peaceful conditions throughout the rest of the night. It was as though the war had ended every day when the dark of night set in. During this time, infantrymen and artillerymen would use the evening hours to prepare for the next day's battle, while the medical teams would continue to treat the wounded and perform surgeries throughout the night. The front-line soldiers and their support personnel would also have time to take in an evening meal, write letters to their loved ones, and get a halfway peaceful night's sleep before repeating the entire process the following day at dawn when the fighting would resume. It was as if both sides had previously negotiated and worked out terms that would apply, to ensure all forms of fighting would cease at the end of each day or when darkness came.

During quieter periods at different encampments where soldiers were between battles, the men could settle in and relax for several days while awaiting their leaders' instructions for the next subsequent battle placement. When paused from the fighting, the men sometimes received letters from home stowed within newly arriving supply wagons. Among the incoming letters, Will had received one from Evie in mid-March of 1864, announcing that he was now the father of a beautiful baby girl named Mary Margaret Glover. Wildly jubilant with the news of a new family addition, he shouted to his other unit mates, "I'm a father! I'm a father! I have a baby girl!" They all gave a rousing cheer of approval to support his step into fatherhood, although there were no traditional cigars nor drinks to be provided to them on such a fitting yet untimely occasion.

But as the realization of this life-changing moment had

sunk in, his paternal thoughts soon turned toward other prospects of making a living for when he would eventually fulfill his enlistment and get out of the Army. As it was, the Army didn't pay much to those serving in its lower ranks to support a family reliably. Also, working the egg farm in Carbondale with his father didn't offer much for a family of three, either. So, reflecting further on that point, he felt that after honorably serving his country in its time of need, it would be time for him to return to the more critical aspects of his newly cultivated life once his enlistment was completed. However, he knew he had to survive this bloody Civil War to make it all possible, ensuring his daughter would have a father involved in her future.

When writing to Evie in response to her previous letter reporting the birth of their new daughter, Will penned the following:

March 28, 1864

Dearest Evie,

It gives my heart great joy to receive your lovely letters, reminding me of my former life in Carbondale, where the love of my life awaits my return from this terrible ongoing conflict. Plus, it excites me to no end to know that our love has given us a daughter, and that I am now a father.

I miss you terribly, much more than words can ever express, as they can only convey sentiment without the real aspect of connection. Regarding how things are right now, our potential return to Camp Butler remains unclear. We are currently hunkered down at a location in western Tennessee, where a significant amount of fighting is taking place. But, we are holding our own, as I have become rather proficient with my assigned cannon.

However, I wanted to report that I am alright now, after be-coming wounded in my left forearm. It wasn't serious, as the field physician took great care in seeing to it properly, and it has now healed and I'm back good as new again. But while I'm again back at my position, please know that I am looking out for myself more now, with the fervent hope of one day falling back into your loving arms again. I have found that war is tragic and messy, and not at all glorious like some have made it out to be. But I want you to know that on each of my days, before taking on my expected duties, I hold tight and say a silent prayer, hoping that you and I and our little one will be reunited again.

With all of my love and devotion,
Your ever-loving husband,
Will

As the war raged on, Will and Henshaw's Artillery Battery of the 3rd Illinois Cavalry progressively moved on to other battlefronts in the south, where men's lives were continually being lost in these bloody, ongoing skirmishes of attrition. At each location where battles took place, a great many bullet and shrapnel-torn bodies from both sides were being left to rot on the battlefield behind them. It was the grim task of a few who remained behind, along with some local citizens thereabouts, to deal with the unceremonial burials of hundreds of former soldiers' twisted rotting remains that lay strewn about the grounds of the now quiet former battlefield, which had previously been just a serene meadow on some farmer's open piece of land. While they worked at digging graves and planting bodies, vultures began to feed on the numerous corpses that lay around them, making the scene even grimmer for those who had to deal with the situation.

On one occasion during battle, Will recalled his mother Margaret's spiritually inspired words to him from when he was just a young child while conveying her thoughts about dying. She would utter the seemingly biblical phrase, *"From where thou cometh, therest ye go."* And while he didn't fully understand its intended meaning, he could never find that little passage anywhere within the pages of the Bible.

For him, these high-casualty-producing battles were never something one's state of mind could ever accept or get used to in any way, as he knew all too well that his chances of surviving this war were becoming slimmer with each engagement. However, given his task as a trained artilleryman, the daily routine of dealing with it was never lost. It was just part of the overall effects of this ongoing conflict between two similar but different cultures and their committed resolve to eventually emerge as the ultimate victor. But with the intense fighting around Will's artillery battery, battle fatigue and the constant adrenalin-filled presence of a heightened sense of fear tended to wear some of them down mentally. In contrast, others were often seen falling around them as a result of incoming Confederate cannon shrapnel and rifle fire. However, again, without fail, soldiers from the rear would be called forward to take their places as part of the front-line support process. But given how things were going, it all boiled down to the fact that anyone and everyone who were situated on the artillery's battleline happened to be vulnerable and possibly subject to either receiving a severe wound or getting killed outright. It was a dark, constant reminder to all who participated and witnessed the resulting carnage.

In the line of Parrott rifled cannon placements, sequentially fired by both sides at several battlefronts, the incoming shrapnel and hails of bullets occasionally rained in and found their mark. In the aftermath, it was found that a dozen or more of Henshaw's battery men had been hit with opposing cannon and small arms fire, suffering severe wounds that ended their involvement in this Civil War that didn't seem so entirely civil. The more severely wounded would eventually be sent home when well enough to travel, either by horse or in the bed of a wagon. Additionally, there were also several others in the battery of cannons who had been gravely wounded or killed instantly, where untrained replacements were then called on to fill the void and learn what they could from the remaining battery mates.

In contrast, the foot soldiers' forward battlefield skirmishes had often taken place well before the line of artillery, where the two lines of opposing infantrymen would commonly clash straight on, out on the battlefield while brandishing their single-shot rifles with fixed bayonets. However, reloading usually took too much time, leaving one exposed for too long during the process. That pause often allowed an opposing soldier to run him through with his bayonet while moving forward. With that being realized, much of the individual clashes on that line depended largely on who could out-perry who with their rifle-mounted bayonets to effectively weaken the opposing strength of either side of the attacking line. Success, either way, would eventually cause the skirmish to shift in one direction or the other, where one side would eventually retreat after suffering many casualties, and the battle would be paused until another organized effort could be mounted, or perhaps be reconstituted on the following day. Will had noticed that this was usually how it all went, according to the existing rules of engagement.

As he allowed his critical mind to occasionally ponder certain things, Will sometimes struggled with why these mutual clashes en-mass, occurring on open battlefields almost daily, were still deemed a practical and purposeful means of fighting a war. The conventional Close-Order Line Formation type of fighting had originated in various parts of Europe, going back several centuries, while commonly utilized in the Prussian wars, the Napoleonic Wars, battles with the British, Scots, and Irish, and the American Revolution when both the British and soon-to-be Americans had faced off.

This particular manner of fighting was commonly regarded for centuries as a more dignified and respectable way of settling differences between nations, straight-up and face-to-face, whether waged with swords and spears from centuries past or with rifles and bayonets. As applied to this country's civil war, it was viewed by commanders in its original form as a more traditional and highly preferred way of fighting while being the only known way of going about it straightforwardly and respectably to collect their rightfully deserved victories. However, from the Napoleonic Wars and the native Indians' involvement in America's Revolutionary War, the observed application of covert 'skirmishers' had also played somewhat of a progressive role on a small scale, as a forward line applying hit-and-run type warfare. It would involve initially engaging the enemy and then retreating to one side while seeking the protection of cover to hide and shoot.

But to Will, the close order line formation style of fighting seemed so archaic and without good meaning while applying and conducting these field engagements in such a way that both sides stood to eventually lose half or more of their armies as a result of the intense clashes. For armies to square off in front of each other in somewhat deep organized formations of human sacrificial flesh and bone, set on opposite sides of a large open concourse, to wage battle until one side emerges victorious while the other retreats to fight another day, seemed like such a waste. However, it was deemed a very prim and proper way for both sides to conduct their battlefield campaigns, which often took place out on open meadows with low-growing field grass thriving among vibrantly colored wildflowers sparsely scattered throughout the grounds. The field's seemingly innocent tranquility would soon be replaced with cannon and musket fire, and blood-curdling screams from the chaos that followed.

Naturally, in the aftermath of these intense skirmishes, regardless of which side may come away as the winner, a mass of carnage was left behind to effectively lessen the number of available men to fight this war. For Will, as he viewed the numerous corpses scattered about the landscape out in front of him, it would give him pause to wonder why it all had to even come to this. For the men from both sides, this very form of open-field warfare had dreadfully frightened many of them at their respective battlefield placements, which at some point may have likely convinced a few of them to pick up and desert their posts. If caught, the punishment for desertion from the battlefront was death by firing squad, which wasn't the sort of punishment to teach them any lesson to be learned. It was otherwise intended to show others considering desertion that there was good reason to abort those thoughts.

Interestingly, if Will were to bring this up and pose all of these questions about the type of warfare they were involved with to his superior officers while converting his thoughts into critical words, he would likely draw their ire and possibly be reprimanded for questioning Army tactics. Quite simply, traditional warfare, as played out on the open battlefields during the 19th century, was not to be questioned nor doubted in any way, as it would tend to raise uncertainty with their leadership while also confusing those within the rank and file.

But, as well orchestrated as it was from both sides of the battlefields, which were more like parade grounds in effect, it all seemed almost ceremonial in form, like a surreal sort of pageantry being played out in a gentlemanly sort of way, with actors performing on a grand stage, although with actual armaments and real blood on display. Because of this antiquated yet very traditional way of respectfully waging war as a proud and honored spectacle while using meadows and farm fields to form epic major productions taking place right out in the open, it can only be surmised that these clashes would eventually be won simply through attrition instead of through skilled tactical fighting and covert maneuvers.

This form of fighting represented the very essence of waging war through attrition by seemingly disregarding the amount of humanity destroyed by it in battle while considering the bigger overall picture instead, with the eventual expected outcome of the war. So, in many cases, these high-casualty battles of attrition would eventually reveal which side could outlast the other in determining the war's ultimate outcome.

Given that the Civil War produced the most casualties of any war in American history, it seems clear this was primarily due to the preferred tactical application of Close-Order Line Formation type fighting.

However, U.S. armed forces have long since abandoned that archaic form of waging war. They now apply more of the 'Skirmishers' covert style of warfare, utilizing the more significant benefits of protective cover and camouflage overall, along with the element of surprise, to serve as a distinct advantage over antiquated battlefield tactics.

Fortunately for Will, having previously been wounded on the battle line, he remained upright and unscathed throughout his involvement with the rest of the war's campaigns. He carried on diligently with his assigned duties as a gunner, manning his post with his 10-lb Parrott cannon while still hoping and yearning to return to his wife Evie some sweet day.

In September of 1864, the 3rd Illinois Regiment found that a significant number of trained men from their ranks had been killed or seriously wounded in combat, including some of Will's close associates and friends from Camp Butler. As a result, while replacements were appointed to help fill the void and keep the battles active, these were largely untrained recruits who were slow to perform as diligently as their trained predecessors had. Because of this, orders soon arrived announcing the 3rd Illinois Regiment's subsequent withdrawal from the battle fronts and their reassignment to their former posts, as new units soon arrived to replace them. As a result, the remaining companies and detachments of the 3rd Illinois then packed up while assembling themselves in formation to march back northwesterly toward St. Louis. Upon their eventual arrival, Will's remaining artillery contingent was allowed to travel back to Camp Butler, where they were again garrisoned in reserve, to either serve the remainder of their time there or be reassigned to the war's theater again at some point, if needed.

Meanwhile, Henshaw's Battery had found themselves involved in further light skirmishes out within areas of southern Kentucky where Will's unit had left them to head back to St. Louis. The Battery unit was then assigned to an established garrison post in eastern Tennessee for the remainder of the war. As it turned out, Will and his unit's 10 lb. Parrott cannons were never called back to the field again, much to his relief. However, he was still required to participate in field maneuvers and range practice with the cannon every few months or so at Camp Butler to help train new incoming personnel.

But for all of the Illinois men who had served there, with earlier enlistments than Will, it was known to them that they would be required to remain past their expected discharge dates while still garrisoned until the eventual end of the war. In short, the Army could not spare them, as the country was still embroiled in turmoil. Because of this, Will had even more reason to hope for the speedy end of the war, as it was all beginning to gnaw on him after a little over four years of service. He just wanted to be finished with the repetitive business of continually drilling with the cannons at the range while constantly being told what to do and always having to follow orders, as if he was still a raw recruit.

It was then becoming more apparent that his time serving as a gunner on the battlelines had hardened him to the point where he was no longer the same person he was before leaving Camp Butler to fight against the Confederates. Quite notably, much of his former light-hearted character had gone missing. He was tired of it all and somewhat scarred in his mind from all he encountered and experienced as an 'executioner' of men. This was how he then began to think of himself, as he fully realized that his cannon projectiles, throughout the many actions he had participated in, had killed or maimed untold hundreds of men. For Will, while not having focused previously on that way of seeing things, it was an entirely unsettling thought to have in his head.

As the new year of 1865 arrived, news involving the war was beginning to reveal more positive signs that the nearly 4-year life-altering conflict had finally worn down much of the resolve of the Confederate forces. From various reports, it was becoming increasingly evident that their ranks were steadily diminishing through battlefield attrition, along with much of their spirit, as desertions were also at an all-time high. Social divisions within Southern society also played a role at the time, as the war's unsatisfactory developments for them had begun to negatively affect their citizens' morale. Given all of these factors, it was becoming more apparent that the Union's tactics were beginning to have more of an impact overall while wearing more heavily on their adversaries to tip the balance of the war in the Union's favor. Part of that effect could be attributed to the Union forces' notable tactic of focusing more on destroying specific infrastructure and disrupting supply lines that commonly delivered goods, materials, and ammunition to the Confederates in the field.

Sherman's Necktie

With that critical development in the war having provided further positive results for the Union and their forces,
it was largely due to locomotives in various southern states
having been seized or destroyed. At the same time, the rails
and ties for their tracks had been partly or entirely disman-
tled. In some cases, the steel rails were then heated red hot
over bonfires while purposely bent into unsalvageable loop-
ing, twisted shapes. The resulting forms of this effective but
insulting tactic were notoriously referred to as 'Sherman's
Neckties.' It was aptly named for Union General William
Tecumseh Sherman, whose scorched-Earth type destruction
of infrastructure, munition manufacturing sites, and township supply stores within the state of Georgia was well
known, if not feared and resented by the area's inhabitants.

"The way to success is strategically along the way of least expectation and tactically along the line of least resistance."
- Union General William Tecumseh Sherman

As a direct result of key tactical developments by General Ulysses Grant, it was on or about April 11th of 1865 when Will had suddenly learned the news that Confederate General Robert E. Lee, with his dwindling forces having been surrounded by the Union Army near Richmond, Virginia, had just surrendered to General Grant. The formal surrender had taken place at the Wilmer McLean family's stately home in the central Virginia township of Appomattox on April 9th, near the famed Appomattox Courthouse. To everyone's surprise, it suddenly and effectively brought the bitter war between the Northern and Southern states to its ultimate conclusion.

Generals Ulysses S. Grant and Robert E. Lee at Appomattox, VA

While tremendously difficult and deeply humiliating, it was a heart-wrenching decision for General Lee to arrive at. However, he felt he had no choice while realizing the futility of continuing in battle. To do so now would be at the expense of further blood being shed from his outnumbered fellow southern countrymen, while it made no sense to fight on only to have them wiped out. As the two Generals met in the parlor of the McLean House, Grant was notably gracious and respectful in accepting Lee's capitulation toward honorably bringing an end to four long years of bitter war that divided the nation and brought so much grief to so many.

While Lee signed the articles of unconditional surrender, Grant pointed out that he remembered they had briefly known each other long before this war, from back in 1848, when they were involved with U.S. forces in the Mexican War. However, in Lee's devastated and depressed state of mind, while in no mood for chit-chat, he said he didn't recall.

"I would rather die a thousand deaths than surrender."
- Confederate General Robert E. Lee

As part of the Articles of Surrender, the Union order stip-ulated that all Confederate prisoners and captured forces were to be released to find their way back home on their own. In addition, their rifles and minimal amounts of am-munition were to be returned to them so they might have the means to hunt for meat. Upon their release, some of these former Confederate soldiers were set free from places that were several hundred miles from their southern homes, which created a travel hardship for them. However, most received no relief, not even a horse to ride, while setting themselves out on the lonely roads toward their home states and towns. Those who had mostly recovered from severe wounds would be placed aboard trains to get them as close as possible to their destinations before having to be helped further by their fellow Southerners while walking or limp-ing the rest of the way.

General U. S. Grant.

"I felt like anything rather than rejoicing at the downfall of a foe who had fought so long and valiantly and had suffered so much for a cause, though that cause was, I believe, one of the worst for which a people ever fought, and one for which there was the least excuse."

- Union General Ulysses S. Grant

Interestingly, with the country's reflections on the war, it was found that Grant's aggressive strategy and crucial successes with the war effort had deservingly exalted him with the American people, as he ultimately became known as ' The man who saved the Union.'

In addition to the surrender at Appomattox, General Joseph Johnston surrendered his Confederate forces to General William Tecumseh Sherman eight days later at the Bennett farmhouse in Durham, North Carolina. When releasing the numerous disheartened soldiers, allowing them to trudge the various distances to their near or far-off localities, some would find nothing left of their homesteads, except for burned-out remnants of what was formerly a farmhouse, and the still-standing rock chimneys on their now mostly barren piece of land. When inquiring whether their family members were still alive or not, some were left with headstones to learn of their fate.

Corporal William Glover still had a little over 14 months remaining on his 5-year enlistment, by which he looked forward to his imminent discharge and re-entry into civilian life now that the war was effectively over. However, for the moment, Will and his Union Army comrades at Camp Butler had taken partial leave of themselves to properly celebrate this joyous occasion, saloon style.

On the evening of April 11th, President Lincoln appeared on the second-story balcony of the north portico of the White House to address a crowd that had gathered there on the lawn, with a brief speech in response to the news of Lee's surrender and the North's great victory. In part, he said, "We meet this evening, not in sorrow, but in gladness of heart. The evacuation of Petersburg and Richmond and the surrender of the principal insurgent army give hope of a righteous and speedy peace, for a day of national thanksgiving."

Then suddenly, just six days after the Confederates' surrender had marked the war's end, shocking news arrived at Camp Butler announcing President Abraham Lincoln's reported assassination at Ford's Theater in Washington. The shooting occurred during the evening hours of April 14th, with his subsequent death coming on the following day.

The news brought a deep sadness and numbing silence to Will and his comrades at the Camp, along with virtually hundreds of thousands of Americans in many other parts of the country. These home-grown soldiers of Illinois at Camp Butler were shaken to the core by the news, as they had observed the career of their President from his former days when serving in Congress. Sadly, they had lost their Commander-in-Chief, who had inspired them to protect the Constitution and preserve the Union. In effect, he led them all to victory over the Confederates while also signing what became a historic 'Emancipation Proclamation' executive order in early 1863 to formally announce or propose the end of slavery within the United States.

For those who had supported the Union's cause in the war, he was an enormously popular figure in Washington whose political and public resolve had moved many of his supporters in such a way as to re-think some previously held political and personal ideals. His inspiring speeches had often left his audiences awe-struck by the meaningful wordage he preferred, which tended to give the people of the United States a deeper and more reflective understanding of life and humanity while helping to change the overall narrative involving the lives and mindsets of all Americans.

He was a complex yet simple man who landed in the right place at a time when his understanding of wisdom and fatherly direction were in dire need toward guiding the American people through an extremely trying evolutionary period of cultural and political upevil. However, his personal evolution also played a significant role in this, given that some of his political and religious positions had changed from before his station in the White House. Having been influenced by the nation's war with the breakaway states and by a few advisors within his inner circle, the President had effectively found the most direct way forward in addressing the critical issues set before him. As to the issue of slavery, it is believed that his close association with former slave Frederick Douglass had helped to turn the tide with him in forcing the problem to become more recognized as the central issue in the war. Even the South had acknowledged, while many hated him all the while, what an effective and feared leader he was. But with his passing, it was widely recognized by all that even though he was not universally known as an abolitionist, he had effectively championed the cause for the abolition of slavery in America.

Soon after his death, his embalmed body was placed in a casket for a short period of viewing in Washington. Afterward, it was put into a railcar on a funeral train that toured various other eastern cities as it eventually rolled westward toward Chicago and ultimately to Springfield, Illinois, where the body was interred. In New York, over 100,000 people turned out to view his body and pay respects to their fallen President. All along the train route west from there, people by the hundreds and thousands came out from each of their hamlets and townships to gather in crowds along the tracks, offering their final farewell to a man most of them had never met, although they felt they knew him well. With nary a dry eye among them, as a mournful expression of their "last full measure of devotion," it became an onward-moving cross-country scene reflecting the nation's deep feelings of unexpected loss.

However, the war between the states was over now, and the Union forces of the United States had won. But in its aftermath, the long-sought victory felt bittersweet for the country, leaving its citizens dumbstruck by the subsequent sudden loss of their revered leader in Washington.

While the war had effectively been settled for both opposing combatants with Lee's surrender on April 9th, the news hadn't promptly reached all areas of the country. Reports of the war's end had notoriously traveled slowly in some far corners of the south, along with the western states and territories. Even when the official news had reached a few of these distant areas, deniers refused to believe what was reported, thinking it to be propaganda. So, while remaining steadfast and persistent in the fighting, the battle for Columbus, Georgia, was fought on the same day Lincoln died, even though Lee's surrender had occurred a week earlier. With a few other pocket skirmishes taking place within other southern states, the last recorded Civil War battle occurred on May 12th and 13th near Brownsville, Texas, known as the Battle of Palmito Ranch. Ironically, the Confederates won that particular battle decisively, leaving them entirely unaware that their war had already been lost.

But, even as all of this came to pass, the war had still not been brought to its official conclusion, as the long delay in declaring its official termination was now simply a means to an end. It came in the form of a detailed administrative process regarding the terms and conditions of surrender for each southern state, as there was a legal process involved with settling things formally after the fighting had ceased. Mostly, it involved each of the former Confederate states having to agree to their reunification with the United States and its constitution before the war could officially come to its ultimate conclusion. But finally, on November 20th of 1866, President Andrew Johnson announced it, after 588 days had passed since the Confederates' surrender at Appomattox. However, for the Union soldiers whose discharges were either imminent or past due, their leave of service was granted to them well ahead of that date.

With the war's end, it would now bring about a new beginning for the country, although in its aftermath, deep scars had been left upon the landscape and in people's minds, which needed much time to heal, for the most part. In reviewing the damage, the losses from both sides were found to be quite staggering. Many hundreds of thousands of men, along with a certain amount of women and children, had been killed or seriously wounded over the eventful course of the war's four-year struggle. Additionally, a great deal of infrastructure had been destroyed or damaged in both the northern and southern regions of the country, where cannon fire had ravaged many homes and businesses into crumbling piles of rubble, ash, and twisted steel. At the crux of this monumental struggle was the driving notion of either maintaining and restoring the Union's constitutional government throughout the entire land or allowing for two different countries to exist within their respective regions of the North American continent.

Before the war, the South had hoped the Confederacy would become a new and separate system of government for the breakaway States. They wanted to independently determine their affairs outside of what they perceived as the oppressive overlord influence of the U.S. Congress and its representative northern unionists, who stood in direct opposition to the practice of keeping slaves. In that regard, the southern states, under the new leadership of the Confederacy, had fully intended to maintain their cherished practice of chattel and plantation slavery while keeping it intact and legally protected through articles within their own newly established Constitution.

In declaring war against the United States, while the southern states had previously represented an integral part of the nation as a whole, they had, in effect, committed a collective seditious act of treason. Quite intentionally, it was the Confederacy's aggressive bombardment of South Carolina's Union-controlled Fort Sumpter on April 14, 1861, that brought about the beginning of the war. Prior to that, the U.S. government in Washington had been focused on fervently holding the entire country together rather than considering any punitive actions for abandoning the Union. Regardless, the Confederates would have no more to do with Washington and its perceived condescending ways.

However, despite the Confederacy's resentful aspirations and intentions, the Union's ultimate military victory four years later, in April of 1865, effectively sealed their fate in disavowing and denying the South's plan to become their own sovereign nation.

As it was, the war had been an open clash of cultures between the two sides, with the abolition of slavery becoming more of the central issue in the North, especially as it pertained to the Federal government in Washington. At the same time, the South had argued that their desire to retain the practice of slavery had become a vital aspect in maintaining and improving their economy, as they did not have much in the way of manufacturing to feed their region's commerce as the Northern states had. Essentially, slavery had become an ingrained part of their storied southern culture, having originated in the deep south through English slave lords arriving from the eastern Caribbean Island of Barbados, as it evolved and developed from earlier colonial times. But with their alleged charge that Washington was interfering with what they termed as 'State's Rights,' those supposed states' rights had centrally included what they felt was their southern culture's sovereign right to keep slaves.

Believing this to be as natural as anything could be, this ingrained aspect of human degradation existing within the radically controlling culture of the South, where black men and women were mistreated by whites and forced into hard labor to bring profitable gains to their holders, it was neither viewed nor perceived by slave owners as anything negative. However, for all who could see it plainly, it was. But even after the war had ended and slaves gained their freedom, there was no remorse...there were no apologies, as the white slave owners had always felt highly superior to the slaves, often regarding them as less than human, while using and manipulating them however they wished, in ways that would make their farm or plantation operations highly profitable.

The stark reality here lies in the fact that these enslaved servants that were purchased on the open market were widely recognized as legalized property to their owners, while the human part of the equation was rarely considered. For the most part, many of these Southerners instead saw them as working animals rather than fellow human beings. Some others were slightly more compassionate but still unrelenting in their ownership positions. Furthermore, while plantation and other business owners kept enslaved people to provide the necessary free labor that made for profitability, the established cultural society within the southern states had fully endorsed and supported this inhumane practice as an inherent part of their highly revered Southern white culture.

To further add to this and leave little doubt as to the South's radically unhinged mindset, Confederate vice-president Alexander Stephens declared in 1861 that **"the cornerstone of the new government rested upon the great truth that the negro is not equal to the white man, that slavery – subordination to the superior race – is his natural and normal condition."**

For most Northerners, understanding the South's position on this was next to impossible, as they could see from a conscienable and humane viewpoint that it made no sense whatsoever. Conveyed quite clearly, the Southern Confederacy's self-righteous attitude toward slavery had reflected transparently on their white supremacist mentality. Notably, the eventual end of the war had only stopped the fighting between the North and South, while even the victorious U.S. government did not have the power to change the cultural attitude of the former Confederates' white supremacist population. That ingrained radical mindset, cultivated over time from the former British colonial Cavalier Royalists would continue to live on as a never-ending cultural curse, serving as an unfortunate but fitting racial malediction for the South.

To that effect, their evolving heritage of abuse and ill regard for the negro race, which had irreverently served their own selfish interests, had effectively placed an indelible black mark upon its society after the war. For many years, it left them bereft, with only their own dark past to serve as a lasting legacy.

However, to further solidify the union's resolve with this matter, when the fighting finally concluded, the U.S. Congress passed the 13th Amendment to the Constitution in December of 1865, after most existing states had ratified it. This amendment ensured that no man, woman, or child shall be brought into forced labor or servitude for any reason or purpose within the influential and geographic confines of the United States. The only exception with this had applied to convicted prisoners whose sentences for working at hard labor had fallen under the very same definition of forced servitude.

Although not entirely related, it was found that many dominant tribes of American Indians had also held enslaved people from rival tribesmen being captured in territorial wars. It was a common traditional practice that went back hundreds or even thousands of years. However, the U.S. Congress had no jurisdiction nor even the desire to involve the country with whatever the Indians might be doing, so long as it didn't affect the white settlers traveling westward. Although, in time, the U.S. government outlawed slavery of all forms and peoples in all of the established states and U.S. territories. But, it seems relatively easy to see, when looking at the Civil War and the Indian Wars, that there were

many remarkably similar parallels between the two tragically his-
toric American conflicts.

With the Confederates' bitter defeat brought to bear after General Lee's surrender at Appomattox, it eventually opened the door for unity to return to the country. Despite the news of President Lincoln's subsequent assassination at the hands of Ford Theater actor and Confederate sympathizer John Wilkes Booth, the formerly untenable impasse on the disputed issue of slavery and state's rights in America had finally been put to rest, once and for all. However, regardless of whichever point of contention may have been observed on slavery, the war's toll had been a costly one for both sides of the conflict, to say the least. All told, in the eventual aftermath, close to 750,000 deaths had occurred over the 4-year course of the war. It was also found that 1.5 million casualties had comprised the overall total of both dead and wounded for both sides in this mind-numbing struggle between the states, to serve quite notably as America's deadliest war on record.

Suddenly, Evie's voice interrupted Will's deeply involved thoughts, having been fully absorbed in them while driving the wagon along this bumpy trail and following through the low clouds of kicked-up dust from the lengthy train of wagons just ahead. She requested they stop so she and Maggie could take a moment to relieve and refresh themselves before moving on. So, he pulled the wagon from their position near the end of the train to grant Evie and Maggie a few moments to regather themselves. The brief stoppage also gave Will pause to draw water from their barrel to quench his thirst and provide some liquid refreshment for their mules before rejoining the trail and catching up with the other wagons.

As they rolled on to rejoin the train, now repositioned at the dustier rear end of it, Evie hopped back up into the jockey box to sit beside her husband on the driver's bench while leaving Maggie in the bed of the wagon to sing her made-up songs and play with her rag doll, Polly. To avoid having to endure the choking dust from the other wagons, Will slowed the mule team's pace to provide further space behind the train, as he had all kinds of room in the rear to create some separation from the others while still keeping them in sight. Effectively positioned at the back of the train, one of the mounted employees had always ridden 'drag' to watch over the rear section and keep it moving. If a wagon within his sight had a wheel problem that would stop the schooner in its tracks, he would stay with that wagon to watch over them while repairs were made. Essentially, it was his job to do whatever he could to get them going again, even to the point of lending a hand physically while continuing to watch for potential signs of trouble.

When traversing some of these particularly bleak areas of prairie land, the scenery tended to be mostly void of anything of interest to look at or appreciate, with even the virtual absence of trees and wildflowers noted in various stretches. So, Evie would sometimes drift off to sleep to relieve her boredom while sitting up front, as she would use her husband's lap as a pillow and drift off to dreamland for a while. But as the wagon eventually hit a bump on the trail, it jolted her awake and caused her to retreat into the wagon bed to rest upon her bunk.

When Maggie would sometimes join her father up on the driver's bench, she would occasionally tell him strange stories that she made up in her head, with Will occasionally looking at her in askance. But when moving through the high prairie country, she would take great delight when seeing a good number of prairie dogs along the way, which neither she nor her father had ever seen before, nor had they even known exactly what they were. She would laugh hysterically while thoroughly captivated by how cute they all were with their quick-moving antics. They would curiously stand up near their communal-type mounds and burrows and watch intently as many of them scurried about, seeming equally amused, as the train of wagons slowly passed their terrestrial prairie-land village.

"Let's go back, Papa. I want to see them again", Maggie pleaded. But her request fell on deaf ears as they continued their westward movement within the train of wagons.

These curious little animals, having looked somewhat like certain varieties of small dogs, were not even related to canines. They were herbivorous short-tailed ground squirrels that burrowed into the Earth to establish their subterranean spacious tunnels, where they would nest and store some of the grasses, seeds, fruits, and insects they managed to gather to serve their mainly vegetarian diet.

While on the move during the morning hours, Evie would occasionally take turns with Will to get them some needed exercise by dropping down from the rear of the wagon to walk beside it for about an hour or so, in keeping with what the wagon master had suggested to everyone at the start of the trip. For a bit of the time, Maggie had even been helped down to walk beside her mother or father, as they all made it a common practice to get in some necessary footwork while traveling with the wagon train.

After passing Independence Rock and climbing the gradually sloping 100-mile trek to cross the Great Divide along the Sweetwater River, Fort Bridger was the next stopping-off point for the wagon train. The fort was established by legendary former trapper and explorer Jim Bridger, who had run the trading post there in earlier years. It served as an Army Fort and trading post where immigrants could replenish some basic supplies at this 'halfway point' in their journeys to Oregon and California.

The Fort had been rebuilt after Mormon militia burned it to the ground during the early 1850's insurrection when opposing and trying to block U.S. troops from descending South Pass to enter Salt Lake City and install the newly appointed U.S. Governor of the territory, in which to remove the existing Mormon Governor, Brigham Young.

Evie was still well stocked with her general supply of dry goods but curiously entered the trading post anyway, with Maggie in tow. Finding salted Elk meat available, she promptly purchased three pounds of it, to cook in her Dutch oven in the coming days.

Directionally, it was near that point where the established southern route veered off from the main wagon trail at South Pass, Wyoming, splitting from the northwesterly path that led to the Oregon country. This was the designated trail for all who were headed down to Salt Lake City or beyond to the Sacramento Valley and the gold fields in northern California. For the Glovers, the new route would take them down through Echo Canyon, into the Salt Lake basin, and ultimately down to Provo.

This southwesterly trail was also more infamously noted a few decades prior as the 'Hastings Cutoff,' an unfamiliar route the Donner-Reed party had taken in 1846 before eventually arriving late in the season to meet their grim, ill-fated misfortune at Donner Lake, near Truckee, California. The trail had been discovered and partly developed earlier by a young man named Lansford Hastings, who had recommended it to Bridger. In turn, he erroneously recommended it to travelers hoping to take a shorter route to California while feeding them misinformation that it was a smooth and relatively easy trail, with only 40 miles further to travel from the Salt Lake basin, across to the Humbolt River in the Nevada desert. But, in reality, it was not an easier route at all, as the Donner Party had to move heavy brush and downed trees to make their way along it. Then, after arriving at Salt Lake and moving through the Nevada desert, they found the distance to the Humbolt River was 80 miles instead of 40. The unfortunate aspect regarding this route, recommended by Jim Bridger, proved that if they had taken a different route, they would have made it through the Sierras in time before the major snowfall event that forced them to hunker down at a forested lake, hauntingly named for them. The advice given had caused them to miss their window of opportunity to cross the Sierra Nevada mountains in eastern California. As a result, it created an untimely and tragic situation for the party, having become stranded while facing an enormous, impassable snowpack, where, eventually, their food ran out, and some degree of cannibalism was involved. But the tragedy later served to remind future travelers to leave early enough in the season before the weather might change in the Sierras.

During the American Civil War, Mr. Hastings served as a Major in the Confederate Army. After the war and his roamings in the west, he moved out of the country to start a new colony of former Confederate immigrants in Brazil, where he later died. However, for all who traveled over the immigrant trail named for him, most had found it more lengthy, with much more difficult terrain to traverse than what they were told.

Faithfully traveling with the California-Oregon bound wagon train for almost nine weeks, the Glovers departed from it at South Pass. From there, they would direct their travel along this improved Hastings Cutoff trail down to the Salt Lake Basin, where they would then be well within the territory of Utah and not far from their ultimate destination. So, after bidding farewell and good luck to their friends, Lyman and Rhonda Morrisey, who were headed up to the Oregon country, they joined another train. This new group was comprised of people from the original train alternately heading to Utah, Nevada, and California, traveling along this southwest detour from the main trail as part of their pre-planned route.

South Pass, Wyoming

Residing farther southwest of South Pass, within the territory of Utah, the northern Shoshone tribes and their related offshoots were the remaining members of a larger group of tribal warriors that U.S. Army Reserve soldiers had nearly wiped out only a few years earlier. The soldiers were temporarily assigned to the territory from their post in California during the infamous Bear River Massacre in 1863. Tucked back within their high prairie and mountainous treaty-protected enclaves, the remaining contingent of these Shoshone, Ute, and other related tribal members were well situated within their designated place of sanctuary. It was where white intruding settlers and the Army tended not to tread.

Interestingly, it was nearly 70 years earlier when Lewis and Clark and their female Shoshone guide, Sacajawea, had traversed through the Bitterroot mountain range in western Montana. They encountered a band of the Shoshones for the first time, as they were given navigational advice while trading with them before traveling farther west.

While no longer traveling with a military escort, the smaller party of about 30 wagons heading down toward the

Salt Lake basin by way of South Pass and Echo Canyon, had then been left to keep a more vigilant watch over themselves as they went.

Part Four

Provo

Upon reaching the Salt Lake basin, the Glovers waved while bidding farewell to the California-bound wagon train before veering directly south along a commonly traveled dusty main road. This was more prominently known then as the Old Mormon Road, where they encountered two-way traffic with freight and hay wagons, stagecoaches, and horseback riders traveling in both directions.

Today's version of the Old Mormon Road is in the form of Interstate Highway 15, which runs from the U.S.-Canadian border at Sweetgrass, Montana, south through Salt Lake City, and with some deviation, down through Provo and other more southerly areas of the state. Directing its route more southwesterly from there, it leads over to the western border at St George, Utah, before heading out through Las Vegas, Nevada, and across the Mojave Desert, to ultimately enter southern California, where it eventually terminates in San Diego. The southern portion of the course had closely followed the old Santa Fe Trail, established in the earlier 1800s by Spanish explorers. The only other deviation from the previous version of the trail revealed that it originally terminated in Los Angeles instead of San Diego. After 1848, the western parts of the trail were used by wagon trains seeking Winter access between Utah and California when other trails to the north were closed by snow. When taking this particular route, it was found that the Mojave Desert was only safe to travel through in the Fall and Winter when water was more accessible, as there was generally little or no water to be found in the desert during the dry Summer months. This path was also much easier to traverse, as there were no mountain passes to scale.

For the first time in their long journey, the Glovers suddenly realized they were completely alone, unguided, and now traveling as a single wagon along this busy earthen roadway south of Salt Lake City. Their new trajectory represented more territory largely unknown to them, although it was more pleasing to the eye than other areas they had recently traveled through. Making their way along this southbound stretch of road, they remained studiously watchful in this interesting part of the territory while still focused on their resolve to reach their ultimate destination, as they looked forward to eventually reuniting with Lucy and Ben.

Rolling through the changing countryside, they took in new sights and passed through small villages and townships where farmland was being established, seeing early crop growth developing all around them. To their delight, it appeared that civilization was beginning to come back into view. After seeing so much of the vast, uninviting prairie country from their journey west that was entirely void of people and development for the most part, it was a welcome sign of relief to see this new country of Utah. Rolling along while taking in the sights around them, they realized they had reached a more promising place where the changing landscape was actively growing and blooming as they progressively moved closer to their ultimate destination.

This old Mormon Road was soon found to be a much smoother surface to ride over than the hilly and somewhat rocky prairie country they left behind. With the wagon's easy movement on the route's surface, Evie occasionally took over the mule team's reins, allowing Will to relax while giving her time to get more acclimated with steering and controlling the team.

At stream crossings, where they occasionally needed to refill their water barrel, Will regularly wandered upstream on foot to inspect the waterway and ensure that nothing was visually contaminating it. On this occasion, he noticed a partially decomposed deer carcass lying fully within the stream. After carefully dragging it to the shore, he returned to the wagon and immediately told Evie not to drink the water there while the mules had already taken their fill. So, he decided to turn the wagon around and backtrack upstream to where he could fill his barrel using one of Evie's pots, just above where he saw the deer in the water. He had learned well from the original wagon master, having paid full attention to his words about watching the waterways to ensure he wouldn't draw up contaminates that could harm his family.

As they approached their destination, they would again stop during the mid-afternoon to water the mules at a stream crossing while unhitching them from the wagon and hobbling their front feet. When making their overnight camp just off the road, where they had a certain amount of tree cover and sufficient grass for the animals to feed on, they found the area quite pleasant compared to the largely uninteresting prairie country. With sparse bunchgrass and mostly treeless open landscape that afforded unenchanting views ahead for nearly as far as the eye could see, the prairie country had left a rather dull impression upon them. The few trees they encountered on the prairie were generally found rooted alongside slow-moving streams and in gulches where minimal water run-off from above would find its gravitational path, offering saplings and poorly grown trees their limited sustenance for survival. However, this new territory they were now traversing was filled with green grass and healthy trees in many areas.

At their camp placement, Will took a walk downstream and located a few deep water holes that would be perfect for bathing, as the entire family was beginning to wreak of accumulated body odor from not bathing over quite a long stretch. So, he returned and reported his finding to Evie, whereby she grabbed a bucket, a bar of soap, and a few towels she had previously sewn together using numerous old flour sacks. While also grabbing Maggie by the hand, they went off to one of the noted downstream spots while later returning to give Will his chance to clean up before dark. Maggie initially protested, saying the water was too cold, although, despite the discomfort, everyone came away a lot cleaner that day.

In the morning, when Evie and Maggie took their dirty cook pots to the stream to wash them out, Will was suddenly alerted to screams. He immediately took sight of a sizeable Grizzly Bear racing through the shallow water, furiously chasing after his wife and daughter. Without hesitating, he grabbed his rifle from the wagon's jockey box and ran down to where he came between Maggie and the bear while hollering to Maggie to "get back to the wagon!" At that point, his actions had stopped the bear in its tracks, as it immediately raised itself onto its hindquarters to appear larger than life before him. That allowed Will to raise his rifle and get off a shot at the aggressive animal, whereby he was sure he hit it in the neck. But it appeared to only enrage the bear further, as it dropped back down onto all fours and quickly charged at Will. He then recalled that he only had one round in the rifle, as the remaining ammo was back within the wagon's jockey box. So, his senses immediately told him to drop his firearm and run. As he ran about 40 yards with the bear in hot pursuit, he looked back to see that it was tiring while breathing hard, with blood steadily draining from its mouth and nostrils. Still moving in advance of the bear, he turned again and noticed the animal had stopped altogether before slowly keeling over onto one side to lie still and silent. With that, there was a long, watchful pause, as Will wasn't sure if the animal was dead or not. But he had never heard of a bear playing dead like possums often do. He then scampered laterally back over to where the wagon was while keeping one eye on the bear and checking with Evie and Maggie to make sure they were alright, which they were. Then he went back over to where the bear had dropped and confirmed that he was indeed dead before returning to the wagon to relate the news. He surmised that he had gotten off a lucky shot, as it was generally rare to bring down a Grizzly with one bullet, although he knew the .44 Spencer rifle packed a powerful punch.

At that point, he got down on both knees and hugged Evie and Maggie for over a minute as the three of them cried together from the frightening ordeal, while he reassured them the bear would no longer be a threat.

After packing up and leaving that campsite, they rolled through more areas of grassy, tree-lined countryside as they moved ever closer to the town of Provo. All three had very little to say that day following the scary, traumatizing incident. However, as they made camp again that night, it still raised Will's concerns enough to where he felt compelled to sleep with his rifle.

When nearly arriving in Provo, Will calculated that it took them an additional four weeks to get from Fort Bridger through South Pass and down to the Salt Lake basin, including the further stretch on the old Mormon Road running down to Provo. This meant that the trip from St. Joseph, Missouri, had taken them just short of 11 weeks to complete as they rolled into Provo to be greeted by Ben Lockhardt at his blacksmith shop on June 20th. Lucy had also exited her fabric shop when hearing Ben hollering for her to "come and see who's here! "

Remarkably, within days of their arrival in the Summer of 1867, the family still managed to purchase a simple two-room log house in northern Provo with sufficient funds that Evie had received from her parents in Carbondale. As Lucy stayed behind in town to look after Maggie, Ben drove Will and Evie up to an area north of there in his buggy to look at a couple of available cabins in the vicinity, and they immediately decided to buy one of them. So, they promptly returned to town and went to the H. W. Lawrence mercantile store, where papers from the cabin's owner were transferred over to William and Evelyn Glover, as payment was made in full in the form of a sizeable bank draft from Evie's father, Charles Proctor.

From that transaction, Will and Evie received a credit for the remaining amount on the draft, which would be held 'on account' to pay for future purchased goods at that store. But that little detail was entirely acceptable to them since it was a market they would be shopping at anyway. This seemingly unusual form of transaction came about because there weren't any institutional banks at that early date in Provo, where paper currency and coinage, along with gold and silver, were otherwise exchanged or deposited. The local merchants and tradespeople at that time had alternately developed their own workable trade and barter system in the absence of local or regional banks, with the exchange of money, appraised jewelry, and certain goods and services being provided as payment for merchandise, in most cases. The only banks in the territory at that time were located in Salt Lake City.

In this case, the mercantile store owner, H. W. Lawrence, had served as a broker to sell a two-room log cabin up in the Little Rock Canyon area of north Provo, where not a penny of cash had been involved. The Mercantile store owner would mail the draft to a bank in Salt Lake City, where the former owner of the cabin had been known to do his banking after moving to that area. The land owner, in turn, sent cash payment back to the mercantile store in the form of the balance from the sale, which would be noted and held on account for the Glovers, to be drawn from as needed.

Provo East Co-op, circa 1890

In 1868, H.W. Lawrence sold his mercantile store and property to another enterprising group, which expanded the operation and changed the name to East Co-op, short for Provo East Cooperative Mercantile Institution. However, all accounts on record were assumed and honored in continuance by the new owners.

So, with a land deed now soon to be in hand and things having been settled as to where they would live, things were beginning to look up for the trio of former mid-westerners. After thanking Lucy & Ben for their hospitality in town for a few days, Will, Evie, and their young daughter pointed their mule team and wagon directly north, traveling over roughly 3 miles to settle into their newly purchased two-room log cabin. As they began to acclimate to their new placement, they slept the first several nights on the floor, upon their thin mattresses from the covered wagon. Immediately, they set about to clean and refurbish the cabin, getting more of a feel for their new surroundings while also having to comport with the newly adopted western sort-of basic backwoods country culture that came with it.

The sturdily built log cabin was located along an old

dusty wagon road north of town within the noted area of Little Rock Canyon. It was fairly remote from the town center of Provo, although still situated within its upper northeastern boundary. Being entirely unaware that the elevation in the Little Rock Canyon area was 6,542 feet above sea level, they at least knew that they were up on higher ground there, where the weather was generally a bit cooler than the surrounding elevations. The area featured a good mix of cottonwood trees, small pines, and some small oak to dot the otherwise rocky landscape of the Little Rock Canyon. The noted trees gave the area a fair measure of shade to shadow and compliment the sparse deposits of scrub grass and wildflowers growing thereabouts. But Evie had taken immediate notice of a particular grassy wildflower plant that stood out and framed much of the surrounding rocky areas, featuring cup-like or trumpeted lavender blooms along with protruding stamens, which she had never seen the likes of before.

As a hearty plant of upwards to two or three feet in height, they appeared to be quite prolific, growing naturally thereabouts in the area, with vibrant flowing sprays spread out on a broad display throughout much of the surrounding area. The enchanting, all-encompassing floral exhibit brought a colorful delight to one's eye when passing through the sparsely populated area. For the local citizens who knew about them, they commonly referred to this variety of wildflowers as 'Beard Tongues' while also pointing out that they come and go with the season, as their blooms only last for six or seven weeks during a yearly cycle, with the increased Summer heat and lack of rain often tending to burn them off too soon. During years when rain may provide them with more sustaining moisture during the

Summer months, their colorful blooms tend to hold up longer, lasting even into the Fall season.

Beardtongue Penstemon

This vibrantly colorful wildflower, known in floriculture as 'Littlecup Beardtongue Penstemon,' is noted as an attractive and unique plant species as a regional variation of the common Penstemon genus. Interestingly, this particular lavender version is only found exclusively in the southeastern areas of Utah, nearer to the range of mountains called Wasatch.

With the Provo River running southward through the area, just to the west of them, and with a backdrop of the impressive Wasatch range prominently standing out to their immediate east, it appeared to be a rather scenic and tranquil area in which to take up a life on the upper northeast side of Provo.

The little pitched-roof log cabin had one small window afforded for each of its rooms, with a standing potbelly stove situated in the main room that served as a living area on one side and an established open kitchen area located at the rear of the room, with a back door leading out to the loosely defined rear yard of the cabin. The other room, which was to serve as a bedroom, was framed off and had a doorway, although without a door. But that was a minor detail that Will would soon remedy. However, it was spacious enough as it was, affording enough room for all three of them for the time being.

In addition to the cabin, there was also a tiny log-constructed barn on the property as well, which could be used to store materials, grain, and hay while even providing a source of shelter in harsh conditions for a few animals like the mule team they still had from their trip west. Plus, the little barn was just the place to store the essential tools that Will brought with him from Carbondale.

When it came to producing furniture for the empty cabin, Will had first constructed a marriage bed for the two of them while already having purchased a suitable mattress in town to determine the size of the bed's frame. After buying an appropriately sized mattress for Maggie, he also built a smaller, single-size bed frame, as they all temporarily occupied the one designated bedroom in the cabin during their quiet hours of pleasant slumber. The former carpenter and animal farmer then constructed a suitable kitchen table with four smartly built chairs from oakwood found at the front of the property. The table top was constructed utilizing several sawn oak boards joined with dowels and coated with linseed oil. The sturdy hand-made furniture filled the kitchen/living room area where they would take their meals, giving the place a more homey feel. When constructing the fourth chair for the kitchen table, Evie had asked Will, in jest, if he was overly optimistic, given the current size of their family.

At the same time, Evie had worked on making some

curtains for the two relatively small windows in the living room and bedroom. Will then moved ahead with his furniture crafting to build a few highback armchairs for the cabin's living area while asking Lucy when she visited if she might sew together some comfy cushions for them.

Having only two small windows in the cabin made for a rather dark interior. However, Evie brought a good supply of candles from Carbondale to help light up the place. But when seeing that, Will took note that he would, at some point, have to cut out larger window openings in the cabin's thick horizontal logs when obtaining more suitable replacement windows. He would have to try to find them in Salt Lake City or order them through the mercantile store where he had an open charge account.

The cabin also had a workable kitchen sink outfitted with a drain line that dropped down through a hole in the wood floor, where their used-up grey water drained off naturally into a ditch beneath the structure, directing the flow as it ran under the log foundation. Evie had marveled that she could more easily wash the family's clothes in that sink, using a washboard and scrub brush. It allowed her to do it all inside the cabin instead of outside before hanging items on the clothesline out back to dry.

However, clear, drinkable water had to be fetched from the nearby river, about 2 miles west of the cabin, which required using the wagon. For that, they would have to make successive trips back and forth to fill up their water barrels for general use, as the Provo River had good, clean-flowing water, well suited for drinking or any other purpose. In time, though, Will would have to dig a well, whereby bucketfuls of water could be more reasonably accessed closer to the cabin, to remedy the inconvenience they were left with when buying the place. However, to help more immediately with the situation, Will stripped down their covered wagon while removing the outer canvas and steel hoops, adding sideboards to serve the family's interests more as a cargo carrier for hauling. This new configuration helped to better facilitate the water fetching problem. He would load several empty barrels onto it when making his river runs and refill them using a metal bucket and a length of rope. This practice would continue until a suitable well could be dug out and established.

But, the central celebrated item and main feature within the kitchen area of their newly purchased log home was a cast iron wood-fired cooktop stove with an oven, which had a stovepipe that went up and out through the upper wall behind it. It was all still in great shape for what it was, considering the numerous years that the previous owners had fired it for their daily cooking needs. But for Evie, it was one of the main reasons for settling there when choosing this rough-hewn, rustic old cabin on the northern outskirts of town. When seeing it, she gleefully envisioned some of the various delicious culinary concoctions that her mother had often created during her childhood, which could be reproduced with this combination of stove and oven. But it struck

Evie when first seeing it how closely it resembled her family's kitchen centerpiece from when she and Lucy had grown up in Carbondale.

In keeping both stoves active during the Winter months for each of their intended purposes, Will had been kept busy every Summer with the necessary task of cutting trees down in the nearby forest and dragging the logs back with the use of one of his mules, to where he could then saw them into burnable lengths and split them accordingly. He created numerous stacks of pine and cedar firewood, which he lined the outside of the cabin with, where it could adequately weather or 'season' for a couple of months before becoming burnable in their cast iron stoves. While both were from conifer trees, Cedar was much preferred if he could find it, as it was found to be denser wood than Pine, burning hotter and longer while putting out more heat for those colder nights in the more elevated area of Little Rock Canyon.

With much of that firewood dedicated to heating the cabin and firing the stove, Will had also procured a large wooden washtub from town for occasional bathing. It appeared as half of a more substantial oaken barrel, considerably larger than common wine or whiskey barrels, as it was designed to hold and age a significant volume of liquid spirits in its original form. The hardware store had acquired it as a surplus item from a cooperage in Salt Lake City before sawing it in half. He also purchased a bung for it, whereby he had to drill a hole at the base of it with his brace and bit, which could properly fit the stopper to hold the filled tub and alternately drain it. He also built a wooden seat inside the barrel, mounting it with two wooden supports to keep it stable. At the time, it was just the thing to fit one's body into comfortably, toward getting it clean and restored to its natural and more presentable state.

Upon seeing it, Evie loved it, as it allowed her to wash with hot water boiled right from the stove, only a couple of steps away. Taking special delight, she enjoyed not only bathing in it but also taking a relaxing soak in the soothingly warmer water. However, in addition to filling it with buckets of cool water, it took numerous potfuls of hot water to get to the temperature level she preferred before stepping into it. For this, it was Will's task to keep the stove fired up and stoked during the tub-filling process, with three large pots of water set to a near boil while rotating, as all of the burn plates were being used. He would keep the hot water coming with Evie nearly submerged in the tub. Maggie was next in line, and then Will, as they all shared the tub water while it remained hot enough. It was then left to Will and Evie the following morning to slowly push the tub to the open doorway after bailing some of the water with a bucket, where he could then pull the bung and drain it to the outside. This was done every month or so, and it tended to eat up more firewood than they typically used. However, it was a luxury item that helped to keep them clean, fresh, and satisfied, for the most part, as they conveniently stored the large bath barrel in the front corner of the room.

As he got more acclimated to the area, Will felt they needed a saddlehorse to serve them better than always riding a mule into town. So he acquired 'Sunshine,' along with a saddle and bridle, for a reasonable price from the owner of the livery stable, who had reluctantly received the 3-year-old dark gray mare as payment for stabling her and four other horses that were left homeless. Their owner's barn had burned down during the previous Fall season, leaving him without proper overhead cover to protect the horses from the harsh Winter months, while intending to erect a new one in the Spring.

The Glover's 3-year-old daughter Maggie, born Mary Margaret Glover, had her mother's curly locks, although somewhat darker in color. She was partly named for Will's late mother, Margaret, whom he had lost while away in the Army, and Evie's mother, Mary Proctor. Maggie was well noted as being fun-loving, as she often jokingly toyed with her father while also constantly asking him that one question that all little children repeatedly ask concerning the world around them, as three years of age is most likely the prime time for a child to continually ask, "Why?" But for both Will and Evie, it was a joy having her around to teach things to and to share their loving relationship with while often wondering and marveling at some of the unusually entertaining comments and observations shared with them, as she would unabashedly say whatever she thought, short of being corrected on occasion.

Given that there was no mail delivery service available for the sparsely populated area of Little Rock Canyon, residents would generally have to drop off and pick up their mail in town a few times every week at the Overland Stage line's express office. In 1860, the heralded Pony Express had come onto the scene to carry the mail by speedy horses over stretches of 15 miles or so before switching to a fresh mount for the next leg of the route, in which to deliver the mail across the far reaches of the country in a speedier manner. But, since their bottom line had never matched up or exceeded the cost of overhead for the service, it only lasted a little over 18 months before going out of business. Mail and packages were then delivered to cities and towns throughout the West through certain express company stage lines and freight service wagons that traveled to and from main distribution points, which in this case was in Salt Lake City.

In addition to the mail, these stagecoaches had transported a limited amount of paying customers to their desired destinations, seated within the enclosed confines of the sturdy wooden coaches. They were commonly driven by a harnessed team of either four or six horses, controlled by a half-crazed driver who generally seemed determined to get to the company's destinations in quicker order than many might have desired. The coaches often traveled over rough and jarring terrain along roads that were sometimes impassable during harsh winter conditions. While traveling along trails previously used by westward wagon trains, the stagecoach drivers had to be particularly wary of potential danger in Indian country. Notably, there were reports of some coaches and all their contents never reaching their destinations. In addition, the stages would occasionally carry essential documents, gold, silver, and other valuables that some banks had entrusted the express companies to transport for them. Those valuables were contained within locked steel strongboxes that were generally kept out of sight from potential armed robbers who would sometimes resort to ambushing the coaches to get them to stop.

But as it pertained to the family's mail, the Glovers would often go into town at a time that coordinated with the inbound stage's estimated arrival from Salt Lake, where they could also drop off any outgoing mail before taking care of other forms of business while there. Otherwise, the express office commonly held onto the local citizen's mail until they would come for it. Letters and parcels were only addressed with the recipient's name and the town of delivery, as there were no numbered street addresses or a mail delivery service in the townships of U.S. territories.

Also, at that time, a relatively new invention called the ' telegraph' had come onto the scene, which was developed in 1838 by renowned portrait painter and noted inventor Samuel Morse. In its widespread application, it gained popularity throughout the country as a trusted means of direct communication. This new telegraph system had previously been applied extensively during the Civil War and was now becoming established in towns within Utah's growing territory. Its wired system of electromagnetic-powered communication lines was extended to Salt Lake City, Provo, and other growing areas in the southern part of the territory to connect with the country's other previously established regions north and east of there. Mr. Morse had found that to make the system work, a series of electromagnetic relays were needed to connect and span the great distances involved when sending and receiving messages to and from all regions of the developing country where the system was in place. Its overhead wires were strung along a network of high-standing timber poles running along the main roads and thoroughfares to where cities and townships were commonly located and where telegraph offices were strategically placed.

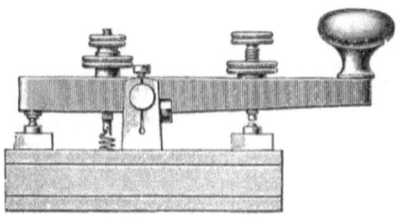

Telegraph Key

Housed within its own 'Telegraph Office,' a Telegraph Key was the desktop instrument used for tapping coded messages over the wire while applying a new method of communication called Morse-Code. It was a system consisting of dot and dash clicking sounds, tapped for each of a word's letters using the key, in which to send these electromagnetically charged coded signals over the live wires. They would be decyphered and spelled out at their point of destination by telegraph office clerks who knew the code. In effect, it was far faster than any letter could travel. Outbound messages and their subsequent replies could be sent and received virtually within minutes. As an interconnected system, it was an unprecedented and unparalleled innovation for its time. Having quickly taken hold, it revolutionized long-distance communication throughout most areas of civilized North America until the first telephone was invented several decades later. Many areas in the wartorn southern states, where they were still going through a reconstruction period, did not have the benefit of the telegraph for their electromagnetic communication over the wires. They would have to wait for new infrastructure to be rebuilt before the telegraph could be of any value to the Southern states.

However, Evie wasn't entirely sold on the telegraph. She preferred to write her letters instead, as the Western Union company charged an itemized fee for their coded messages according to the number of words, letters, and numbers involved. Plus, to her, it seemed far too short of a message to send anyway while being much less personal than the selected wordage within her lengthy letters. The postage for her letters was based on weight, which might have only cost her less than one cent at that time.

But to her smug-filled satisfaction, she knew that her former school Marm, Mrs. Johnson, from her earlier years back in Carbondale, would indeed have been proud of her for choosing to write her letters instead of using the telegraph. She thought it was probably suitable for specific emergencies or notifications where only a few words would suffice. However, it would not replace an all-encompassing, descriptive, and elaborative communique with the preferred wordage within her letters.

With the constant 'water runs' out to the river becoming more of a chore and a nuisance to Will, he knew it was finally time to begin digging a well. Luckily for him, his new neighbor and friend, Riley Atkinson, offered to lend him a hand with it as a neighborly gesture. They decided the placement for it, just to the right front of the cabin, would keep it within a short walk from the front door, as the two of them began carving out a six-foot circle to start work on the shaft. They took turns digging and piling up the extracted soil and rock before eventually deploying a rope for one to drop down into it and to later ascend from the well's progressing depth. The other would feed the digger with empty buckets to fill before pulling full ones back to the surface using a length of rope to effectively dump them and continue the cycle. It was an arduous process, as they would manage to run the shaft depth down about 8 or 10 feet each day while sometimes dealing with relatively large stones that were difficult to remove, which tended to slow the progress. For that, a rope end would be tied around them in a cross pattern, whereby the heavier stones could be pulled to the surface with the urging of Will's horse.

It took them five days to dig down to where water finally began to seep into the pit at 46 feet, steadily rising above Will's boots as he stood in amazement while trying to fill the last bucket with muddy soil. Eventually, as he stood there, laughing and reveling at the sight of his new resource, the water rose to the height of his knees before he realized that he should head back to the surface. Again, with the aid of his horse 'Sunshine,' Riley tied off his end of the rope to the saddle horn and urged the horse forward as she steadily pulled on the rope. Will then stepped into the other end's loop, with bucket and shovel in hand, to ride upwards quite effortlessly, finally emerging at the top with a big muddy-faced grin as he and Riley celebrated the moment.

The project's next step involved spreading a thick layer of gravel from the river to cover about a foot of depth at the base of the shaft. It effectively served as a filter to keep the mud factor down, which would help make the water much clearer and more drinkable. Once those significant parts of the process had been accomplished, Will finished the exterior with a 4-foot circular rock barrier and a pitched roof covering.

The cement used in solidifying the stonework was something the earlier Spaniards had commonly utilized since the 16th century to fuse rock and to help seal between the logs on cabins, as it became exceptionally strong when dried in place. It was known to them as ' Tapia,' consisting of a mixture of lime, sand, and aggregate (small gravel) blended with water to form a thickly made gray-colored mud with great sticking power. The American pioneers of the 19th century, referred to this gritty mixture that was used well before modern concrete mix eventually came onto the scene in the latter part of the century as ' Tabby.' It was probably a result of not fully remembering its original Hispanic name. Fortunately, while sacks of lime were readily available at the dry goods store in town, the sand and pebble-sized gravel could be gathered easily along the shores of the nearby Provo River.

During their second year living in this place they had

come to call home, Will decided to cut down some similarly sized pine trees to serve as suitable timber for the addition of another room for the cabin since Maggie was getting to the point where a separate bedroom for her would be needed fairly soon. But he had to allow the cut timberwood to sit and weather for about half a year after stripping off all the branches and bark on them to where they looked like large poles lying about on the ground. The Sun would then be asked to beat down on them, effectively drying them out, where they would eventually be much lighter and easier to deal with altogether.

In the meantime, something else was in greater need of his attention, as it became quite evident to all who used the existing outhouse out back that the old structure was rotting and falling apart. It had noticeably tilted to one side due to time and the elements having their way with it. So, Will decided to dig a new crap shaft nearby and put it down about 15 feet before splitting some dead tree logs from the nearby forest into roughly 2-inch x 4-inch boards. It provided him with what he could use to form the framework of the new little building. It also allowed him to assemble and secure the framework of the single-pitched roof, which slanted back to the rear of the structure. He then split a few cedar logs into planks for the siding and roof cover while also building the interior box where the hole for the seat was to be cut out so that it was centered over the pit. A lantern perch was also installed, and a sturdy door was built and fastened for the new outhouse, using leather for its hinges. The only thing left to complete the structure was to install the toilet seat, which was sentimentally reclaimed from the old outhouse.

In an almost ritualistic manner, Will then decided that

the best method to do away with the old crapper was to set fire to it and allow it to burn to the ground, whereby afterward, multiple small pieces of burnt wood and ashes remained. It allowed the burned-up material to be more conveniently shoveled right back into the old, smelly pit before filling it in further with most of the soil and rocks recently extracted from the new pit nearby. All in all, everything came together quite nicely in Will's estimation, as he stood back proudly to assess the newly finished product, with Maggie insisting that she should be the first to use it.

In addition to the new outhouse, with further necessities called for at the homestead, Will had also constructed a small chicken coop with nesting boxes and rear access doors. He then bought five hens at the grain store in town, as well as a good supply of feed for them. From his interactions with the townfolk, he also acquired a Hereford milk cow named 'Violet' from a nearby farmer in a straight-up trade for one of his Missouri mules. With these additions, he wanted his family to enjoy the rich nourishment of milk in their diet, along with the added protein from chicken eggs, to go with the essential bread, cookies, and fruit pies that Evie would so lovingly bake in her much-celebrated cast iron oven.

Violet

Hereford cattle were imported into the United States from Hereford, England, in 1817. Recognized for their exceptional cuts of meat and ample milk production, they became quite a familiar breed of cattle seen out on the open landscape in many of the existing states, including the western territory of Utah.

In addition to Will's resourceful upgrades to what was then becoming a small family farm, there were cuts of fresh deer and antelope meat that he would occasionally acquire and put on the family's table whenever he found those flighty animals within rifle range in the nearby woods. He would also acquire cottontail rabbits, sometimes seen thereabouts, along with a few gray squirrels he could occasionally put a bead on. Plus, now and then, he would take Maggie out to the river with him, where they would generally have good luck in landing a stringer of trout to bring back to Evie's kitchen. Since he knew they couldn't possibly eat them all, while these fish wouldn't stay fresh for long, they would stop at the Atkinson's cabin on the way home and present a few to Riley and Betty.

When Will went to town to buy necessary supplies, such as fruits, vegetables, hardware items, and tools like shovels and picks, he would also pick up a copy of the only newspaper available, the 'Salt Lake City Deseret News.' This little newspaper, brought in regularly from Salt Lake City, had been established as a local news source in 1850 when the area gained territorial status. It allowed Will to exercise his mind a bit by learning more about this U.S. territory of Utah he was now acclimating himself and his family to while still knowing so little about it. But, he would now have the opportunity to learn more about some of the 'goings on' in the areas around Salt Lake and other places, including Provo. This Mormon-influenced periodical also covered national news and world events for those wanting to hear about what was happening outside their settlement within the territory.

Among the wonders of the day that he came to learn about when reading editions of this paper was a report that various laborers for the Union Pacific Railroad, working to lay tracks for the country's attempt at establishing a transcontinental railroad, had completed 10 miles of track in one day during April of 1869. On that note, it would soon be announced that the railroad would finally be completed at Promontory Summit in northern Utah in May of that year. For this, a ceremonial golden spike would be driven into the last section of rail, connecting the Union Pacific train tracks from the east with the Central Pacific's tracks from the west. The completion of this project would bring rail passenger and freight service to new heights. Trains would be able to run from the East Coast of the United States to the West Coast and back, marking an unprecedented achievement for the time. This development would also spell the eventual end of the pioneer days and their covered wagons while opening up new opportunities for easier travel across the country, with little or no hardship and significantly reduced travel time.

A much earlier edition of the Deseret News, dated August 31, 1850

When reading further, the news story pointed out that in the years immediately following the American Civil War, many people of all races, from most of the existing northern states at the time and some from the southern states, had increasingly desired to move West. Most had felt that uprooting themselves and their families from their unworkable and untenable situations, in which to find new beginnings elsewhere, would become their newfound salvation. Lengthy wagon trains continued transporting pioneering settlers across the country to their territorial destinations, as that antiquated mode of travel continued for a while, even as the railroad took passengers westward. It was primarily due to these migrants needing to transport their sizeable and cherished belongings, as they could not convey everything by rail. However, as the wagon trains eventually decreased in volume with the railroad's increasing popularity, most travelers who could afford rail passage preferred to shed much of their unneeded possessions and travel West aboard the 'Iron Horse' steam train.

But, prior to that, Chinese laborers were on the move from the West. Because they were diligent and hard-working, while also being cheaper than other workers, a few thousand were gainfully employed in 1863 by the Central Pacific railroad. Their task was to create a rail line from where ferry service from San Francisco regularly served Oakland's 'Long Wharf' on the eastern side of San Francisco Bay in northern California. They then ran the tracks from that point in Oakland, northeast through Sacramento, and across the remaining width of the state. When progressing through the rugged Sierra Nevada mountains, these Chinese immigrant workers blasted their way through areas of solid granite with nitroglycerin to clear the way, laying track while also blasting through more precipitous areas with black powder to create lengthy tunnels for the tracks to run through where mountains could not be brought down. From there, they extended the line further east through Reno, which was no longer known as Truckee Meadows, and ran it out through the Nevada desert into northern Utah.

However, because nitroglycerin was a highly sensitive liquid chemical form of explosive, the occasional accidental mishandling of this extremely volatile mixture resulted in premature detonations, with quite a few of these Chinese workers suffering severe injury or even death as a result. In addition, some others had lost their lives when climbing up precipices to place explosives, only to slip and fall to their deaths. It was found that laying track through the rugged Sierra Nevada mountain range had become their greatest challenge as the process surged further eastward.

The work crews that placed the ties and rails while driving the spikes for the Union Pacific line from the east were comprised of German and Irish laborers, along with Civil War veterans, formerly enslaved Black men, and some native Indians. The UP railroad paid their workers well for the arduous labor they put in every day. But they also impressed upon them the expectation that they would be dedicated to this task while remaining fit and ready to put in a full measure of hard labor each day. This prerequisite was also to be observed without alcohol or anything else that might deter them from their task. However, the alcohol still flowed within their temporary nocturnal 'tent city' train towns. Although, it didn't prevent them from losing much progress with their given task.

While laying track from the east, these laborers would sometimes run into situations across the great plains, which forced them to stop work and take up their arms to defend themselves against attacking tribes of angry indigenous warriors who did not want the white man's Iron Horse trains running through their sacred land. In some cases, when it was known they were going through a notoriously dangerous area within Indian country, the government provided cavalry soldiers to stay with the work crew and watch over them, which tended to lessen those incidents overall.

The laying of tracks from the West would eventually culminate above the Great Salt Lake within the Utah territory, as the Central Pacific railroad would eventually meet up at the Union Pacific rail worker's tent city locality of Promontory Summit in May of 1869.

From the West, the work crew of hard-working Chinese immigrant laborers did not need to be warned about their vices getting in the way of providing an honest day's work for their given pay. Plus, they were not similarly delayed by any attacking indigenous tribes. Nevertheless, in both cases, with the two determined railroads pushing from both directions, the overall mix of laborers would not disappoint, as they would eventually meet up at Promontory Summit to ceremonially complete an epic undertaking that would forever change the country's direction. The conjoined tracks from the two rail companies would then span the newly established distance from Council Bluffs, Iowa, to the bay shores of Oakland, California, covering 1,911 miles.

On May 10, 1869, East meets West at Promontory Summit, Utah.

In other news reports within this periodical, Will was also intrigued to learn that in November of that year, Egypt was to begin its ambitious shipping project by building the Suez Canal, which was designed to link the Mediterranean Sea with the Red Sea. It would allow commercial shipping to go through areas where they had previously been forced to sail way around to deliver and take on goods at various ports in that part of the world. He also read about the outlaw Jesse James holding up his first bank in Gallatin, Missouri, after becoming more notorious in recent years for train robberies.

So, this little newspaper, even though it was often four or five days late by the time Will could grab a copy, had become a vital source of information where he could keep tabs on world and local events from his relatively remote location in north Provo. Evie also enjoyed reading the paper, as there wasn't much else available to inform and exercise her mind with the written word, apart from her Bible or her mother's letters. So, it was found to be a bright new source of information for them in which to keep up with events of the time, while finding it as such a rare pleasure to now be able to read various news stories within their remote locality, making them feel much more in touch while acclimating to their new life away from Illinois.

The three of them occasionally enjoyed shopping in Provo, often buying fresh fruits and vegetables at the grocery market when they were in season. But because these items were seasonal, Evie would 'can' a good amount of it, putting it all down in vacuum-sealed jars for Winter use by par-boiling everything and heat-capping the jars. It was a thoughtful food-saving process she had learned from her mother, Mary, in her earlier years. They also purchased meat from the nearby butcher when venison was unavailable in Little Rock Canyon. However, this local meat vendor only had portions of beef and pork available, as far as red meat goes, while only offering it in large roasts. If anyone had desired steaks or chops to be cut from it, they would be left to do that on their own while still being stuck with having to buy the entire sizeable roast. In addition, he also had whole chickens for sale much of the time.

When purchasing a whole chicken, Evie also inquired if he had any lard available, which he did, presenting her with a tin of it. Lard was actually what clarified animal fat was called. It was commonly rendered from the abdomen of pigs, and then clarified to be set up in solid form for cooking. Many folks of the day used it exclusively to fry with. But Evie mainly applied it when making her pies and biscuits, adding it to the dough to give her baked creations more flavor and flakiness.

While still in the butcher shop, Will noticed that the butcher's white apron had been almost entirely spattered with animal blood, as he oddly continued to wear it while working the counter. But of course, for Will, it brought back an unpleasantly haunting memory from years ago when, during a Civil War battle, a Union Army surgeon with spattered human blood similarly displayed on his chest apron had extracted a rifle ball from Will's left arm. He also remembered, all too vividly, the mix of Union and Confederate soldiers inside that medical tent, suffering from battle-inflicted wounds, some of whom were struggling and dying on operating tables while emitting their eerie groans, gurgles, and screams that tended to linger inside of his head. However, that disturbingly haunting moment soon vanished with the jingle of the shopkeeper's bell atop the front door, as another customer entered the store.

While still in town, he and Evie walked to the dry goods store across the street. While there, she purchased salt, sugar, flour, and a package of double-acting baking powder, which would effectively activate the leavening process. With yeast's unavailability apparent within the territories at that time, it was found that double-acting baking powder still performed quite well in its absence, perhaps even better. These ingredients would be used for baking fruit pies, loaves of bread, and her lovingly created flaky biscuits. In addition, she would buy a few variations of dried beans by the pound, an everyday staple found within everyone's pantry. At that point, Will would remind her that she had probably spent enough of their meager income for one day while they should take their sacks of goods and get back on the road toward home in their openly converted former covered wagon that was now light enough for their one remaining mule to pull.

On a day when Evie was using her cast iron oven to bake fresh bread for the family's supper, Will sauntered into the cabin carrying a bucket of freshly drawn milk. He had convinced Violet to cooperate while locking her head within a makeshift stanchion. It allowed him to work her apparatus before bringing the resulting product into the kitchen to separate the cream from the raw milk for the family's daily consumption of this wondrous white liquid.

The naturally occurring concentration of fat globules rising to the top of a container in freshly drawn milk was commonly separated from the raw milk while alternately used in making butter. During this period in America, pasteurization had not yet been introduced, nor even recommended, by simply cooking the milk to keep bacteria from infecting its raw form. However, as long as the raw milk was sufficiently covered and consumed on the same day it was drawn, it was generally considered safe to drink.

While enjoying the sweet smell of bread baking as he worked at the counter nearby, he opened the oven door to briefly peek at it out of curiosity, while Evie quickly took notice and scolded him for it. She exclaimed that one should never look into the oven while something is baking, as it can interfere with the leavening process that allows the dough to rise and become a consistent loaf of bread. Otherwise, she pointed out, the cooked dough would appear more like a dense, lifeless clump, more closely resembling a dried-up remnant from Violet's backside than anything else. Will thoroughly understood her point, and with that, he quickly exited the cabin to gather his ax and chop up some more wood while sporting a rather amused grin.

When constructing various things for the cabin and the surrounding property, Will also, at some point, made good use of a solid upper branch that protruded from one of the more sizeable cottonwood trees standing in the rear yard of the cabin. He tied two rope sections onto it by applying and securing slip knots to each. With both lengths of rope dangling down, he pushed them through holes drilled with his brace and bit on a suitable little wooden platform. He then tied knots to the rope ends on each underside of this assembly to form and serve as a sturdy seat for a nice little girl to sit on and swing back and forth to her heart's content. It was a fun little diversion to add joy to her outside playtime activities.

Evie was busy cooking dinner late one afternoon, noticing earlier that Maggie was happily swinging back and forth on her new diversion out in the backyard. She had the stove fired up, baking a batch of biscuits while simmering a pot of aromatic beef stew on the stovetop. Tasting the stew, she found it quite pleasing, with a good beefy flavor and just the right amount of spice. As it was getting dark outside with ominous cloud formations and thunder heard overhead, she opened the rear door of the cabin to call out to Maggie and noticed that she was no longer at her swing. Immediately, she descended the steps and wandered throughout the rear yard, calling out for her until her voice began to turn frantic. Maggie was nowhere in sight.

Remembering her biscuits, she quickly retraced her steps and pulled them from the oven before returning to the rear yard to search for her little girl. As she continued to call out, Will's voice suddenly called back to say, "Evie, is that you?" He had been working at the side of the cabin and immediately came around to see what all the commotion was about.

"She's not here, Will. I can't find her anywhere." Acknowledging, Will instructed her to stay calm; he would search for her, as he didn't believe she could go far. So, they both went to the front of the cabin and out to the road to see if she might have wandered out in either direction, as they repeatedly called out to her. But there was no one around and nothing in sight that was moving, with nary a sound to be heard.

From the rear yard again, Will made his way in the low light from the threatening dark clouds overhead, moving directly into the forested area beyond the rear of his property. He walked the forest floor, with conifers of various sizes standing all around him, calling out his daughter's name. As he kept at it, a flash of light was seen overhead, and a loud clap of thunder was heard while light sprinkles of rain had already begun to fall on him. He had advanced nearly 1,000 yards into the forest before suddenly hearing Maggie's voice calling back to him. With her father moving toward the sound of her words, she was found sitting under a tree, thoroughly disappointed that she couldn't catch a fuzzy cottontail rabbit she had followed from the yard. Will was both relieved and exasperated at the same time as he gathered her up and took her back to her mother.

Because of that worrisome incident, Will decided to fence off the cabin's rear yard with cedar logs that he split into suitable posts and rails. He placed several rails between each planted post, with siding boards covering them, to help keep Maggie inside of it and certain undesirable critters out. It turned out to be a good move, as he later discovered some fresh bear scat and tracks across the road from the cabin while looking for dead or dying timber to render into firewood.

When celebrating Maggie's 5th birthday, Evie baked a cake for the occasion, which delighted her little girl. As a special present, Will gave her a very nicely carved and honed wooden horse that he had been working on in his spare time, which was quite artfully done, and she loved it. As much as her mother suggested that it should be placed on a shelf near her bed, she protested and would have none of that while preferring to keep it with her as a constant companion to play with...at least for a few weeks or so, anyway, until somehow it found it's way up onto that shelf, although as a 3-legged horse.

During that same year, Will set himself to the task of building an additional room adjoining the cabin to serve as Maggie's new bedroom, as it was becoming rather difficult for the three of them to continue sharing sleeping quarters.

Plus, he and Evie could do without Maggie's utterings to the Atkinsons or Evie's sister Lucy that "mommy and daddy sometimes like to wrestle at night."

To begin the process, he dug holes in the ground next to the cabin's kitchen/living room side. He then sunk log posts 3 feet into the holes and stabilized them by adding gravel around them from the river bank before pouring a slurried form of 'Tabby' over the gravel to help solidify it. This would provide the foundational support for the horizontal logs mounted atop the vertical posts that would form the basis and support for the planked bedroom floor. He planned to interlock the logs for the exterior walls while aligning them with the cabin. Additionally, he needed to ensure that the height of the floor matched that of the cabin. After he got the walls up to a certain height, he marked the cabin where a doorway would be established while slowly but surely sawing it out before constructing a dowel-conjoined cedar door for the opening.

From there, while continuing with the erection of the new bedroom addition, he finished off the new roof for it. For that part of the process, he had to build a couple of sturdy ladders to reach the heights of the project as it escalated, which helped to ease his strained efforts in getting the higher logs up and in place. After buying three large framed windows during a trip to Salt Lake City, he cut out the opening on the new room's front wall and set one in place before framing it off while adding jute material around the frame and between the logs to block out outside air. This made the window frame airtight. To finish it off, batches of ' Tabby' were mixed up and applied over the jute to further seal the gaps around the frame, making it water-tight and giving it lastability. This would also block out any insects from entering the cabin.

As the family of three stood out in the front of the yard to view the completed addition, Will knew it wasn't a perfect accomplishment. But it did match up quite nicely for all appearances while fusing the new addition with the existing structure. It effectively gave his little girl her own space at a time when it was sorely needed. She would also enjoy the added benefit of having a much larger window to gaze out onto the area's natural beauty while filling the room with a good amount of needed daylight. The other two windows to be installed would follow in due course.

After completing Maggie's new bedroom and installing the windows, Will responded to Evie's earlier request that they establish a root cellar where the cooler temperatures below ground level would provide better preservation for meats, eggs, fruits, and vegetables. It was where those goods could be safely stored for longer periods while maintaining the freshness of perishable items for several more days than what was experienced within the warmer room-temperature confines of the cabin. The cellar also had to be strong enough to keep bears from breaking into it. So, after digging it out and framing it with cedar posts and planks, he added the roof covering and a solid door that was thicker and heavier, to fit the opening and help to keep bears out. For that resolve, Will drilled holes into the door frame with his brace & bit while also drilling into the side edge of the thick wooden door, where he then fashioned two large wooden slide pieces that could be pushed into the door near the top and the bottom of the door jamb to effectively lock and unlock the door from the outside.

With several wooden racks added, it was complete and ready for Evie to use. When depositing her perishable items onto the secured racks, she found that they indeed remained fresh for a more extended period, comparatively. She estimated that it provided them with an extra three to four days of storage time before vegetables and fruit began to turn while finding that meat, when covered, was more sensitive and would only remain fresh for just a day. However, eggs could stay fresh for at least ten days, while milk contained in jars only lasted a day or two at best. This little root cellar, with its commonly cooler temperatures found beneath the ground, represented the early pioneer's crude and limited version of what would eventually follow in the form of an ice box or refrigerator. During the Fall, Winter, and early Spring, the lower temperatures with fallen snow would help to increase the duration and lastability of their fresh food supplies even more.

In their new locale, the Glovers observed that Utah's predominantly Mormon faith had influenced most of the townspeople and the surrounding farmers and ranchers in the Provo area. They noted that their faithful had regularly attended services and meetings near them at a small church in the north section of town. They also had access to a larger congregational church in the central part of town where most of their local population resided. While seen as caring and welcoming people in general, they represented a different sort of Christian philosophy than what Will and Evie were accustomed to, having been raised as Presbyterians in southern Illinois. So, as described, this clan-like Mormon community, with its unusual Christian-based religion, had recognized Jesus as the son of God, along with what they referred to as Latter-Day Saints. However, this didn't quite align with what Will and Evie were used to with their more traditional established form of Christianity. Additionally, Evie had heard that some of these Latter-Day Saint followers were involved in the objectionable practice of polygamy, as some of their menfolk tended to take more than one wife.

Because there were likely only a few others who might share in the Glover's faith, they still did not have a Presbyterian church in their area to support their own religious beliefs. Oddly, even other similar Christian denominations were not represented by having established churches nearby, with much of the territory mainly populated by Mormons. However, Evie, who kept her Bible by her side for spiritual guidance, regularly read passages from it to maintain her faith while helping her husband with the chores and upkeep of the cabin and its pleasant surroundings.

At some point, after having taken care of much of the domestic needs at their new homestead, Will took part-time work as a clerk in the dry goods store in Provo proper, where he worked for about two and a half months, even though he never really enjoyed it. He regarded it as extra earnings that helped the family supplement their income, although in a limited fashion, as wages were considerably lower there compared with Illinois. After that, he found work at a local mining company north of town and close to home, which paid him a bit of a higher wage than the dry goods store, although it still wasn't entirely permanent employment.

The Glover family's next-door neighbor, Riley Atkinson, lived a bit farther out along the same earthen road, nearer the junction of the Little Rock Canyon road that leads westerly to Orem. His similarly constructed cabin, standing out amongst a sparse stand of pines, was built on rockier ground. He had originally emigrated to Utah with his folks in 1851 from the Ohio River town of Covington, Kentucky.

More recently, he resided with his folks farther south of Provo in the smaller town of Spanish Fork before eventually migrating north for work. In Provo, he met his wife, Betty, after finding a job at a local mining company where Will had also come to be employed more recently. In fact, Riley was good enough to have recommended him to his foreman for the job at the Atlas Mine, and Will was most appreciative of that. This man, who had sported a thin black Amish-like wrap-around beard minus the mustache, was mostly bald-headed except for the sides and was considerably shorter than Will at 5′ 7.

He and Betty had tried to have children in the few years after arriving in Provo, but she miscarried twice. This left them with only a glimmer of hope that she may yet conceive again and bring forth the life of a child to create the makings of a family. However, Betty had regularly exhibited signs of relatively poor health after she lost their second child. Specifically, she was unable to fully digest much of what she could eat while vomiting frequently, which caused her to become somewhat weakened and dispirited while looking gaunt, having lost significant weight as a result. This rather odd health condition had become most worrisome to both her and Riley, although they were at a loss as to how to treat it. Betty regularly experienced these episodes of nausea and vomiting that tended to drain her of energy. She also suffered from mood swings and signs of depression, seemingly due to this digestive disorder. In support, her mother, Nora, would come from across town to help cook and take care of the cabin and their animals while offering comfort to her daughter in her time of need.

Dr. Hiram Hutchins, the town's practicing physician, had scheduled a stop at the Atkinson's cabin in Little Rock

Canyon after Riley had requested his services. It was a day of heavy rainfall, causing muddy conditions that made it difficult for his single horse-drawn buggy to navigate the softened and slippery earthen roadway. Dr. Hutchins, at 74 years of age, also covered the nearby town and vicinity of Orem with his practice in serving both nearby communities. However, due to his age and declining health, he was not as nimble as he had been five or six years earlier. Despite his poor eyesight and struggles with alcoholism, he continued to serve as the only general practitioner for the two local communities. When more serious medical issues arose on occasion, Dr. Hutchins would recommend his local friend, Dr. Ira Phillips of Orem, who was a noted surgeon. Interestingly, Dr. Phillips had gained respectable recognition from serving with the Confederate Army's medical corps during the Civil War, often dealing with amputations and abdominal surgeries.

When Betty's mother, Nora, opened the front door of their cabin to let Dr. Hutchins in, she could smell the presence of liquor on his breath. He had previously treated Betty for her miscarriages and was familiar with her. However, as a diagnosis in this case, he could only speculate that her current digestive disorder was probably related to her depression and that she would do well by trying to raise her spirits, if possible. He prescribed a diet of soups for a week's time before retaking solid food and suggested that she chew her food longer before swallowing. In addition to his advice, he supplied her with a bottle of castor oil to take daily, theorizing that it would help lubricate her throat, esophagus, and stomach lining, making it easier for food to pass through while ultimately helping her get back on track. He charged a fee of $2.00 for this service, which was a significant amount of money at that time, particularly considering that most laborers were earning about a dollar a day for their work. However, over time, Betty's condition would improve, along with her disposition involving depression and anxiety. Riley also did his part in helping to bring her back around by expressing his undying love while reassuring her that their life together would still be worth living.

Riley had kept himself reasonably busy working part-time, with odd-job tasks being called for at the mine, while also having a certain amount of free time to go out hunting the countryside and nearby forests for available meat, which was not all that plentiful in the vicinity of Little Rock Canyon during certain months of the year. But at other times, he would ride on horseback due east, up into the higher reaches of the Little Rock Canyon, as the trail rose and cleaved its way between the slopes of the Wasatch range, where he would look for the signs and presence of deer and antelope. He would detect their fresh scat and tracks before laying for them well above the water-filled creekbed that meandered down the snaking canyon. Opportunities in that vicinity were few and far between, although he would occasionally get lucky with his lever-action Henry rifle, chambered in .44-40 rim-fire, and bag an animal to drape over the front of his saddle while making his way back home triumphantly.

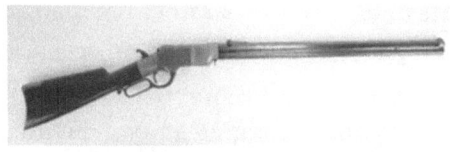

1860 Henry .44 Repeating Rifle

At the time, the Henry repeating rifle was one of the costliest to purchase. It was commonly available in the West, although the asking price was generally found to be around $45. to $50., making it a rather pricey investment during the 1860s for frontiersmen to plunk down their hard-earned cash for. However, as a lever-action repeating rifle, it was the most reliable and the best there was at the time for frontier life during the decade of the 1860s. Plus, the .44-40 caliber was large enough to take down any animal known to man in North America.

Will and Riley's friend, Otto Olinger, was from the little settlement of Orem, which was about 5 miles north of Provo and just 3 miles west of the residential area of Little Rock Canyon. He was from Germany and lived in a particular section of the town where quite a few of these immigrant families had established their little cultural enclaves while primarily residing in tenements. Many of these former Eastern European immigrants, as in this case, were still speaking fluid German as if they had entirely forgotten they were now living in the United States. Otto's association, in joining up with Will and Riley, was from having become another one of their fellow part-time mine workers in Provo, who had traveled the 3-mile trek from Orem to find part-time work he heard was available at the Atlas Mine near Little Rock Canyon, where both Riley and Will lived and worked.

At 29 years of age, he was a rather big man, just 6 feet in height but carrying 255 lbs of mostly muscle. Clean-shaven with a full head of curly blonde hair, he was hearty and stout, gregarious and strong as an ox. Having emigrated from Stuttgart in southern Germany, he still managed to learn and speak English fluently enough since coming over, although he retained his homeland's signature accent to give himself away.

Will Glover was a somewhat taller man at 6'1, who at that point sported a full darkish brown-colored beard that draped down to just below his neck while still carrying a full head of the same dark-shaded hair under his preferred western slouch hat. Being of slim build and still rather muscular in appearance for his 33 years of life, he had kept himself rather fit for most of those years, while some of his more recent strenuous activities had been spent around his homestead in north Provo. He was already almost three years removed from an unsettled life in the mid-west before acclimating to the more rugged and rocky landscape of this new growing territory.

As the like-minded bond among these three part-time miners had grown stronger, they became good friends and occasionally met at the local saloon in town to have a few beers and swap stories. The beer was brought in by wagon from a brewery in Springville, just south of Provo, as the Mormon proprietors catered to outsiders and non-believers while knowing that their brethren did not consume beer or any other alcoholic beverage. But they were still enterprising enough to put aside their religious disdain for it and profit by selling it to non-believers at their locally owned and operated saloon.

On occasion, Will's brother-in-law, Ben Lockhardt, would come over from the Blacksmith's shop to join them for a beer while taking in some lively conversations with the trio, offering up a few stories of his own about his unusual and sometimes comical experiences serving as the town's blacksmith. But as the conversation sometimes shifted to prospecting for gold and silver, Ben tended to give dire warnings that there were still some unfriendly break-away tribes of Indians living up in the higher elevations of the nearby Wasatch range. He pointed out that a few other prospectors in recent years had ventured up into those lofty areas and were never seen nor heard from again. In addition, he would suggest that there wasn't much of the two precious metals of silver and gold still awaiting them up in the high country at this late date anyway, as it was his impression that earlier miners and prospectors had already cleaned out much of it. The truth was, he had no use for prospecting, thinking it to be a waste of time, as the very mention of it would generally prompt him to take his last gulp of beer and head back to his nearby home, where Lucy would be waiting after buttoning things up at their respective shops for the night. He was pretty content with the life he had cultivated for himself and Lucy in Provo, where the town's Blacksmith was just as important as its Undertaker, although hopefully more active. For both he and Lucy, it was an easier way of living, with most everything available right there, within short walking distance between their home and the two shops. Having grown up in Carbondale, where she was accustomed to being in close proximity to all of the town's shops, markets, the postal office, and the schoolhouse, it didn't take much for her to convince Ben that this type of close, in-town living would suit them both.

While already nearly four years removed from their former lives in Illinois, he and Lucy had thoroughly enjoyed seeing Will, Evie, Maggie, and Polly fairly often, as they were their only relatives living this side of Carbondale. Plus, they appreciated having several other nearby friends who had become not-so-far-away neighbors in and around their community.

In north Provo and the nearby locale of Orem, the changing four seasons tended to bring different weather patterns to those higher elevations each year. Springtime was generally noted as being mild and cool for the most part, with a mix of showers and sunshine. Summers were commonly hot, clear, and dry, with temperatures ranging from the mid-80s to the 90s. The existing flora tended to remain mostly green and vibrant for an extended period before eventually burning off in mid-summer. Fall would generally see a cooling off, with colder overnight temperatures felt as winter would make its noted approach, with varying winds commonly occurring during the day. When winter arrives, temperatures tend to drop to 20 degrees and lower, with occasional frigid days and nights not rising much higher than 5 degrees Fahrenheit. However, it would sometimes get even colder. Snow often tended to fall and accumulate, sometimes causing traffic disruptions, although solo horses with their riders seemed less affected by it. On rare occasions, the snowfall may even amount to several feet of coverage, which tended to halt all wheeled traffic on the roadways, whereby only horses could navigate their way into town and back, provided the heavier snow hadn't made the way ahead unrecognizable.

For many people around the country in the more rural areas, farmers and some others would generally rely on the

Old Farmer's Almanac during the 18th and 19th centuries, which tended to forecast the approximated regional weather conditions around the country. Originally published and distributed from New Jersey, it was a widely observed periodical that was thought to be a somewhat accurate assessment of weather conditions throughout the United States and Canada. However, for many, it was hit or miss, as the weather was found to be largely unpredictable around many parts of the country. But without anything for farmers to go by, the almanac at least gave them something to scornfully complain about when the periodical's forecast was wrong.

The Provo area usually enjoyed or endured these typical seasonal conditions every year. However, occasionally, rare blizzards would also occur to test the citizens' overall endurance levels. During these times, Will had to house the horse, mule, and Violet together in the small, sturdy log barn to protect them from the biting cold and high winds. The barn was quite cramped as it was for the three large animals, and Violet protested being packed in with the horse and mule standing close beside her. But it kept them safe while the structure was strong enough to withstand the rare storm conditions and keep the snow out. Whenever he needed to feed the animals or get milk from Violet during a snowstorm or blizzard, he would look for the rope previously strung from the cabin to the barn. It helped to guide him during these blinding snow events, as he would grab hold to make his way from one structure to the other without getting lost due to the near complete lack of visibility caused by the blowing snow in the form of a 'white out.' Because the blizzard had also brought much lower extreme temperatures to the area, Will would take three of their older, moth-eaten wool blankets with him to drape over the animals and tie them in place with lengths of rope.

As a new Winter arrived in Provo, with snow steadily falling, along with the expected frigid temperatures, Lucy Lockhardt had extended invitations to Will, Evie, and Maggie, along with Riley and Betty Atkinson, Otto Olinger, and his friend Helga Schmitt, to join her and Ben, along with a couple of their other friends for an afternoon Christmas dinner at their spacious home in town. It served as their traditional end-of-year event: a social gathering with close friends and family while observing the winter season and Solstice, along with the merriment of Christmas.

Fortunately, when the day before Christmas arrived, it brought abundant sunshine, although the area still exhibited rather cold temperatures without much snow on the roadway leading to town, making for a safer buggy ride for everyone. It was the one time during the year when all of Will and Evie's friends and Ben and Lucy's friends could come together in one place to observe, celebrate, and enjoy a seasonal tradition that's been around practically forever.

But, it also served as a special time for Ben and Lucy to announce their entrance into parenthood, as Lucy was quite pleased to relate to all that she was now with child. Dr. Hutchins had recently given her the good news that she was definitely ' in a family way.'

Part Five

The Telegram

On a day in early June of 1869, while Evie was in town shopping for a few supplies, she walked by the telegraph office on her way to the dry goods store when the telegraph clerk happened to spot her through his window and quickly stepped outside to call her back. When she returned, wondering what he wanted, he presented a sealed envelope to her and said, "Here's a telegram that came in yesterday for your husband." She looked at it with some puzzlement for a second or two before stuffing it into her dress pocket, thanking the clerk before resuming her circuit, as she still needed to pick up several small containers of cooking spices before visiting with Lucy at her fabric shop.

When she and Sunshine returned to the homestead in the early afternoon, Will was busy working on the chicken coop in the backyard while also looking after Maggie. But at some point, as he detected that Evie was back, he thought he'd take a break, get a drink from the well, and ask her how things were in town. With that, she immediately remembered the telegram she had put in her pocket and quickly retrieved it while handing it to Will, saying, " Oh, you got a telegram." Well, this was all new to him, as he'd never gotten a telegram before, even feeling a little gleeful as he opened the envelope to see the words that told him his father, John Glover, had died. As he lowered his hand that held the telegram, his arm fell by his side, and he just stood there with a blank look on his face while staring into nothing at all for at least a minute until Evie looked up from what she was doing at the kitchen sink to ask him who it was from. He placed it on the table as he walked past her, out the door, and into the backyard again, trying to sort out or come to terms with what he had just read. As another minute or so passed, Evie quickly exited the cabin and grabbed hold of him to express her deep sorrow and empathy for his sudden loss.

He had only read the first line of the telegram. But when he regained himself with Evie's help, he then learned that John had died of a heart attack and was found over a week later on his kitchen floor by one of his regular egg customers who had wondered why the steady egg distribution had stopped. It went on to say that the area had gone without eggs for many more days than anyone had known in the past, with the townspeople feeling that something may have happened. So, when dealing with John's already decomposing body, the town of Carbondale went ahead and buried him right afterward in the cemetery there, as they didn't have the means to preserve him for a later burial. They placed him beside his wife Margaret, which was entirely fitting and proper. The telegram also reported that at least three potential buyers had inquired about possibly purchasing the family's farmhouse and chicken/egg operation. However, that would depend entirely on what John's son and only living relative might decide.

In his grief, Will thought it to be quite odd that he felt so bad about losing a father whom he almost came to hate when leaving for Utah; a man he had great respect for when he was growing up as a child, but whom he had lost all connection with after his mother's death, along with the time he spent fighting the Confederates.

As the next day began, Evie decided to give him some room to grieve and sort things out on his own while she went about her regular daily chores: feeding and watering the horse, mule, and chickens, along with the homestead's primadonna, Violet. She then took in the clothes on the line and drew successive buckets of water from the well to boil on the stove, as it was time again for Maggie to take her bi-monthly bath.

Over dinner that night, Will finally opened up and told Evie that because of the circumstances regarding the loose ends left to him with John's passing, he would need to go back to Carbondale for a short period. Essentially, he would have to sell off the family farm and take care of any outstanding bills where payment may still be expected before returning on the train, now that the trans-continental railroad had been connected to allow for faster travel east and west across the country.

But for Will to catch the train in Salt Lake, given that there wasn't any rail service from Provo to get him there, he would have to ask his friend Riley to drive him to the Salt Lake City train station in his buggy over a distance of 45 miles. He worked out a means of payment to Riley that was agreeable while telling him that on his return trip, he would send a telegram with details of the date and the train's arrival time in Salt Lake from the east. After boarding the train at the Salt Lake station, he would then get off when it eventually reached Springfield, Illinois, and catch the southbound Central Illinois Railroad's daily train from there down to Carbondale. It would all be most unfamiliar to him, as he would have to acclimate to this new progressive mode of transportation now available in this new adventurous age. Even while fully aware of train service to other localities from Carbondale when Will lived there, he never bothered to check it out and see what train travel was all about.

So, at around 5 a.m. on June 11th, Will bid goodbye to Evie and Maggie while stepping into Riley's buggy with a small suitcase in hand, and with enough daylight in which to see their way, off they went. The trip up to Salt Lake took just over 4 hours, leaving Riley with another 4 hours of travel to return home the following day after resting overnight at a hotel while parking the buggy and his horse at the nearby livery stable.

Will had worn his only suit, which was dark gray, while sporting a light gray vest and stylish white wing-collared shirt, along with a black ribbon-like bow tie that was fairly fashionable at the time. When prepping him for the trip, Evie had told him that everyone dresses 'proper' when they ride the train. She had previously recalled seeing travelers dressed up at the train station in Carbondale, noting that it was the usual classy way people traveled these days when riding trains and visiting big cities. The vest, shirt, and tie were of her choosing from a men's haberdashery shop in town, where Lucy often ordered various types of buttons for her dressmakers. However, she noticed that Will's tie was partially obscured by his dark beard draping down to cover the front of his collar.

Also, Evie had previously wanted him to buy a nice black bowler hat to complete his outfit. But he much preferred a western gray slouch hat instead, as he didn't care for the eastern 'city slicker' type hats that the "high-falutin folks" of Chicago and New York tended to wear these days.

At the station in Salt Lake, he had purchased a second-class ticket to Springfield for $27.00, which placed him in a standard wood and steel-constructed coach car for the duration of the trip. But it wasn't luxuriously comfortable as it applied to the lightly padded seating, although he would soon find it far more relaxing and inviting than what his covered wagon had offered him on the trip west. Initially, he thought $27.00 was an exorbitant amount to pay for the journey, especially without an appointed sleeping arrangement. But he soon came to realize how quickly this train would take him to his destination while covering great distances at higher speeds. With that in mind, he appreciated the shorter duration of a trip that now only took days while previously enduring all that he did on the California/Oregon and Mormon trails over a little less than eleven weeks of travel out to Provo. Plus, in this case, there were likely no difficulties or potential conflicts with Indians involved.

As the locomotive chugged to build up steam while leaving the station, he sat by a window that afforded a great view of the towns, cities, and prairie lands he would pass through, taking it all in while seeing how some places had grown a bit more in just a few short years since he had previously gone through there with his covered wagon.

The train route was to take him from the station at Salt Lake, running northeasterly, up to Fort Bridger, and due east from there, through Green River, Wyoming, out to Laramie and Cheyenne, before heading into Nebraska, with stops at Fort Kearney, Lincoln, and Omaha scheduled. After crossing the Missouri River at Omaha by ferry, a different train would then carry the passengers through to Davenport, Iowa, and down to Galesburg, Peoria, and Springfield, Illinois. It was a lengthy trip that covered 1,400 miles of countryside with varying landscapes, although the overall duration was phenomenally quite shorter compared with the wagon train that carried him out west. It took the appointed 'Iron Horse' locomotive just over four days to complete the route east to Springfield.

He brought his old cloth-covered Army canteen filled with water and a couple of large sandwiches that Evie made for him with her excellent homemade bread, along with two hard-boiled eggs, so as not to go hungry, as he didn't know the food situation on the train. So, he spaced out his supply of food and water while ever mindful of the duration of the trip, only consuming a little at a time. However, the Conductor later pointed out to him that the train had an ample supply of fresh potable water available, where he could freely refill his canteen. He also related to him that the train tended to stop along the route at different intervals in towns where restaurant dining would be available during the mid-morning and early evening hours of each day. At the same time, supplies of firewood and water would be replenished, and engine maintenance would be observed as the train would await the passenger's return from the restaurant. At that early date, the transcontinental trains weren't equipped with such an onboard luxury where they could provide passengers with their own accessible dining car service.

When stopping at mid-morning in a town where most of the passengers filed out to fill their bellies with some breakfast at a nearby restaurant, Will decided to throw in with everyone else and enjoy a satisfying meal of bacon, eggs, and a biscuit, with a generous cup of black coffee to wash it all down, before getting back aboard the waiting steam train. These optional meals en route weren't included in one's fare, having become additional minor expenses for each passenger.

If somehow a passenger might unmindfully dally a bit too long away from the train at these stops, the train personnel would not wait for them to get back aboard. It was the passenger's responsibility to ensure they kept themselves fully aware of the train's schedule while paying close attention to the Engineer's whistle and the conductor's subsequent call of "All Aboard!" Otherwise, the train would proceed on its way when the signal was given, leaving behind anyone who may have missed the final call. Those who were left behind would then be saddled with finding an alternate mode of transportation or perhaps a seat on the next day's train for another nominal fee, plus whatever their overnight lodging might have cost them. In addition, they would find themselves having to retrieve whatever baggage was left onboard at Union Station in Chicago. So, as it pertained to riding the rails, the message here was that, much like time itself, the railroad waits for no one.

At some point in the initial part of the trip, Will felt the natural urge to relieve himself, and upon learning where the train's outhouse was, he found that it was at the very end of the last railcar. As he made his way to the trailing coach car, he had to walk on a short platform outside between the railcars to move about from car to car. But when entering the

last car, the 'inside outhouse' was found to be located in a
small enclosed room with a locking door and a raised metal
conical type housing protruding from the floor, with an outhouse seat perched atop it in which to sit on and do one's
duty in the usual manner. However, when Will looked
down into it, he was quite astonished to notice that there
wasn't a bottom to it, as he could see the rail ties and tracks
below in somewhat of a blur as the train moved along while
issuing the familiar clickety-clack sound from below. It
quickly made him realize that everything was meant to drop
down onto the tracks as the train sped along. Although this
all seemed quite astonishing and entirely unconventional to
him, as he wondered how everything eventually got cleaned
up from the tracks or if anyone even bothered with it.

Sometime later, he learned that the unusual outhouse-
like raised seat he used, with the hole in the bottom, was
commonly called a Hooper Toilet. Plus, the exact way the
waste was deposited was deemed perfectly normal at the
time. He also learned that the conductor always locked the
door to that little room whenever the train stopped, to keep
people from soiling the tracks at the stations along the route.

So, after using it for the first time, he returned to his seat
with a bit of a smile, as if he'd just experienced something
entirely unusual, if not amazing.

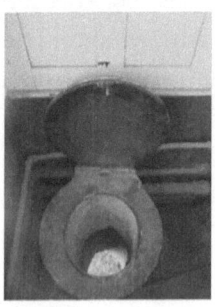

Hooper Toilet

As the train made scheduled stops to pick up other passengers or drop them off, the steam-powered locomotive would often take on more water to refill the boiler. It also afforded an opportunity to load an additional supply of firewood for the firebox that was situated directly below the boiler, whereby the stoked-up firebox would serve to boil the water, making pressurized steam. This essential source powered the train. These steam-powered locomotives were primarily steel-constructed tractors, having large steel wheels that were placed upon a laid-out system of tracks, with the power and torque to pull heavy loads in the form of rail cars trailing behind them. So, from that perspective, they could be considered another variation of a tractor, although configured differently on a larger scale.

In the early years of service, large quantities of seasoned split firewood were used as the raw source for firing the boilers on these steam trains while later giving way to Bituminous and Anthracite coal, which burned hotter and longer than firewood, allowing for further distances traveled before replenishing the supply within the train's 'tender' car, or coal/wood box that trailed right behind the engine. When seeing a wood-fired train in the distance, the stack's plume of grayish-white smoke always gave it away, while the coal-fired trains billowed their signature black smoke behind them as they got their steam up. The train engineer up front, who was the watchful eye in helping to guide the locomotive along the rails and keep a look-out for obstructions on the track and whatever else, had another man up there with him who monitored the firebox to keep it well stoked with shovelfuls of coal or split pieces of firewood. As the train moved down the tracks, the engineer occasionally checked the steam pressure gauge to ensure the reading remained normal, keeping the train performing as it should while maintaining optimum speed levels over the terrain ahead.

After drifting off in slumber for a while, Will awoke to hear the Conductor announce the next stop in Cheyenne, Wyoming, as he looked out to see a heavily overcast sky with the station quickly coming into view. At different stops where water and wood or coal had to be loaded, the passengers had time to step off at the station to stretch their legs, smoke their pipe, and take in the view of the surrounding area to get a brief feel for the place. It also allowed some to stand back and away from the train platform to appreciate a fuller view of the monstrosity's entire interconnected assemblage. The steam engine and fuel tender car featured up front were followed by the baggage car and four or five coach cars trailing that offered different seating according to one's ticket class. For Will, he was situated in the third coach car as a second-class passenger. The railroad had initially adopted the class system for their passenger trains, borrowing the formerly European concept from steamships and other oceanic passenger lines. These passenger trains did not feature a Caboose serving as the end car, as the caboose was more noted on freight trains to serve as an office and rest area for the conductor, and a temporary shelter for a few of the train's crew who would watch for any possible load shifting of their heavy freight within the railcars in front of them.

As they all reboarded from the Cheyenne platform, the train slowly rolled away from the station, building up steam while soon high-balling its way into Nebraska as it covered long, flat stretches of countryside where vast cornfields and plowed farmlands could be seen for miles. Will had noticed the overcast skies had become significantly darker, with billowing dark clouds forming, to suggest that rain may be in the immediate forecast. After about 20 minutes, he looked out again and suddenly spotted a sizeable raging tornado touching the ground while seemingly moving in the train's direction from the southwest as it quickly angled its way. Some sizeable loose debris from a few houses and barns was observed being lifted within its vortex while being strewn about as it aimlessly twisted its furious way across the plain. By then, many of the other passengers had also noticed it, as they exhibited a good measure of anxiety with all that was going on while hoping that the train might outrun it, which it did, but not by much. From a short distance ahead, a few passengers could look back and see the twister crossing over the train tracks where they had just been, less than a minute before.

As nightfall came, the next brief stop was at Grand Island, Nebraska, with Lincoln and Omaha to follow, as it would be the morning of the next day when the train would eventually roll into Omaha. At Omaha station, the passengers deboarded with their luggage and crossed the Missouri River by way of a ferry boat, leaving the Central Pacific train behind while then boarding a waiting Union Pacific steam train on the other bank in Council Bluffs, Iowa. From there, the train headed northeast toward stops in Des Moines and Davenport, Iowa, where it crossed over the Mississippi River by way of the Chicago & Rock Island Railroad Bridge that was built in 1856. With that, the train finally entered the state of Illinois, with its next stop placing it in Galesburg. By now, Will was starting to anticipate his upcoming junction in Springfield, where he could then catch the southbound Illinois Central train down to Carbondale.

As all of that came to pass, he soon found himself walking through the Carbondale station and out to the street with his suitcase in hand. Taking in the town's familiarity from his previous life there, he found that it hadn't changed much in the few years while he was away, much the same as when he returned from the war and Camp Butler. It was late afternoon, and he needed to make his way back over to the farm, as he didn't have any other place to stay while back in town, preferring not to impose on the Proctors. So, after grabbing some dinner at a restaurant in town, Will stepped just as lively as he did when Mrs. Johnson would open the schoolhouse door at 3 O'clock to allow her students to return to their homes. He again covered the 20-minute distance from there to his parents' former egg farm, with still enough daylight to spare. When he arrived, he found that the skeleton key they had always hidden on a ledge near the front door was still there, as if nothing had changed. But he found that the place had collected a goodly amount of dust while standing idle, so he set about to clean things up a bit to make it more presentable.

In the morning, because there wasn't any food left in the house, he again retraced his steps and walked back into town to grab some breakfast at the café before heading over to the bank to talk with a man named Cletus Judson, who had sent him the telegram.

By 9 a.m., the bank had opened for business, as Will finished his last bit of coffee before paying for his meal and walking across to see Mr. Judson. He had suspected that the name Judson had sounded a bit familiar to him, but he couldn't place it until he met Cletus and recalled an old red-headed schoolmate by the name of Simon Judson, who was this man's son. As President of the Bank of Carbondale, Cletus Judson was a pleasant sort of man in his mid to late fifties, rather rotund and on the shorter side of six feet. He had a high forehead and a receding red-headed comb-over hairstyle to complete his outward appearance.

After exchanging pleasantries, he mentioned to Will that soon after John's passing, the townspeople had become curious about the status and future of the farm, as there had been no local egg distribution around town since his death. They were hoping that someone would revive the farm's operations so everyone could once again purchase locally sourced eggs. "You know how small townspeople like to talk and speculate when things change." Will nodded in acknowledgment while wondering where Cletus was going with this.

Mr. Judson, the town's banker, was deeply concerned about the sudden failure of Glover's Farm after the owner's passing. He felt that this would not be in the best interest of the town or the bank, while having a negative effect on the overall commerce within Jackson County. Throughout the years, both John and Margaret had been making weekly deposits to their savings account as their egg operation flourished and became an integral part of the town's economy. Seeing the farm lying fallow without generating any income was concerning enough for Cletus to send off the telegram to Will out in Provo while announcing John's passing. But in addition to that announcement, he wanted to see if he could prod Will into returning to rerun the family farm or sell it outright to someone else who could bring it back to its old form while re-establishing the business at the Carbondale Bank...naturally.

As Cletus went on, he said, "Since your father's passing, there have been limited supplies of eggs brought in from outside the county, but they never satisfied the area's needs as much as your father's supplies always had. Plus, there was some question as to just how fresh they were." Cletus also mentioned that he had learned about some locals who were interested in buying the farm if it were available. He retained their contact information "in case anyone might hear from you, as John's son and his only surviving relative. Are you now interested in coming back to restart the egg farm?" asked Cletus. "No, replied Will. I have other interests and obligations elsewhere that are more important to me now. I've had my time here, but I'd rather enjoy my new life out in Utah. So, I'd really like to sell the place and cut my ties with Carbondale...No offense". "None taken, son," replied Cletus, as he gave Will a sheet of paper containing the names and addresses of three prospective buyers who had expressed their interest in purchasing the farm.

Incidentally, all three happened to be account holders at the Bank of Carbondale.

Then he presented Will with his parents' account information, pointing out that there was still a sizeable amount of funds that accrued from their egg sales over the past several years, after withdrawals in the past for farm equipment and repair parts, etc., along with other withdrawals for their basic needs. However, several thousand dollars remained in the account, which would be left to Will, should he decide to close it and take the funds. Since he knew that his business was all but finished in Carbondale, he closed the account and accepted a bank draft from Mr. Judson for the full amount.

After presenting the draft to Will and giving him information about the potential buyers for the farm, all of whom were local residents, they shook hands, and Will left with the intention of contacting them immediately. But first, he wanted to make a point of stopping by the Proctor's house to visit Evie's folks and catch up with things so that he could provide his wife with some heartwarming conversation and news of the town upon his return. As overjoyed as the Proctors were to see him, they invited him to stay for dinner before heading back up to the farm. He accepted, but first, he had to take care of some unfinished business, including paying the undertaker and cemetery administrator for John's burial and headstone, before locating the farm's potential buyers.

But while visiting with Charles and Mary Proctor in their spacious and well-appointed Victorian home, he had the sudden urge to relieve himself and started for the back door to head out toward the outhouse, only to find that it was no longer there. Puzzled, he looked back at Mary, who flashed him a knowing smile and said, "Oh, we had some construction done since you and Evie left for Utah, which brought water right into the house, with a small hand pump now mounted right next to the kitchen sink. It also allowed for an indoor outhouse, but in the form of what is now called a 'water closet.' "So, it's all right inside the house now, and it's simply the latest thing, you know...from France. Some of the most prominent folks in the east have one now, as it works with the use of water to flush everything out to what they call a cesspit that's in the ground, and it makes things less offensive and more sanitary with how it works."

Suddenly struck by this new development, Will proceeded to enter the "Water Closet" to take care of his necessary business. After finishing, he pulled the chain and watched as the gravity-fed water from the tank above cleared everything from the white porcelain bowl and refilled it with a clear reservoir of standing water. He momentarily wondered how to turn it off until he noticed it somehow shuts itself off. It was all quite phenomenal to him, as he never saw the likes of that flushing mechanism that went with it, with water being used in such a way. He chuckled and thought, this is even more impressive than what he experienced on the train, as he washed his hands and resumed his visit with Evie's folks. But, while he didn't rightly understand how the thing moved water through it like it did, he marveled at what a fine working contraption it truly was.

After visiting briefly with the Proctors, he made contact with the aforementioned town officials to pay his debts, then walked to Morton Dailey's address, as he was the first on the list of prospective buyers. Dailey was interested in purchasing the farm and its egg operation as an investment while intending to appoint a couple from nearby Carterville to reside there and run it. Mr. Dailey wanted to broaden the operation by adding more henhouses to increase egg production and expand distributional coverage to both nearby Murphysboro and Carterville townships. Plus, he was interested in creating softer cushioning within the flats of eggs so that they could be distributed more safely to ensure there would be less breakage involved.

Will thought that was all fine with him, as it sounded like Mr. Dailey was truly interested in taking the egg business to new and greater heights. He felt that his family's previous operation would live on with the townsfolk as a legacy to John and Margaret anyway, as the only egg business the people of Carbondale had ever known, going back through a few generations of Glovers. However, the place's name would likely be changed to the 'Dailey Farm' or something other than Glover's if he decided to sell to this man.

He arranged to meet Mr. Dailey at the farm the next day at 10 a.m. so he could inspect the place and get a better understanding of its layout for the potential purchase. Will had also spoken with another interested buyer named Norm Edwards. Mr. Edwards' initial inspection would follow Mr.

Dailey's visit, starting at 1 p.m., serving as his appointed time to see the place.

As it turned out, they both had positive things to say about the farmhouse and its still serviceable henhouses and barn. They noted that the house had been well cared for, given that it was a little over ninety years old, and the six chicken houses containing many nesting boxes were all in good condition. Both men concurred that the hen houses would still be quite suitable for starting again by immediately adding new batches of hens, as John's chickens had all died due to lack of care after his passing.

These two potential buyers, who were eager to revive the egg business in Carbondale, had each submitted their written offers to Will, stating what they believed the property, along with the house and business upon it, was worth. They then left, giving Will some time to review their offers and make a decision on whether to accept one of them or reject both and wait for a higher bid. As he sat while taking in what they had written, he thought it was all so very strange that he was left in this position, to have to decide the fate of his father's, grandfather's, and great-grandfather's farm and egg business as it was, while already deciding not to carry on with the family tradition by walking away from it. He carried bitter memories and resentments from his struggles there with John, leaving a negative imprint on his mind. Plus, he just wanted something more liberating for himself and his family, which he believed he had found out in Provo.

When considering the two offers, Will remembered Mr. Judson telling him that the property was considerably more valuable being sold as a viable business than simply a house on 4 acres of land. Plus, the close proximity to the town had some further value to consider. But, while Mr. Edwards had given what Will thought was a respectable offer, Mr. Dailey's offer was notably higher. So, he decided to accept Morton Dailey's generous proposal.

The following day, he took his routine walk back into town to have breakfast before acquiring the family's recorded deed. Cletus Judson later presented the deed to Mr. Dailey after Will signed off on it to complete the transaction. To that effect, the former Glover Farm would be transferred to Morton Dailey in its current condition for the sum of money that was agreed upon. After both parties signed the bill of sale, it was noted and approved with another signature showing that Mr. Judson had witnessed the transaction. A handshake sealed the deal, and the new owner drew sufficient cash out of his account at the bank before handing full payment to Will. He thanked him for accepting his offer, allowing him to become the new owner of the now-former Glover's Farm.

In turn, Will paid Mr. Judson an acceptable sum for all he did to help broker the deal while also providing him guidance and professional advice, despite effectively being maneuvered into it. Unsurprisingly, as a more significant aspect of the deal, Mr. Judson was quite pleased to know that one of his more notable account holders now owned the egg farm. This ensured that a formerly successful business in Carbondale, which had been serving the area's consumers for many decades, would be revived and restored to its former prominence and potential. It would again benefit the town's consumers while raising the level of commerce in the Little Egypt area of southern Illinois. Before leaving, Will turned the large sum of cash over to Mr. Judson in exchange for another bank draft that would be much easier to carry.

So, with a feeling of finality, Will muttered to himself, "Well, that ends that," as he departed from the bank and again grabbed a meal in town before walking back up to the farmhouse for his last night in Carbondale. In reminiscing, he realized it was the only home he had ever known before serving in the Union Army. The more he thought about it, he found that he had a lot of old childhood memories from growing up while living in that little farmhouse on Murphysboro Road with John and Margaret. In a sense, it was hard for him to bring the final curtain down on his former life there, which was what all of this represented. But as he had always been a practical-minded sort, he knew that it had to be done to move forward with things, even as bittersweet as it was, to serve the better interests of his family life in Utah. After the farm sale, the money would provide them with a sizeable nest egg for the future, allowing them to live a better life together without worrying much about money. Plus, he was pretty sure that it would likely make Violet a lot happier as well.

The next morning, he closed the front door of the house behind him and walked out to the road. Turning back, he paused to take in a final farewell view of the old place before heading back into town to catch his northbound train to Springfield, where he would board the westbound back to Salt Lake City. As he walked the old Murphysboro road for the last time to wind his way back into town, he could see the old schoolhouse off in the distance, next to the Livery Stable. It had been abandoned a few years prior in favor of a larger facility with multiple classrooms to accommodate the town's growing student population. However, it still stood there with a certain prominence, serving as a notable icon from earlier times. As he paused to look upon it for the last time, Will fondly recalled an unforgotten teacher who had provided her students with something that went well beyond the curriculum she taught: the timeless and enduring gifts of awareness and understanding. For him, this represented a deeper and more advanced level of academic learning from which he and all of his fellow students had benefited.

After breakfast at the cafe, he had some time to spare, so he decided to stop by the telegraph office and send a message to Riley in Provo, informing him of the expected day and time of arrival in Salt Lake City. Again, he stopped briefly to say goodbye to Charles and Mary Proctor, who presented him with some fresh fruit to eat on the return trip. But before heading to the station to catch his train, he stopped by the cemetery to visit his parents for what he felt was the very last time.

Upon Will's return to the homestead in North Provo, Evie and Maggie just happened to be doing chores in the cabin's front yard when he and Riley surprisingly rolled up in the buggy. They rushed over as he stepped out, embracing him tightly and shedding tears of joy at the reunion. It was an exciting surprise for them, as Riley hadn't informed them of Will's return date.

After freshening up from the long journey, he told Evie that her parents were still healthy and doing quite well at their home in Carbondale. They had entrusted Will with expressing their love for their daughters, whom they missed terribly, along with their lovely curly-headed granddaughter. He also surprised her by relating about their new indoor "Water Closet," which he was very excited about when visiting. He remarked that it was "the most innovative and amazing thing he had ever seen in terms of an outhouse," which, in this case, was brought right into the house. "Your mother said it was the latest thing, and they just had to have one."

He then told her that he managed to sell the farm for a nice sum while paying the undertaker and the cemetery for John's burial. Filling her in with all the details, he then presented her with two sizeable bank drafts to deposit into their account at the bank in Salt Lake City through the mercantile store in Provo. This would allow them to draw on it, as needed, from the mercantile store. When she saw all the numbers on the drafts, she didn't know what to say. She was quite surprised and thoroughly overwhelmed by it, although still exceedingly thrilled with the realization of getting her husband back after being away for nearly two weeks. He then proceeded to tell her about the train ride, describing what it was like to sit comfortably next to a window in the coach car and watch the rapidly changing landscape without the discomfort that often came with riding in a covered wagon. He also mentioned the rather close tornado sighting, of which she had always heard stories about the tremendous damage they tended to cause and the deaths that often accompany their presence while only having seen one from afar.

In summing up his trip, he suggested that if she and her sister Lucy, and perhaps even Maggie, may ever consider returning for a visit to Carbondale to see their parents, and for Maggie to see her grandparents, they would only have to travel for a little over four days in which to get there aboard the train. This was nearly incomprehensible to her compared with the eleven weeks they all endured by covered wagon. Finally, when elaborating on his unusual discovery within the train's inside outhouse, Evie fell into hysterical laughter while learning about Will's observations and his all too vivid descriptions of how things are to be done nowadays aboard a train.

Part Six

Prospecting

While resuming his usual activities in and around Provo, Will continued to occasionally put in some time working at the nearby Atlas Mine. The same applied to Riley and Otto, as they all enjoyed the decent wages paid during more active periods when they were called on to provide their labor, even if it was only temporary. Although satisfied that he now had a large sum of money in the bank from the sale of his deceased father's egg farm and its accrued income, he figured he could always work to earn a little more while still young enough and able to do so. In his idle time, he also entertained the idea of prospecting for gold and silver while having some adventurous outdoor activities to potentially increase his savings. However, he was very aware of the possible hazards involved with such adventures within the territory of Utah.

Some of the more stimulating stories the trio shared as they occasionally gathered in Provo's only saloon had involved the existence of gold in certain areas, as some reports were still rumored to that effect. But whether they were true or were spread in the form of hearsay and hyperbole, nobody knew for sure. However, as a mutual hobby, these three all shared the common goal and desire of trying to locate some of it for their own self-interest, to help improve their family's lot when not working at the mine. So, after a few beers, they made a pact, agreeing that any gold or silver they found while prospecting together would be divided equally among the three of them, regardless of who found it. In that respect, it made the three of them equal sharing partners.

Their progressive involvement in prospecting, influenced by the saloon gatherings, led to several short expeditions fairly close to home, involving overnight camping and hours of stream panning. On those nearby excursions, they were fortunate to find a bit of glittery dust in their pans to further fuel their ambitions, but not enough to get excited about. So, they planned to go farther from the Provo area during the summer of 1870 to head northeast up and into the Big Cottonwood Creek canyon, roughly 15 miles southeast of Salt Lake City. It was a noteworthy mining area within the high hills of the western slopes of the Wasatch Mountain range, where they could pan the highly regarded and more hopeful headwaters of the Big Cottonwood Creek.

Right away, Evie was nervous and anxious, as she had difficulty with the notion that her man was planning to go off into unknown high country areas with his two friends for an extended period. She didn't care about the prospect of finding any amount of precious ore in the backcountry, as she just didn't want her husband to leave her and Maggie alone on the homestead for such a long time. Will had suggested they would be away for roughly three to four weeks unless they somehow got lucky sooner. But, while explaining things to her, he said that Betty Atkinson would come by on occasion to visit and look in on them, as this excursion and what it represented would be good for the family's future if they might find a fair amount of either gold or silver.

She knew that while they still had much of the money from the sale of Glover's Farm, Will was always interested in adding to it, if possible, to help ensure their future in Provo, while the lack of work there left him idle and bored at this time of the year. He told her not to worry, as the three of them would be sure to look out for each other throughout their time away. Pleading with him, she soon relented and resigned herself to at least secure his promise that he would return as soon as he could. He agreed and gave her his solemn promise that he would return to her, as the two hugged and kissed each other before saying goodbye. For her, this was different from Will's time away in Carbondale, as it was just a little under two weeks compared with this newly hatched prospecting trip. But, as this seemed important to her husband, she reluctantly acquiesced while allowing him to follow his own path with such things. As a faithful wife, she would have to trust his judgment on whatever he would decide, even though, unlike most other women of the day, she was often allowed to give her preferred views on things.

It took them a few days of constant travel with their three horses and two pack mules in tow while moving at a horse-walk, going north up along the main dusty thoroughfare known as the old Mormon Road. As they moved along the shoulder of the road, they joined company with the passing traffic of freight wagons headed up to Salt Lake City, making camp for the night in a tree-lined area away from the road, as dusk then came upon them. At some point the following day, the three turned off to the east, riding along a farm wagon road stretching for several miles toward the Wasatch range before it ultimately took them up an escarpment into the higher mountainous country. At the end of that wagon road, there was only a narrow trail to follow as they left the valley to wind their way up onto a high plateau leading through the southern outskirts of the well-noted Shoshone tribal wilderness area. The further rise in elevation on this lengthy mountainous trail eventually brought them to their ultimate destination, higher up within the namesake canyon, along the upper stretch of the Big Cottonwood Creek. Once there, they noticed wildflowers were still bursting with color even at this mid-summer time of the year.

Before their departure on this trek into the high country, others warned them to be on alert when traversing through a strip of the trail that was generally recognized as being a bordering section of it, lying within designated Indian land. The area in question was part of the more remote southern portion of the Shoshone wilderness, where it was well noted that there were occasionally a few bands of renegade tribesmen roaming those parts from time to time, who would make their presence known while commonly not being of a friendly nature. The Big Cottonwood Creek, which carved its waters right through that section of the canyon trail, would likely be drawn from, on occasion, by tribesmen roaming in that area while hunting for game.

The three enthusiasts set up their tents near the creek at the established site to form their mining encampment. They created a stone fire ring to cook their meals and warm themselves during the evening while devoting the rest of their time to investigating the area's rock formations for clues of silver or gold deposits. The camp's placement also allowed them easy access to pan the nearby creek for gold. When deciding to set up camp there, they luckily found another spot nearby with plenty of green grass for their animals to graze on. This unexpected find helped them stay at the campsite longer without having to use up their limited supply of grain for the horses and pack mules.

But while camped at that site, they amassed only a small poke of gold dust and tiny nuggets to show for all their efforts over three weeks' worth of work while traversing a good distance overland and upward into that canyon. The hopeful trio kept busy every day with the work that went into it to see if any precious metals might have formed deposits thereabouts or if anything may be collecting in their pans. With daily persistence, they came up with only small amounts of ore before electing to spread out and pan the creek in both directions. That redirected effort brought about better results, yielding a fair amount of glittering gold dust and tiny nuggets to add to their leather poke.

But after nearly four weeks of panning and digging throughout the area, the prospectors began to see their hopes dimming at that location. To add to their woes of having a relatively lean yield from their efforts, they found their food supplies rapidly dwindling, with little or no prospect of finding any game to shoot within that canyon. Additionally, the supplemental grain for the horses and mules began running quite low after the animals had already consumed what was naturally available in the previously noted grassy area. So, after a certain amount of shared handwringing, they resigned themselves while deciding it was probably time to pack up and head back to their families in the Provo area to check on the activity at the mine and see if their part-time labor there might be needed again.

The decision to return home hadn't come easy for the three of them. They had hoped to find a halfway significant ore deposit to further support their family's livelihood. It would have made their efforts more worthwhile in helping to afford additional food, new clothes, and shoes. Additionally, it would allow them to buy more ammunition to hunt fresh meat from the nearby forest. Although, for all of their efforts and time put in at that mining site, they did manage to accumulate enough gold dust and small nuggets to make the expedition at least worthwhile, if not entirely fruitful.

So, the following morning, all three men took down their tents and rolled them up tightly, strapping them to their pack mules, along with their prospecting tools and other remaining provisions. They would soon break camp and set out down the mountainous slope beside the canyon to plot their simple course back to Provo. The three prospectors followed the same trail they came in on, along the meandering Big Cottonwood Creek, flowing westerly toward the lower elevations. They also knew they would again have to pass through the southern edge of the Shoshone Wilderness before eventually dropping down into the Salt Lake Valley below.

At a more precipitous section of the canyon trail, Will descended into a steep hillside draw on foot while leading his horse 'Sunshine.' His two prospecting companions followed along at a fair distance with their horses and two pack mules in tow, ladened with their essential gear and remaining supplies. As Will continued with his gradual descent, the others kept him in view while trailing from a lightly forested section of ground located considerably above and behind him.

It was a thoroughly overcast day in the area, with relatively mild temperatures felt by the traveling party while experiencing no rain, which might otherwise dampen their footing to make for slippery conditions on their downward trek. None of the three would have been able to say what day of the week it was at the time, as each day was generally seen as just the next day in that remote mountainous environment. However, they all knew they were actively moving along through mid to late August on the calendar in their journey back home to Orem and Provo.

As Will continued to make his way to lower ground to lead the way back for the party, he found himself in an open area where the slope was beginning to flatten out to some extent. Nearby, there were natural grooves in the landscape that had noticeably been formed in the ground over time from erosion. It was due to yearly water runoff produced by the snow melt on the mountain above. Interestingly, they appeared like small, narrow creekbeds that carried the melted snow from above in a gravitational flow down to the creek below. They naturally created somewhat deep erosional scars over time. However, at this time of the year, the runoff trails were completely dry, only showing as slotted, vein-like lines trailing down the hilly and mountainous landscape as natural telltale creases from above.

While making further progress down the draw, Will stopped briefly to turn around and see where the rest of his party was situated in the distance behind him, when suddenly the ground beneath his feet began to violently shake back and forth, throwing him to the ground while spooking Sunshine and causing her to rear up and dash away from his grip on the reins. Finding himself halfway sitting on the ground as the tremor subsided, Will immediately realized he had just experienced a sizeable earthquake. He quickly arose to take stock of things while noticing Sunshine had scampered off, down and well out of range from him.

Then he heard a strange clatter and rumbling sound coming from behind him. He quickly turned around to see a large cloud of dust with various-sized boulders rolling ahead of it, tumbling down toward him from the mountain above. Alarmed, he could see that it was all headed straight down in his direction at an accelerated rate of speed. While realizing he had no time to move laterally in either direction in which to avoid this swiftly moving rocky avalanche that involved quite a few boulders of varying size, he immediately looked at one of the slotted drainage ditches nearby and frantically ran toward it in a desperate attempt to seek refuge there. In his frightful haste, he felt that even in that moment of extreme chaos, the lower ground within the hillside trench might possibly save him from these large rocky boulders. As he quickly dove into it and lowered his body face-down into the narrow recess of the dry rock and earthen creekbed, he could hear and feel the impacts of the heavy boulders bounding overhead and around him. It all pounded the nearby ground with a deafening barrage from these large and heavy rocks and stones that tumbled chaotically down the mountainside draw.

As this was all unfolding in full view below, from where Riley and Otto were positioned above, they could see Will hunkered down in the narrow trench-like creekbed, with the avalanche of boulders moving steadily, and rolling at a good clip all around him, as an immense blast of dust came trailing down behind it. But then they both suddenly cringed and shuddered at the sight of one of the largest of the boulders tumbling end over end with its enormous oblong shape, headed right down in Will's line of direction, as it tumbled one last time and landed right on top of where he was situated. To their horror, as they watched, it covered him completely while the sheer tonnage of this rock had embedded the huge, heavy stone a few inches into the ground with its final impact. As the dust was clearing, Riley and Otto faced each other in shocked disbelief while shrieking at what they had just witnessed before them.

As everything finally subsided, with the billowing dust from this sudden ground-shaking calamity having cleared, Otto tied the horses and mules to a nearby tree. Immediately, the two scampered down to where the giant boulder had landed and where Will, with what may or may not be left of him, was situated beneath it. They both wandered around the massive stone to see if there might be anything they could do to help their friend and partner as they hollered out to him in this seemingly impossible situation. However, as things soon became more evident that this was potentially a grave situation, they feared their friend may now be gone, or otherwise likely doomed, while entombed beneath this enormous stone. Nervously rationalizing as they stood by the giant boulder, they surmised that if he might somehow still be alive, his oxygen may soon run out, and then he would be done for sure.

So, with that realization, Otto frantically ran back up the draw, grabbed a pick and shovel from atop one of the pack mules, and made his way back to the big stone, slipping and falling a few times as he hurriedly descended back into the draw. He then began to work the pick into the ground on one side of the enormous boulder while Riley used the shovel to scoop away the loosened soil and rock. Soon, Otto hit solid rock at about a foot below the ground level, and without pausing, moved laterally a few feet, only to find more of the same rocky subsurface, and it began to frustrate him as he worked. Stymied by this impasse on one side of the stone, they decided to move to the other side and dig there, only to discover the same problem. At the rear of the stone, where it settled over the drainage ditch, there was a good amount of soil that they managed to remove until running into compacted gravel and large embedded stones. These stones and pressed gravel were extremely difficult and next to impossible to extract, given their size and the compressed weight from the giant boulder. So they then tried the very front part of this gigantic boulder and found the same situation there. Exhausted and thoroughly frustrated, the two of them had worked frantically for well over an hour, having spent all their efforts on possibly freeing their friend while disappointingly falling short. They just could not find a way to gain access under that huge rock, and it thoroughly destroyed them as they sat in shock and disbelief at their failed effort and what it would mean.

Sadly, as they hated the thought of leaving Will or even his body behind, it now appeared to them that this gigantic stone would become their friend's grave marker by default.

The utter shock from this unbelievable tragedy, having unfolded right before their eyes, was written on both men's faces. The full realization of what had just occurred soon began to settle into their psyches as they reluctantly abandoned their efforts toward possibly digging him out. In this utterly helpless situation, it left them feeling as if they had suddenly lost a close family member. Tears of grief had streamed steadily down both their faces once they knew nothing further could be done to help their friend.

As Otto and Riley painfully resigned themselves to losing their close friend and mining partner, they soon realized they still had to hike back up the draw to retrieve the horses and mules before making camp farther down the canyon for the night. They would then have to move on through the Shoshone country farther west of there the following day before returning to the Salt Lake Valley and home. In planning the way back, Riley had reckoned the overall distance from their campsite on the Big Cottonwood had been judged to be roughly a 40-45 mile journey to get back to Little Rock Canyon, which would take them a little over two days.

Meanwhile, from within the dark recess of the narrow and shallow creek bed beneath that huge boulder, a sound heard by no one was suddenly expressed by a still-alive Will Glover, who desperately cried out with a banshee-like scream.

It was followed resoundingly by, "NO, NO, NO!"

But no matter how loudly reported, his cries fell silent while completely contained within the enormous stone covering above and the sound-deadening ground below.

In the moments immediately following this bizarre and unexpected development, with the realization that a giant boulder had suddenly covered him over, Will frightfully found himself in great distress, going into shock with what had just occurred. He lay there helpless within the 30 – 36 inch deep trench with this huge stone now covering him completely, having blocked out all light, with no prospect of getting out to see daylight or his family ever again. But, it was somewhat fortunate for him that this gigantic stone, with its tremendous girth and weight, did not compress on him, while the depth of the shallow trench still allowed him to move his arms and legs.

In his travels and experiences, Will encountered odd and unusual situations that he could always deal with. Whenever he encountered an obstacle or a challenge to his stamina and mental skills, he usually found a workable solution to overcome it and move on. However, this situation seemed entirely different. Suddenly, when thinking about the possibility of backing out of this drainage ditch to quickly resolve the problem and escape this scary situation, he desperately kicked with his legs, feeling around behind him in the darkness with his feet while pressing himself rearward as best as he could. However, with that effort, he finally reached a point where he found there was a solid build-up of compacted soil, gravel, and large rock now blocking the way. Thoroughly disheartened, he concluded that the ditch had collapsed behind him, pressing more gravel and rock into it to block that exit. Plus, he knew he couldn't possibly dig himself out with his feet, and couldn't even turn himself around within the narrow trench to address it straight-on. So, at that point, he began to realize this was an entirely unconventional and altogether different type of situation, being perhaps unworkable as a problem to be solved. Not knowing what to do next, he resigned himself while figuring that this situation was inescapable now, and his heart sank with that hopeless thought as he fully realized in his frightened state of mind that he was trapped and, as a result, was likely going to die.

But when finally calming himself down and coming more to grips with his futile situation while lying there on his belly, knowing full well that there can be no escape from this earthly stone coffin, Will thinks of his family, his wife and now 6-year-old daughter back in Provo, as he begins to weep. In his grief, he thinks of all of what he was unable to accomplish for his family while believing that he had failed them in his efforts to make a steady living. He then dreaded what might now lay ahead for his soon-to-be widowed wife, Evelyn, and their sweet daughter, Maggie.

As he and Otto moved on down the canyon trail, Riley struggled mightily with the sudden realization that he and Betty would have to break the news to Evie when getting back home. He knew that it would devastate and break her heart even more than his own heart was broken by this.

After descending from the higher elevations of the Big Cottonwood Canyon, they finally made camp for the night about six miles below where the rock slide occurred, back within a somewhat sparse piney-wood forest. They hobbled the horses and mules to keep them from wandering off while setting up their overnight camp. With nightfall closing in, they suddenly heard the rustling sound of some nearby movement and grabbed up their rifles to check it out while slowly moving out toward where it was coming from, only to discover that Will's horse 'Sunshine' had gotten onto their trail and followed them to their overnight encampment.

Reclined within their bedrolls and blankets, splayed out next to the roaring campfire, Riley and Otto, in dealing with their grief from the day's tragedy, could not speak at all as they stretched out in total silence, going over things in their minds while staring up at the multitude of stars in the night sky. The eerie silence was only broken by the distinct crackle from the fire heard in the cool night air, along with an occasional nearby hoot from the familiar Great Horned Owl with its deep, almost baritonal report.

To them, Will wasn't just a prospecting partner. He was a close friend, which was somewhat of an uncommon find in the mostly uncaring early western territory of Utah. He was also vital in keeping the trio's interest in mining for their shared profit alive. Although, with all that transpired that day, none of that mattered anymore. They both only knew that they lost a very good friend.

Being a survivalist by nature, while not one to give up so easily when in difficult or next-to-impossible situations, Will felt for his hunting knife down at his right side within the dark and cramped space of the ditch, as he pulled it from its leather sheath and began to apply it while picking at the soil and rock that lay in the black void before him. Noting the combination of soil and rock, he found the ground somewhat workable, even without any light to see what he was doing, as it was all done according to feel. However, he didn't know exactly how much length or width this heavy rock on top of him had left him with in determining how far he may have to dig to get past it. Plus, he was well aware that his oxygen would likely run out at some point. So, instead of waiting for that to occur, which seemed to be what would happen anyway, he felt like he just needed to stay busy, to keep his mind occupied while refusing to give up.

As he worked at possibly digging himself out of this situation, he desperately stabbed and carved at the ground in front of him, blindly shaping the walls into a crude sort of tunnel wide enough to accommodate the forward movement of his body. He began to feel better with the new activity, which he realized may or may not hold merit in this seemingly futile situation. But it kept him from focusing on the inevitable. As dirt and small stones began to pile up in front of him, he pulled the accumulated leavings down past his legs, where he could push and kick it all farther behind him and out of the way. It made room for more of it as he continued to dig at the ground ahead of him. Steadily digging and scraping at the compacted soil with his knife in total darkness, he found that he could inch himself forward with each little degree of progress while repeating the cycle as he continued to pass the loose material down beside him and kick it to the rear.

He was beginning to develop some rhythm with the process while being able to systematically push his body a little bit further into this crude little tunnel until his knife blade suddenly hit solid compacted gravel and larger impacted stones in his path ahead. When using his hands to feel around where this newfound gravel and rock was now blocking the progress, he discovered that these larger stones were firmly embedded in the ditch as the compacted rock went all the way up to the top, where it met with the bottom of the enormous stone to seal off the way ahead. Frustrated, he rested with that new obstacle while contemplating a possible alternative.

Then suddenly, he turned to his left and plunged the knife blade into the soil beside him to begin carving away at the earth and rock combination there, where it was still workable. Now, he was moving in a decidedly diagonal direction, hoping to resume the forward progress, although he still didn't know if that was the right tack. Again, while carving and clearing the soil and rock away to accommodate his body, he wriggled and inched himself further forward, feeling that he was making some progress, although at a snail's pace.

But in his desperation with this new prospect of possibly digging himself out of an otherwise impossible situation, even as methodic as he was with the process, he became easily exhausted while seeming to be low on oxygen. This caused him at some point to drop his knife and cease all activity as he labored to breathe, while then becoming increasingly light-headed and disoriented to the point of finally passing out.

After regaining consciousness, when waking after an unknown amount of time, he found that he could now breathe a little easier than before and couldn't figure out why. Surely, he thought, he should have run out of oxygen by now, to where his troubles would have been over, where it would have otherwise designated the small carved-out space that he now occupied beneath the huge boulder as his body's final resting place. But with new energy and determination, he continued to dig and dig with the knife, again pushing the loose dirt and small stones down beside him, and to the rear, as he progressively moved forward once again.

Inch by inch underground, while taking his mind off of everything else and just focusing on digging through the dark void beneath the boulder that entombed him, he began to feel a degree of hope with all of his efforts. He would again use his hands to shape the size of this tunnel while measuring and gauging it to accommodate his body size as he inched and stretched himself forward like a giant, overgrown earthworm. At that point, his entire body was no longer positioned within the lineal drainage ditch. His diagonal trajectory now found him actively moving within this newly carved-out tunnel, with renewed hope and energy, although still without knowing whether it might save him from this dire situation.

Then, while making further progress, he suddenly sees a strange and confusing faint light right out in front of him at the base of where he had been digging...or thinks that he sees something. So, while managing to thrust himself farther forward in which to move closer to it, he turned his head sideways to the left to look and peer upward toward where the light seemed to be coming from, into what looked like a small tunnel where oddly a few stars in the firmament could be seen, and where some degree of moonlight appeared to be shining through. Oddly, it was almost as if he was viewing the idiomatic expression of *the light at the end of the tunnel*, which made him wonder just what it was he was looking at. He then paused and thought that whatever it was just couldn't possibly be real and that his mind was likely playing tricks on him. While nearly dismissing it, he assumed he must be getting delirious at this point of his adrenalin-filled ordeal. Then, as it all suddenly dawned on him that it *was* real, with the vision coming more into focus, he suddenly knew in excited amazement the reason why. It was no wonder that he was able to breathe easier, as fresh air was now coming in through this little tunnel he uncovered, which he finally came to realize was a "Goddamned gopher hole!"

That new gleeful discovery had spurred him on further, to start digging in more of an upward direction from there while continuing to carve away and widen the walls of this crude tunnel with his knife. The discovery had changed his digging direction again, this time toward following the line of sight through the beautiful little gopher hole he found. His new upward activity would eventually fit his body into and up through another phase of the tunnel as he snaked and shimmied it forward and upward with every few inches of progress. He thought, what a superbly great placement this newly appreciated varmint had provided him with, as an unbelievable underground navigational pathway that could not be underappreciated in any way, coming from an otherwise pesky little creature. However, unfortunately, the little fella was not around in which to properly thank him.

With this odd but exciting discovery, Will quickly developed a new-found appreciation for the little subterranean furry varmint responsible for carving out the tiny tunnel, which helped to possibly solve an otherwise impossible situation while helping to save his life, just by chance.

So, all thoughts and actions were now fervently on directing the dig upwards to where stars could still be seen in the night sky through this little 2-inch tunnel that suddenly turned Will's dire situation around to give him renewed hope and energy. While continuing to dig, he followed and expanded the gopher's hole by carving away the soil and rock around it. At some point, the ground had become noticeably softer and more workable as he inched closer to the surface before it all suddenly collapsed in on him. However, with only minimal amounts of soil and rock dumping on him, it was a minor setback and didn't cause much of a problem, as gravity allowed it all to drop down beside him and out of his way. Incredibly, as Will spit dirt from his mouth, he could see that his passage up through the tunnel he dug was now entirely achievable, if only for what remaining strength he may still have within himself to pull his nearly exhausted body upwards to effectively extricate himself from it. The tunnel's glorious completion had placed him just about three feet beyond the influence of that giant stone as he breached the surface and prepared to see the world again.

While it still took him a few more hours of digging and carving from the point where the gopher hole was first discovered, he then managed to thrust his body up and through the newly reshaped opening to pull himself out of the cramped tunnel he carved out so methodically in his desperation. Oddly, it almost appeared like the Earth was giving birth to a new life. But it immediately fed an unbelievable moment for him as he emerged, while now realizing that his life was not over and that he could still see his family again and get on with almost everything that he still wanted to do and accomplish in this world, as he drew in a much welcomed deep breath of abundant fresh air.

Now that he was entirely out of that critical predicament, his senses began to return, as his head started to clear from the adrenalin and fear-driven anxiety that this ordeal had left him with. He was then struck with amazement regarding how fantastic it was to smell and suck in the cooler and abundant fresh pine-scented mountain air again. At the same time, he felt deliriously ecstatic while marveling at the previously underappreciated starry heavens, shining brilliantly above him in full spectrum splendor. In his exhausted state, the enormity of this accomplishment could not be fully realized at that moment. He could only appreciate his newfound freedom, achieved triumphantly through his desperate escape from certain death. Tears of joy streamed down Will's face when taking in all that lay before him as he splayed himself flat out on his back, fully exhausted physically and emotionally. Quite amazingly, it was as if he had died and suddenly came back to life again, with no one but himself having witnessed it, nor even to have understood what it took to press on under the circumstances. Given his ordeal's fear-driven level of adrenalin, it helped to keep him actively involved in the digging process, as he refused to give in to the situation, even as dire and seemingly hopeless as it was.

After the stunning initial relief from this ordeal had then turned into unexpected euphoria, Will had regained himself somewhat as he felt the deepening chill in the night air and quickly realized that Sunshine had his warm coat and bedroll tied onto her saddle, and she was nowhere to be found out there in the cold partial dark of night. So, he knew immediately that he had to quickly find some form of makeshift shelter nearby where he could keep his body heat up and out of harm from hypothermia, as this was becoming another potential life-threatening challenge.

With a waxing gibbous phase of the moon now shining a fair degree of light on things, he was then able to carefully and methodically make his way down the draw while having to step and move around several of the various-sized boulders from the landslide. As he went, while slipping and falling on occasion, he soon made it down to the bottom of the draw, where the ground leveled out and where a thickly forested partial tree line came immediately into view next to the trail. The nearby flowing creek had then awarded Will with a much-needed drink to replenish what he had lost when stuck beneath that giant boulder.

With all of what occurred that day, from when the earthquake had set things in motion, Will had been near-hopelessly trapped underground for roughly eleven or twelve hours before finally coming to grips with the situation to eventually emerge from his former tomb below the Earth's surface. But with all his stoic efforts and some fortuitous luck, he triumphantly arose from the impossible like a Phoenix, although perhaps more like a giant gopher... again referencing the furry little subterranean dirt-boring varmint that Will Glover now had the greatest respect for.

Part Seven

Survival

With his surprising escape and survival from the impossible, Will Glover had resourcefully managed to free himself from beneath the enormous boulder that entrapped him in the aftermath of the earthquake-induced rock slide. But he now faced a new critical situation. Realizing that his horse and companions were nowhere to be found, he was now suddenly at the mercy of the area's notably low overnight temperatures within the higher elevation of the Wasatch range, with little or no personal insulation to protect and keep him from going hypothermic. Plus, he had no means in which to build a fire, leaving him entirely at the mercy of the higher elevation's overnight conditions. This was nearly as dire a situation to him as the entombment he had miraculously escaped from only minutes before, which, in this case, threatened to lead to certain death by way of the cold overnight mountain air. Without a campfire to help solve this problem, Will knew that he had to do something if he was hoping to survive the situation.

Knowing that he had to act immediately while using the existing moonlight and his now somewhat dull hunting knife, he cut and broke numerous branches containing thick boughs of pine needles from the abundant trees at the edge of the woodline. With his hands now feeling the bite of cold that set in, he chose an open spot of ground just inside the line of trees, where he placed layers of the thickly-needled boughs while crisscrossing them as he went. He surmised that it would provide a degree of insulation from the cold ground and the air above, with some adequate support for his body. The use of these pine boughs, in this way, served theoretically as a partial measure of protection against the cold from below and above to keep him from losing too much body heat. Layer after layer, these pine boughs were placed accordingly to create a five or six-foot-high pile. Once completed, Will then lifted the boughs in the middle of the pile and slowly pressed his body into it while managing to wriggle to the pile's center and curl up in a fetal position. He could feel the extra weight of it all, which only added to the hardship he knew he had to endure throughout the night. But as he shook and shivered uncontrollably inside this pine-bough mound, he tried to get as comfortable as possible. However, as cold as he was, there was no comforting aspect to this, although he knew it would be his only chance of surviving this critical situation. While the outside temperature didn't quite feel like it was at freezing or below, he knew that it was somewhere close to that mark, which could still bring on hypothermia and death by way of exposure if not addressed with some additional insulating factor to stave off the bitter cold in the night air. At that point, Will's thoughts turned to Evie and Maggie, knowing that he needed to stay as vigilant as possible to endure this situation for one night before safely returning to Little Rock Canyon.

So, despite his continued discomfort throughout the night, he remained steadfast but shivering while lying there within the pile, although staying true to what he believed would ward off enough of the chill to ultimately keep him alive. Getting some overnight sleep was an entirely different story, even as tired and nearly exhausted as his body was from his previous activity underground. In his mind, he knew that sleep would have to come later, after possibly surviving the cold overnight situation he had been left with. The only other resource he would have available to him throughout the night was his faith in God, which would help give him spiritual sanctuary and hope in this critical situation.

At some point, after lying there while shivering throughout the night, Will suddenly noticed a faint, glint of light coming through the pine boughs from above, while also finding that his teeth-chattering and shaking had lessened somewhat. He quickly realized that a new day was upon him, where the Sun's promising rays would soon bring the temperature back up to a more tolerable and comfortable level. As things eventually warmed up, he emerged from his pine-bough nest and felt relieved and jubilant to have survived the cold night. He was ecstatic to find that his quick-thinking, theoretical survival trick had worked. Now, he realized, he could get on with trying to make his way back down the meandering trail along the Big Cottonwood Creek canyon toward home. However, as cramped as he was during the night, he found that his body felt stiff all over, and he needed to warm up and stretch a bit to get himself right again.

From both of his harrowing experiences over the past day, where he spent a great deal of fervent energy mixed with high levels of anxiety and adrenalin, in escaping certain death from under that massive boulder, after which enduring the pain and discomfort of the overnight chill, Will had miraculously recovered from those travails to now point himself down the canyon trail. Through it all, he found that he could still regain a good amount of stamina once he had sufficiently warmed up, as the morning Sun began to bring the temperature for the day into a more comfortable range. Soon, he felt warm and fit enough to set out on foot over the roughly 40-mile trek back to Provo and his family, for whom he now held an even deeper feeling of love and devotion.

As he walked the winding trail with the Big Cottonwood Creek flowing beside it, he would occasionally descend from the bank to get his fill of the clear, cold water before climbing back up and resuming his steps along the beaten path of this earthen trail. Its snake-like form wound its familiar way down the forested canyon, meandering westward in its gradual descent toward the eastern farmland region of the greater Salt Lake basin.

But before he could get to where the landscape would ultimately open up and drop down into flatter terrain where the mostly Mormon-owned farmland would lie all around him, he would have to traverse the area through where there might still be some active breakaway bands of Indians present within treaty territory belonging to the northern Shoshone tribe or their related offshoots. On the journey up to the Big Cottonwood a little over a month prior, the trio of prospectors had not encountered anyone when coming through that tribal section of land to get up to their prospecting site. As Will approached that sovereign tribal area again on this trail leading back to the west, he assumed that it would be the same for him this time as well, as he dismissed the thought from his mind, although still reserving a certain degree of normal apprehension.

As he wandered along this serpentine canyon trail, he still felt strong enough to keep going, although he had occasional hunger pangs from time to time. But, by being able to at least satisfy his thirst from the waters of the nearby flowing creek, he still didn't seem overly affected by the fact that he hadn't eaten anything or slept in over 24 hours. Regarding his last meal, he recalled sitting by the campfire with his two friends the previous morning, devouring several flapjacks, along with a hot cup of coffee to wash them down.

As it was still Summertime in the region, daytime temperatures were mainly in the low to mid-seventies in the high country. He found that making his way back toward the Salt Lake Valley in late August was still quite comfortable, as it made the descent somewhat easier, with the established path also being mostly downhill. As Will stretched his distance farther from the higher elevated site where he began in the morning, the temperature range had noticeably increased by a few more degrees. With his constant movement on the trail, he began to exhibit some degree of sweat developing upon his head and brow while also showing signs of wetness on his green plaid wool shirt, just around the armpits, as the day was increasingly heating up around him.

Alertly, he tried to gauge his progress as he went, with the warm afternoon Sun then being more on the wane in the western sky and with nightfall promising to be only three or four hours away at that point. He figured that he had only covered some 8 to 10 miles that day while noting his slow progress had also raised his chances of having to endure another night without adequate shelter and a warm fire. At some point, he stopped beside the creek, where he descended the bank and drank some more water while just sitting there to give his body a brief respite. As he lounged there, suddenly, a fish jumped into the air, just out from the opposite bank, quickly splashing back into the flowing waters to disappear and leave ripples wavering on the surface.

It seemingly taunted the hungry man sitting there, having observed such a precious moment. At that point, Will could have eaten a dozen of them if presented with that imagined scenario, as his degree of hunger had grown significantly. But as it was, he had nothing in which to make a try for one of these all-too-familiar, slippery, but quite tasty freshwater critters called Trout.

Sitting there a while longer, while contemplating things, he looked down at his boots, which were the lace-up variety of leather hiking boots he had preferred over slip-on western-type boots that many men tended to wear regularly during that period out in backcountry areas. So, while unlacing one of his boots, he proceeded to also remove one of the steel lacing rings from the leather while noticing that it had somehow cracked, as it was then relatively easy to break it on one side and bend one of the open ends of it over and onto the shoelace end to serve as a crude sort of hook that was effectively crimped tightly to the lace by biting down on it with one of his eye teeth. However, he still needed to take his knife to it and scrape the other end of the little curved eye to create a somewhat sharp point in fashioning the makings of a small hook. He then stripped the other boot as well to utilize the other long bootlace while tying the two together to give some length to this crude little, almost laughable fishing line that he affixed to a lengthy, dried-out tree branch found nearby.

The only thing he didn't have, in completing this halfway foolish bid to catch some food, was something suitable to serve as bait. So, immediately, Will looked at the semi-wet soil near the edge of the creek and began to dig at it with his hands to see if there might be a grub or some other type of insect or worm around in which to run the makeshift hook through it to complete this half-baked attempt at possibly catching a fish. But when digging around as he did, he came up with nothing and wondered if he were to try it while offering just the crude empty hook, if it might still work....until suddenly, as if by providence, a green grasshopper flew in close by and alighted on a large rock next to him. Will was able to quickly grab it while keeping it locked within the closed palm of his hand. Instantly, he thought nothing could have been more fortuitous than that at such a crucial moment. As odd as it was, he knew that no one would believe such a thing if he were to tell about it. So, as he worked the fingers of his free hand to slide in and get a hold of this active little bug from the closed palm of his other hand, he quickly took up the crude hook and stuck it into the grasshopper's upper body while bringing it through to leave the insect stuck there, as it furiously flailed its legs about in desperation.

Then, the actual moment of truth was at hand as he stood up and tossed the crude shoe-laced fishing line into the water out in front of him to see if it might entice and bring about a possible response. As this ridiculous shoelace line halfway bobbed in the slow-moving stream, it floated past and came up against the shore on the first attempt, with the grasshopper still hanging on the hook. The second cast turned out to be just like the first. However, on the third cast, he suddenly got a solid strike and immediately jerked and pulled the line up fast, to where this somewhat medium-sized trout had then been launched out of the water and into the air, where it flung off of the hook as it flew back over Will's head and landed on the upper part of the bank behind him. He then quickly scampered back to grab it as it flopped around, holding a tight grip on the wriggly little fish while taking out his hunting knife again to promptly knock it over the head with the handle, killing it, before gleefully slicing open its underside to clear all of its entrails. The next step was to rinse it off with the stream water to flush all of what might have remained after gutting it before presenting the prized catch before him as his supper for the day.

As starved as Will was at that point, it didn't take him but about a second or two to sink his teeth into this 10-inch trout while not giving much thought to the fact that he was eating raw meat. But he found that he enjoyed the flavor of it anyway, as he ate all that he could find possible to ingest, short of the tail, the flippers, and the head, all of which he left in a pile on the bank for some local scavenger to find while spitting out some of the thin little bones contained within the meat.

Feeling quite satisfied as he arose from his position by the creek, he turned and thanked the little dead grasshopper for making it all possible as if expecting it to say, "Oh, think nothing of it." He then gathered up his bootlaces from the makeshift fishing line, untying them, before re-lacing his boots and climbing the few steps back up to where the trail was still waiting for him to resume his progress. By then, the Sun had sunk lower in the western sky.

While feeling much better after getting some food in his belly, even if it wasn't all that much, he made some further progress, covering about four or five more miles down the trail before the eventual arrival of dusk, stopping to cut pine boughs once again and lay them to serve as his bedding for the night, much in the same manner as the previous night. But not so many were needed for the top covering now, given that the area's night air was warmer and not perceived to be as biting as what was experienced the previous night at a much higher elevation.

As he lay in his makeshift bed, taking in the scent of pine all around him, Will thought of his two friends who must have had a hard time with what occurred in the aftermath of the rocky avalanche. He realized that they thought they had witnessed his death firsthand while likely feeling help-less in their belief that something further could have been done to save the situation. He understood this was why they left, as they would never have done so under other circum-stances. On the trail back home, he had calculated that they were a good day to a day and a half ahead of him without any chance for him to catch up.

With that, he shifted his thoughts to Evie and Maggie while imagining himself back at the homefront in Little Rock Canyon, spending his time again with those he loved and deeply cared for. But less importantly, he knew he also still had chores to take care of, along with ongoing projects that he had put on the back burn-plate when returning to the homestead. While away, Evie was good enough to maintain things for him by watering and feeding the chick-ens, mule, and Violet, whom she also milked daily for their consumption of nutritiously enriched milk.

Running through his many thoughts about other things, he soon drifted off with them as the restorative sleep that he needed so badly finally came.

Part Eight

A Rude Awakening

Quite suddenly, Will was awakened from his peaceful slumber by an unknown commotion nearby, as light filtering through the pine boughs had again indicated that a new day had begun. But, a significant rustling sound and a quick movement of the bough-branch assembly alarmed him, with voices heard as the boughs were all completely thrown off him. Will was now exposed while facing several Indigenous men out in front of him as he sat up to take notice. Whichever tribe it was that stood before him, he did not know, although these young men didn't appear to be at all friendly by any means. They all carried black zig-zag patterns of what appeared to be war paint on each of their faces while aggressively taunting him as he sat there. He counted seven of them, and they didn't look Shoshone to him, as he'd previously seen pictures and character drawings of Shoshone people in certain publications when stationed at Camp Butler with the Union Army.

They immediately seized him up by both arms and walked him to a nearby tree as he briefly struggled with their forceful grip on him. Then they tied ropes around his wrist and ankle on one side of his body while wrapping the ropes around the back of the tree to tie off each section of rope to the other ankle and wrist before letting loose of him. Stretched out tightly around the tree trunk, he was left entirely incapable of doing anything to help his cause while being taunted and poked by these young, terrorizing tribesmen.

While feeling their threatening intimidation, he wondered just what this was all about while also not knowing what they intended to do with him. But he knew he couldn't speak or even understand their language in which to ask why they were mistreating him. After vehemently yelling insults while laughing and jeering at him, they then took turns beating him with their fists and sticks before ripping off his green plaid wool shirt to reveal his bare chest and arms while confiscating his dull hunting knife and sheath. When examining it, they all had a good laugh amongst themselves before cutting and stripping him of his denim pants and laced-up leather boots to leave him standing tied to the tree in nothing more than what God had given him upon his birth. As they continued to beat him, one of them struck a hard blow to his genitals, which made him scream in excruciating pain. Then, suddenly, they stopped with the punishment and stepped back to confer on what they would collectively do next.

This was all great fun for this little band of wild natives, who were a small group of young renegades that most likely broke away from their main tribe to terrorize and kill any white men they might come across, including, as in Will's case, those who were caught traveling through their designated tribal lands, uninvited. As this little band of seven jubilantly raved with their new-found captive, they seemed disappointed that he had no weapons except for the rather dull hunting knife.

Seeing that he wasn't much of a threat to them, they weren't quite sure what to do with him, while they also wondered what he was even doing there, without even a horse to make his way. But by his very presence in their country, he had violated the sanctity of what was considered to be their jurisdiction. So, they decided to turn him loose just as he was and let him fend for himself. With this decision, he had now become part of a predatory race for survival, in which he would be hunted for sport by this clan of seven young braves. It was a customary cat-and-mouse sporting event for those who were confirmed as enemies of their people. In their estimation, it also allowed their captives an opportunity for what the natives felt was a fair sporting chance of escaping by possibly outrunning their opposition or outsmarting them somehow. By their biased interpretation of this so-called sport, all able whites and other enemies were generally qualified to meet the largely unfair and ever-changing terms by which these Indigenous ruffians had held a clear disadvantage.

As Will was still standing upright with his face bloodied, while leaning back against the tree with arms and legs tightly bound to render him entirely helpless, he was frightened for his life, feeling that finally, this was likely to be the end for him. Then, one of the tribesmen wandered over his way, brandishing a knife in a threatening manner, only to cut both ropes from behind to effectively release him from the tree. Dumbfounded, Will just stood there frozen and confused, not knowing what to do next. The other tribal members moved in closer, taunting him further while motioning for him to run away. So, he took their cue and did just that, as his naked form soon scampered off into the distance with ropes still dangling from each appendage as he ran while occasionally looking back at the amused young tribesmen.

After a few minutes of running, he stopped momentarily to untie the ropes before pushing on in this race to escape these crazy, wild-eyed Indians. As he ran, he quickly took to the woods while getting off the beaten path, but with the mindful thought of trying to stay parallel with that definitive trail that ran westerly toward the Salt Lake basin. He figured that it would at least help him keep his bearings in that given direction while trying to elude these savages by going out through the more wooded terrain in this new, potentially life-threatening situation that was presented to him. He now realized that it was a serious game they were playing, and he was the object of it, whereby if caught, they would kill him and take his scalp as a trophy.

But the way forward was problematic, to say the least, for a man running naked in the woods without any footwear. As he continued to run the undefined course while occasionally stepping on hard objects along the way, his bare feet took a beating. Turning his head as he went, he looked back to see several of the tribe's braves had set out together in following his course. Notably, their much stronger running skills had made up a fair amount of the ground that Will thought he had gained from them. He looked back again and noticed they were only less than a minute behind him while still gaining ground. Will had then slowed his pace up a bit from the effects of sheer exhaustion, trying to catch his breath, as these desperate and frenzied tribesmen had nearly caught up with him before he quickly picked up the pace again to remain somewhat in advance of their determined charge.

Just then, Will nearly ran right into a tiny bear cub that wandered into his path, alertly evading it as he passed by. He also noticed another cub and their mother standing in some berry bushes nearby as he sped past. At that point, further fear had engulfed him with what possibly represented another threat to his life, as he knew all about Grizzly bears. But when he looked back again, he noticed that the mother Grizzly had gotten hold of one of the braves who was in hot pursuit, with the others trying to beat the bear off with sticks and their tomahawks, as the maternally instinctive bear also grabbed and bloodied another of their tribesmen in the process. With that ugly and surprisingly providential scene in clear view to his rear, Will faced himself forward again and kept moving while taking full advantage of the tribal members' misfortune. In his ongoing attempt at fleeing this critical situation, he desperately pushed on with extra effort, furiously making his way toward the freedom awaiting him in the Salt Lake Valley.

Tired and nearly worn out as he was, he continued to run through the wooded landscape while soon finding it safer for him to then move laterally back over onto the old original beaten path where it would ensure that he could more easily make his way back down into the valley and onto the notable farm wagon road. Slowing himself to a trot and then back to a walking stride, he found that he had developed a limp in his right leg from rolling his ankle when stepping partially into a hole in the forest floor. The painful effects of bruising from the beating he took had also slowed him down somewhat after fleeing from this dire situation he had landed himself in.

Now recognizing where he was, he knew that the valley would soon be coming back into full view, out in the distance from where he was actively moving, up on the hilly plateau. Trying to regain himself somewhat while still breathing quite heavily, he stopped momentarily and then walked on while giving a long look back to see if his former captors may still be in pursuit. Then, when rounding a more familiar bend in the trail, he quickly recalled that the forest suddenly opened up from that point as the treelines moved outward and away from the barren trail to reveal the cultivated and level terrain of the Salt Lake Valley below.

Taking it all in from the plateau's edge, he experienced an added rush of adrenalin when seeing the vast Salt Lake Valley again. Feeling thoroughly overjoyed at its familiar sight while also knowing that he was now probably out of danger, he then began his descent down the plateau's escarpment portion of the trail, leading to the familiar farm wagon road below. While now seemingly relieved of the ordeal that had him believing his life would be over, Will allowed his anxiety to die down, with his rapid heartbeat returning to near normal again, as a new feeling of calm enveloped him when finding his way to safer ground. Triumphant in his opportune flight to freedom, through good fortune and some sheer luck, he was able to foil his captors while inadvertently diffusing the life-threatening situation the young tribesmen had so vehemently presented to him.

However, there still seemed to be one particular detail that remained from that little encounter involving those wild savages, with concern to the fact that Will was still rendered 'naked as a jaybird', as he descended into the valley below where it mattered. Once the upper pathway finally flowed down the hillside to merge onto the wagon road at the base of the valley, Will was then left with the desperate hope of finding something in which to cover his nakedness. However, nothing appeared to be available or forthcoming in the treeless landscape that lay before him.

As he now limped his way along this old wagon road, he couldn't help but wonder why it was that he had been tested with so many life-threatening predicaments over the past two days. It was as if the Grim Reaper himself was out there on the trail stalking him and setting the stage for these odd and unusual hair-raising events that he somehow still managed to escape from. While he had gotten out of certain predicaments in the past when growing up in Carbondale, they were small in comparison and not life-threatening like these of late, which had oddly occurred only hours apart from when the sudden earthquake up in the Big Cottonwood Canyon had seemingly set them all in motion.

While noting that the Sun was directly overhead at this point in his now unclothed journey back home, Will was getting hungry again, although without any means this time by which to acquire anything that could satisfy that nagging condition. Walking due-west along this crude soil and rock-compacted farm wagon road, he couldn't see much of anything ahead except for the relatively straight line of the wagon wheel-marked route that extended far into the distance. But, he at least knew that he was heading in the right direction, toward where he would eventually turn left on the old Mormon Road, which had initially been established as the main artery and supply route from Salt Lake down to the areas south of there.

Fortunately, he still had the Big Cottonwood Creek flowing immediately next to him, running parallel with the road on its north side, streaming in that same westerly direction.

The day's increasing heat had forced him to occasionally partake of its convenient sweet-tasting water again. It was a much-welcomed resource that appeared to accompany him on this journey toward the old Mormon Road. At one point, he jumped into its shallow waters to clean all the accumulated dust and residual dried blood from his body while refreshing himself with the stream's wonderous cooling effects, in countering the day's opposing heat from the afternoon Sun overhead.

Returning to the road to resume his pace, a newly refreshed but still naked Will Glover continued on his way. He soon spotted a large field of green foliage off in the distance that somewhat perplexed him in identifying exactly what it was. As he approached, he came to find that, of all things, it was a cornfield with tall stalks of growth that featured green husk-covered ears with golden tassels protruding from much of the crop. Without hesitation, he immediately ran forward and grabbed one up while furiously stripping away the husk from it to reveal the cob's goodness within. He ate the raw corn as if it were candy before grabbing up another and another, which he ate in rapid succession. When breaking off one more to take with him, he suddenly realized he no longer had pockets for storing such things. But he hung onto it anyway, as he couldn't be sure when or where his next meal or snack might come from again. It was just what Will needed to help restore his energy levels and satisfy his hunger, as he hadn't eaten anything since consuming that little trout up in the higher elevated area of the Big Cottonwood Canyon.

As he continued walking the road, he noticed that the creek was now taking a decidedly new directional turn to the northwest while the road was leading due west. With that new development, he realized he would soon lose the benefit of having this convenient water source nearby. So, in bidding a final farewell to that broader version of the Big Cottonwood Creek, he again immersed himself in its shallow cool waters while filling his belly with it to keep hydrated for as long as possible before resuming progress back on the wagon road. As he looked back to cast his last gaze upon it, he couldn't help but wonder where his next good drink of water may now come from.

By now, the Sun was hanging much lower in the western sky, with nothing ahead to offer him relief in the way of shelter or the possible covering of his nakedness. Day's end would soon cast its darkness upon the road, although Will was more bent on maintaining his pedestrian progress as the light of day was approaching dusk. He was more concerned with getting closer to the expected junction with the old Mormon Road. Surprisingly, after spending the entire afternoon walking that nearly straight-line route on this eastern wagon road, it hadn't offered anything in the way of human movement or activity of any kind in which to ask for help. Not even as much as a single farmer was out and about to possibly help Will with his situation. It all seemed odd to him, now that he was back in civilized territory again, as he wondered if his nakedness might have scared everyone off.

But as the promise of dusk was coming on, he suddenly noticed a strange dark movement against the northwestern sky, just off to his right, oddly swirling around in different lively patterns and shapes, almost appearing as a sort of animated dance on display against the sky. Upon closer study, he discovered it was created by a large swarm of birds, moving in unity while seemingly dancing in flight. When stopping to observe this unusual activity before him, Will became overly captivated while impressed with the close synchronization of these little blackbirds as they flew together in close formation. They moved around in perfect harmony as if they had all rehearsed or choreographed their quick turns and undulating patterns of flight while flowing together in entertaining unison about the early evening sky. This rather bizarre assembly of birds had instinctively come together to present their unusual shared flight as a single unit, while ever-so-smoothly executing their mesmerizing ballet-like aviary performance. As strange and beautiful as it was, Will struggled to grasp any possible meaning it might otherwise hold. However, he could certainly appreciate the sheer, almost other-worldly movements on display before him, as it was such an oddly delightful sight for his tired eyes to take in. This unusual performance he witnessed while heading back to the Little Rock Canyon homestead was a much-appreciated distraction from his current plight.

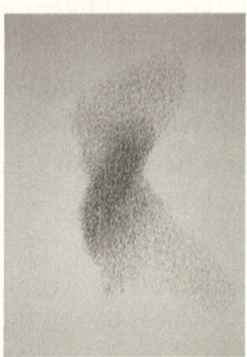

The rare phenomenon at work with these bird swarms is commonly referred to as a 'murmuration,' which is thought to be a means for these birds to protect themselves from predators like hawks and owls when night approaches.

As the swarm dispersed and the sky was darkening further, he again picked up his step on the wagon road while spotting a colorful sunset in the far-off distance, low in the western sky, where clouds above it were thoroughly saturated with darkening beams of red and orange. As it eventually faded in the lower light of dusk, darkness soon came upon the road, while the Moon hadn't presented itself yet in the night sky to help light his way. But by now, Will was entirely used to finding his way in the dark anyway, as it didn't phase him much. He just kept on with his progress, moving steadily along this road with each step that he took while bearing the nagging soreness from tender soles on both of his feet, along with the pain that stayed with him from suffering bruised ribs and a sore jaw.

He thought that if only he hadn't stopped the previous night to get some rest and had kept going instead, he wouldn't have been left with the predicament he was now in and wouldn't have had to endure and escape the harrowing experience involving the obsessed band of natives up on the plateau. But his worst regret was that he felt it was partly his fault anyway, for building his pine-bough bed right along the trail, just inside the treeline, where it could be seen.

With the onset of nightfall, a noticeable coolness had fallen over the valley, as Will's complete lack of clothing had left him feeling the discomforting chill. In total darkness with only a very faint view of the way ahead and without the benefit of anything with which to cover himself, Will again feared the possibility of becoming hypothermic. At the same time, he was frustrated that, in this case, there was absolutely nothing he could do about it. So, he had to rely on a quicker walking pace to allow his heart to pump more warming blood throughout his body's arteries to keep the chill from affecting him too much. But fortunately, it was not as cold in the valley that night compared with what he had to endure up on the Big Cottonwood. However, with his ongoing anxiety, it was still a concern to him.

The night sky above him was entirely clear that night, with many of the various illuminated constellations on display overhead, which his former school teacher, Mrs. Johnson, had familiarized him with some years before. An occasional shooting star was also spotted streaking through the night sky as he continued to amble his way while favoring his limp, out along this seemingly endless road.

Then, just off to his left in the distance, Will suddenly spotted a lantern light emanating from a faint silhouette of a house or structure of some sort, and he reasoned that it must be a farmhouse, given the relative location out along this road. So, when eventually reaching where the supposed farmhouse was situated, he wandered up the short dusty lane leading into it and found that his assumption had been correct.

When knocking on the front door, he immediately sought refuge behind some bushes at the base of the wooden porch, so as not to scare the inhabitants with the sudden appearance of him standing about in his altogether. But nobody answered the door, which moved Will to try knocking again before scooting back down behind the bushes. Again, no response. So, he tried it a third time with the same results before hollering out to whoever lived there, saying he needed their help. Again, no response, as only crickets could be heard chirping nearby.

With that, he decided to wander around the place to see if they might be out in their barn, although no light was emanating from that structure. But he noticed the lantern shining from the kitchen window when heading back there. As he got to the rear of the farmhouse, while aided by the low light now emanating from the rising moon, along with the lantern light from the kitchen window, Will suddenly caught sight of the farmer's family clothesline, still ladened with freshly laundered garments. But it seemed quite odd, though being rather lucky for Will, that its contents had not yet been taken in for the night. Looking things over on the line, he found a pair of denim overalls hanging there, along with a white cotton long-sleeved shirt, which could help resolve his uninsulated and embarrassing situation concerning the necessary coverage of his birthday suit. Surely, he thought, the farmer wouldn't miss a few clothing items from the line. Although, as it pertained to footwear, he couldn't expect to be that lucky in solving that other aspect of exposure. So, he donned his newly acquired duds, finding the overalls to fit well enough in the chest and seat, although the trouser legs were quite short. The shirt was much the same while rather loose in the chest and shoulders, but with shorter sleeves. Seeing this, he realized that the farmer was somewhat wide in his torso and tail but shorter than Will by several inches in the shirtsleeves and the leggings of his breeches.

As he turned to go, he immediately spotted a human leg and foot sticking out from the base of one of the bushes there and cautiously went over to check it out, finding the farmer's wife lying there dead with her throat cut and much of her scalp missing. Her half-empty laundry basket was turned over and lying just nearby. Half shocked at the grim sight of this, Will immediately went over to the farmhouse's back door, where he found it wide open, with the lantern light from within shining over the kitchen area to reveal the place as having been recently ransacked. So, he grabbed the lantern and set about to find the farmer and anyone else who may have lived there.

After a search in and around the barn, he soon discovered the farmer's bludgeoned body out behind the structure while noting that he, too, was missing the scalp on his head, to a cowardly savage ritual that was nothing short of evil. With these senseless slayings, Will could only surmise that it may have been that same band of Indians he encountered much earlier in the day who had threatened him with his life in no uncertain terms, even though they were unable to communicate their intentions in so many words.

Over the next hour or so, Will put himself to work, going about the business of digging graves for the two. He found a shovel standing up in the barn and dug two plots, placing the two of them side by side in an area at the back of the house, laying them both in, and covering them over accordingly. When finished, he had no words to offer them as he just stood there, while only affording a brief moment of silence, in respect for whomever they may have been as fellow human beings. Also, he could not come up with anything that might suffice as crosses or stones to mark their graves. So he just left it at that, without anything marking their placement there. As he departed, he put the lantern aside and thanked the farmer for the clothes he would no longer need, while Will's need for them was indeed a high priority that was greatly appreciated.

In addition, after earlier finding the farmer out behind the barn, Will had removed his slip-on boots before burying him, and with a knife he found in the barn, he made the undersized boots fit well enough for his intended purpose by cutting out the top of the toe box to where Will's toes then hung out the front a bit to look somewhat unusual, if not downright silly. It rendered them completely open to the air while they rested just beyond the tip of the sole. However, it made the newly found footwear that otherwise didn't fit his feet at all, quite functional and comfortable enough for Will's current needs, despite appearances.

Now that he was outfitted much better for travel through Mormon country, he set himself back on the wagon road again, sporting a custom pair of boots to cover and protect most of his bare feet. He now strode forward more confidently with his telltale limp, moving toward the wagon road's ultimate junction ahead with the old Mormon Road.

As near as Will could figure, after finding the slain bodies of the farmer and his wife, while noting that rigor-mortise had fully set in, he surmised that they must have been killed at least a day earlier, and apparently later in the day, given that there was a lantern still shining from within the kitchen. It also appeared to him that the farmer was probably still working in the barn while his wife was busy taking in the laundry. Plus, with the kitchen ransacked as it was, it was likely that the perpetrators were looking for food to take with them, as Will had also looked around the room to see if there might be anything to eat. But they had likely taken it anyway, if there was much to be pilfered. He also noted that no animals were present around the farmhouse or the barn. It suggested to him that whatever horses or mules or cattle they may have had were likely stolen by the savage predators who had destroyed the productive lives of these two innocent farmsteaders.

Ambling along in the moonlight now, while still in its waxing gibbous phase, somewhere between a half crescent and a full sphere, there was enough abundant low light emanating from overhead to keep Will's pathway well-lit. It allowed him to see the ground just ahead to prevent him from tripping over rocks that were noticeably embedded in the compressed soil that comprised much of the general makeup of this old farming road.

After walking continuously for nearly an hour further, he suddenly arrived where it stopped at a T to merge with another much wider roadway running perpendicular in a north and southward direction. At that point, Will acknowledged that he had finally reached the long sought-after junction point of the old Mormon Road. So he then knowingly took the route to the left, heading southward toward Provo and to the Little Rock Canyon area where he lived, just due east of Orem.

It was still fairly dark along this Mormon road while also being notably quiet for a major thoroughfare, as all traffic on it tended to cease with the setting of the Sun, even though some freight haulers believed they could still see well enough in the moonlight. But for that night, all was lonesomely quiet and uneventful, much like what Will had encountered on the eastern wagon road.

From the day's taxing activities in making his desperate escape from the wild-eyed tribesmen he encountered up in the Shoshone country, he still managed to cover most of the distance traveled by way of his aching bare feet out along the eastern farm road. But now that he had protective footwear, even as crude and unusual as it was, he felt the distances in front of him would be much more manageable. However, despite that, Will was beginning to show signs of fatigue and soreness, as he had slowed his stride and pace significantly in the late night hours to what seemed more like a trudge. He soon realized that his worn-out body desperately needed some well-deserved rest, water to rehydrate himself, and a little food, most of which seemed entirely out of the question, considering where he was.

At that late night hour, with the air still being on the cool side, although not as uncomfortably so, he noticed a spot up ahead with an open area of thickly grown, greenish-brown grass showing. It was about 3 to 4 feet in height, just off to his right side, where he thought it could help by offering him some form of respite, providing protection from the night air, for at least a few hours before moving on. Settling into that grassy area about twenty feet from the road, he laid himself down, halfway collapsing into it, to fall fast asleep, with these tall grasses helping to serve as an effective measure of cover all around him.

He didn't know what time it was when he awoke and stretched while yawning to greet a new day. The morning Sun had already cast its considerable warmth upon where he was lounging, which stirred him toward getting himself back up and onto his feet again to scan the area in the light of day. As he squinted in the bright sunlight, he could visually make out some far-off activity on the road, with a few approaching wagons being noticed way back in the distance to the north. But, as nature then called on him to make an offering, he took full advantage of the tall grasses around him to privately add his generous contribution to the soil composition there, after which he pulled up and rebuttoned his newly acquired overalls before lighting out and getting back on his way again.

Walking along the now more active roadway leading south, he noticed right away that his limp, which had been quite bothersome to him on the previous day, had now shown itself to be much less of a hindrance, to give him a little more added drive with his steps as he went. He recalled that he had always been somewhat of a quick healer when it came to minor injuries, finding it to be the case in this instance.

At this point in his travel, he calculated that he had covered a lot of ground since escaping from the dire situation he faced up in the Shoshone country. From there, he had managed to put roughly 15 miles behind him since that unforgettable and unfortunate encounter with the savagely obsessed band of Indians. He estimated he still had about ten or more miles in front of him before finally returning home to Provo's Little Rock Canyon area. However, by now, he knew that he would make it, or at least felt that he would, as he couldn't foresee any other problems or obstacles that might deter him from returning to his homefront. In that regard, he was entirely resolute in his further determination to reach his destination. Within his focused mindset, he resolved that nothing or no one would keep him from it, as he remembered his solemn promise made to Evie when departing from the homestead in Little Rock Canyon.

In his river of thoughts, as he made his way along the grassy right edge of the Mormon road, he believed that his two companions had most likely arrived back home by now, while he hoped they hadn't related their mistaken news of his passing to Evie yet. He knew that would devastate her and cause a whole string of unnecessary, deep, dark emotions to arise. She would also have to deal with her counter-reaction in a highly emotional way when surprisingly seeing him upon his return. It was too much for Will to imagine as a possible unfolding scenario for when he would finally reappear on his return home. He knew that such initial mental anguish and grief from her being misinformed of his death would then be followed by shocking relief, with even some frustrating anger involved with it, as he feared the very thought of it having to be put upon his wife like that before he might at least have a chance to keep it from her. Although en route as he was, while still being several miles away from home and his dear sweet Evie, there was absolutely nothing he could do to prevent it from happening, as he knew that his friends had to say something to her at some point, to provide some explanation for her husband's absence. Plus, the very thought of Maggie possibly hearing about the falsely reported demise of her father in this way had also disturbed Will greatly. All of this weighed heavily on his mind, becoming entirely unsettling to him in his determined and near-obsessive efforts to return home as soon as possible.

But, just as Will had feared, both Riley and Betty drove their buggy over the short distance to the Glover's cabin, with Sunshine in tow, just a day after Riley and Otto's return from the mountains, and immediately grabbed hold of Evie to tell her the news of her husband's passing. In complete shock, she could not believe it and thought they must have been mistaken, as it had to have been someone else instead, not her man Will. But when explaining further about the details of the accident that came in the aftermath of

the earthquake, she burst into tears and buried her head while
coming to realize that Will's friends would certainly not make up
such a story.

With his mouth and throat now being quite dry, without
having had even a drop of water to drink since the previous
night, after waking and returning to the road again, Will
soon came upon a small creek, flowing out immediately to
the west. Leaving the road, he walked in through several
stands of sizeable trees to soon emerge onto a mildly sloping
grassy and rocky landscape that led to a section of the creek
where he could take his fill to replenish and rehydrate himself. He lay prone at the water's edge to scoop up several
successive palmfuls of the cool, clear water as it trickled by,
sufficiently satisfying his thirst before raising himself up and
heading back to the road again. He knew that while he
didn't have a jug or a canteen to carry water with him, he
would have to look for another water source when his thirst
might get the best of him again.

On the way back to the road, he noticed a sturdy tree
branch lying about, which had weathered significantly from
the elements over time. Finding that it had a good shape, he
gathered it up to be used for support as a staff-like walking
stick while wandering back up and over to the road's edge
to resume his journey. By then, it appeared to be sometime
during the afternoon hours of the day, as Will had followed
the position of the Sun overhead to calculate with some degree of approximation as to what time it may have been getting to be. He estimated it to be somewhere around 2
O'clock, or thereabouts, as the Sun's glaring heat was beginning to draw beads of sweat upon his hatless head, with a
significant portion of this roadway yet to travel down and
put behind him.

He noted that several freight wagons had passed him as he continued to walk down this road, with only respectful acknowledgment shown by their drivers as they passed by. Will had inquired with a few as they rolled past if they might have room aboard for him, as he said he was only headed to Orem. But none of the drivers stopped for him. They hadn't much space available anyway, even for the relatively short trip ahead to his destination, and they also weren't about to allow anyone to sit back where their crops or goods were situated in the load bed of their wagons. These were primarily large freight wagons traveling from Salt Lake City, hauling goods and materials down to Provo or other points south on this busy route. Curiously, only very few wagons or horseback riders from the opposite direction had passed by.

Zorger.com

When noticing a large wagon approaching containing harvested corn, Will hailed it and hollered out to the driver, asking if he could spare a single ear of it to help a starving man. The driver obliged by stopping and turning his body around to grab up one ear, tossing it down, and giving him a respectful head nod as if to say, "Good luck," before continuing on his way. Will thanked him profusely as he rolled past before ripping into the husk to reveal the fresh, sweet kernels on the cob within. He ate all that was there while also biting off small sections of the cob and chewing on them to get the full value of that single ear of corn before spitting out much of the remaining roughage from it. Pleased with that, he found that it immediately satisfied his hunger again, for the most part, as it relieved his mind of worry about not knowing where his next meal or food item may be coming from, if at all forthcoming.

Now that his hunger and thirst had been sufficiently satisfied, he more heartily picked up his pace as he continued hiking along this Mormon road thoroughfare. For him, this road was found to at least be active and somewhat accommodating, as compared with the old farm wagon road, where there wasn't a soul around over the full miserable stretch of it to provide help of any kind. But it did seem odd to him, as he remembered encountering a few farm wagons passing by when he and his friends had previously traveled eastward on it to get up to the Big Cottonwood. Then he wondered if perhaps on this return trip when hiking back through again, if it might have been on a Sunday(?), as he knew that Mormons and other Christians had always observed that day of the week as their Sabbath, signified as their one day of rest according to the Book of Mormon and the Christian Bible. Or could it have had something to do with Indians having been out along that road, as evidenced by Will's discovery and subsequent burials of the unfortunate farmer and his wife? In his thoughts, it bothered him that he could not make sense of that portion of his trek.

But to add to this, Will still had no clue what day of the week it was. He was only left with the reality of actively moving along in the present moment, on another day in his newly reclaimed life. Still, upon his upcoming arrival back at the Little Rock Canyon homestead, he knew the prospect of tomorrow for him would become his own day of deserved rest.

Part Nine

Homeward Bound

As Will continued southward on the old Mormon road, he could see he was getting closer to the town of Orem. After a few more miles, he noticed more farmhouses and established crop fields along the way until Orem's familiar little farming town finally came into view. From there, he immediately came upon the Little Rock Canyon road, his more favorable shortcut from the north, which would take him in an easterly direction to his home in north Provo. The landmark roadway stretched a little over three miles toward another section of the Wasatch range. It would carry him on for most of that distance before the access road to his cabin would lead him to turn south again to where his homestead was situated and where his family was waiting for him. He was now overjoyed to be at this point in his journey, knowing that he would soon be home again and back in the welcoming arms of Evie and Maggie.

As he continued along this stretch of the Little Rock Canyon road while still limping, he soon found himself again at the end of another long day of walking, with nightfall soon to darken the tree-lined roadway and with only the moonlight to guide him. Then, from just ahead, he heard the sound of water flowing and remembered that the Provo River was up ahead. It was where the familiar waterway flowed under a wooden crossing bridge that spanned about 80 feet to the other side. As he approached, he still managed to see well enough to cross over the bridge and descend the river's bank to get a needed drink before realizing he still had well over a mile to go. Feeling exhausted at that point, he thought it best to arrive at the cabin in the morning with the bright light of day instead of at this late hour. So, again, he found some tall grass in the moonlit night when wandering a few hundred yards upstream and away from the road to again lay himself down in. As tired as he was, he quickly fell asleep.

Then, after several hours of restful sleep, he suddenly awoke with a resounding scream while suffering excruciating pain, as a coyote had found him there and was biting and tugging vigorously at his left leg. The aggressive predator had opened up a wound in his leg, just above the top of his boot. As he repeatedly kicked the wolf-like creature hard with his other foot, he got the animal off of him while then being more capable of rising to his feet to readily address the situation. Remembering the walking stick beside him, he quickly grabbed it up, swinging it like a club while smacking this snarling animal in the head a few times. Painful yelps were expressed, causing it to immediately give up its aggression toward Will, as it quickly turned to run away.

With the situation now under control after the animal fled the scene, Will then tried to assess the damage in the tree-filtered moonlight, noting that there was a fair amount of blood all around, along with the fact that he was feeling a goodly amount of throbbing pain from the open puncture wounds. But, as the bleeding soon stopped, he was then able to apply a temporary bandage of sorts from his shirt's cotton fabric, after removing it and ripping part of the back side of it into a few large strips to get what he needed. He wrapped one of the strips around his lower leg, covering the puncture marks several times to sufficiently protect it before loosely tying it off.

By then, it was nearly dawn, and as he put what was left of his shirt back on and re-buttoned his overalls, he felt it necessary to immediately clean the wound before applying another wrap. So, as he hurriedly limped and hopped down and over to where the river was, he quickly descended the bank with uncontrolled momentum before reaching an unforeseen natural spring flowing down into the river. Suddenly, he slipped and fell, sliding through the slick grassy patch where the spring run-off flowed while helplessly going right off the river's edge into a section of its deep, fast-moving waters. As the current quickly began to carry him downstream, he struggled to keep his head above water while remaining close to the bank, seemingly astonished that he could stay somewhat afloat, knowing that he had never learned to swim. As the current carried him along, he oddly no longer felt the cold from it. But with the luck of a stationary downed tree lying prone in the water, Will was able to grab hold and use its branches while pulling himself out of the current to eventually get back up to shore. He stood himself back upright again at the shoreline without much effort, to where he seemed to be ok and none too worse for the wear or the wetness. Oddly, his leg felt better at that point, as he no longer exhibited any pain from it like he had previously, and marveled at how miraculous that seemed to be.

So, after recovering from that unusual little double mishap, he shook it all off and trudged back up the river's bank and over to where the bridge was. He felt well enough to resume his short journey homeward at that point, as the Sun was beginning to cast its morning light upon the road.

He felt better now as he walked, no longer sporting any limp and moving along steadily without the nagging fatigue he had experienced when back out on the old farm wagon road. It now felt like such an easy walk for him as the morning Sun had brought forth its abundant light along this partially shaded roadway.

When Will eventually came upon his noted side road, off of the Little Rock Canyon road, he turned south on it and went about a quarter of a mile farther in, where he could see his family's cabin in the distance.

Back in the area of the Little Rock Canyon bridge, at the site of the Provo River, a farmer heading into Orem had pulled his lightweight buckboard wagon off to the side of the road to fill his jug with water. When descending to the flowing stream, he suddenly came across a bearded man's body dressed in ill-fitting denim overalls, with a white shirt, floating face-down against the bank. As he pulled the man's lifeless body from the cold, rippling waters, he noticed a few open puncture wounds on his left leg, as the man's shortened pant leg was high enough to reveal it. He immediately laid him down on the shoreline before dragging the body back up to the roadway to place it onto the back of his single horse-drawn buckboard, to carry it on into Orem and drop it off with the Undertaker there. He also stopped to relate things to the town's Sheriff, who asked him a few mostly unanswerable questions before heading out to take care of his intended business in town.

Both Sheriff Ray Whitaker and Orem's Undertaker Ralph Potts had looked the body over closely as it was laid out on the undertaker's examination table. They began by checking the pockets of the denim overalls for any possible means of identification or clues that might lead to finding out just who this unfortunate drowning victim was. But his pockets contained nothing in which to lead them to any conclusions. Upon further inspection of the body, they noticed the open bite wound on his left leg. However, while it appeared that it was a curious and somewhat fresh-looking wound, they quickly dismissed it as possibly being related to the victim's cause of death, as it was pretty clear to them that he had drowned in the river.

When examining his facial features, he didn't appear to look at all familiar to either of them as a possible citizen of their locale, although they noted that he appeared to have been beaten, with bruising and small lacerations noted on the man's cheek and jaw areas. At the same time, they agreed that his clothing suggested he might be a farmer or even a wagon driver hauling crops or goods from some other locality. But no wagon of any kind, nor even a horse, was located or even seen anywhere around the broad vicinity of where the man's body was found. However, they thought it was entirely unusual, if not odd, that his clothes didn't fit him all that well. Plus, no one out on the main street of Orem knew of any farmer or anyone else in the area who may have recently gone missing, as the Sheriff made the extra effort of inquiring with the locals who were out and about that day. But what seemed to be the queerest thing of all about this unidentified drowning victim, in their eyes, was the perplexing sight of the open-toed boots he was wearing.

As Will ambled on and approached the front of the cabin, he went up the steps to the porch, noticing the front door had been left wide open, where he could see Evie sitting inside at the dining table with a raised hand to her head and a kerchief pressed to her eye with the other hand, as she was exhibiting sure signs of grief and deep sorrow. When eventually looking up from the table while wiping away tears, she shockingly took sight of Will's semi-transparent apparition standing in the doorway. She blinked wildly a few times while wiping away tears and wondering if she might be seeing things. But immediately, she saw that it was indeed him and that he was trying to say something that was not audible to her. But she was quickly able to read his lips, as she realized he was saying, "I Love you, Evie, I love you." With that, Evie immediately jumped to her feet, shrieking at the top of her lungs, with uncontrollable tears flowing steadily down her cheeks, as she hysterically screamed, "I love **you**, Will! I love **you**!". Hearing her mother scream like that, 6-year-old Maggie quickly raced across the room to her side and wrapped herself tightly around her dress, still unsure what the commotion was all about. But upon seeing her father standing there in the doorway, she naturally let loose of her mother and gravitated over to him to give him a big welcome home hug, only to eerily find that she was hugging nothing at all, before quickly moving back to stand alongside her mother, as shivers began to run up her spine in frightful confusion and utter disbelief.

At that point, Will suddenly realized while in their presence that something had happened when trying to get home, and he felt that somehow he was no longer engaged with this world as he had been, while still gazing at the two of them from the open doorway. With that, he immediately knew he was looking at his family for the last time. As mother and daughter, the two stood frozen, side by side, completely fixated on his sudden non-material presence. In those tragically precious moments, they knew they were witnessing the very sight of Will Glover's ghost, with tears of grief flowing equally down both of their faces. As an un-expected supernatural visitation, it became what would be his last meaningful appearance, in which to lovingly bid them his final farewell. His lingering semi-transparent image then slowly faded out and disappeared entirely into the partial morning sunlight beyond the doorway, leaving them with only themselves to carry on and wonder about what had just occurred.

They both cried and cried throughout the day and well into the night until no more tears could come, while know-ing that their loving source of strength and direction was now truly gone, and they didn't know just where it now left them.

Evie had later reasoned in her mind that what she saw could not be a figment of her imagination, as it was con-firmed between them that both mother and daughter had shockingly viewed Will's ghostly image together. However, the clothing he wore in the sighting didn't match with any-thing he had ever worn in the past, as he appeared in ill-fit-ting denim overalls and a white long-sleeved shirt. But also, his face appeared to have been beaten and bloodied, as a few cuts and bruises were quite visible to them in the semi-transparent image that filled the doorway of the cabin dur-ing the visitation.

According to Riley's recollections from that fateful day up in the Big Cottonwood Creek Canyon, after Evie related the sighting to him only a day later, "Will had been wearing regular denim dungaree trousers along with a green, black, and white plaid wool shirt with the sleeves rolled up." But whether any of this was of particular importance, no one knew, as this related supernatural manifestation that both Evie and Maggie had witnessed first-hand had left them all with a disturbingly haunting mystery where no immediate answers could be found. However, Evie & Maggie both knew it was a farewell sighting that would stay with them for as long as they lived.

Two days later, over in Orem, the Undertaker had delivered the drowning victim's body to the local cemetery for burial, where a simple wooden coffin was laid into a freshly dug grave and covered over with fine reddish-brown soil. It featured a simple 2-foot wooden cross at the head of it. This was all the little town of Orem could offer this unidentified drowning victim, to at least provide him with a decent burial. For that matter, no one had attended the closing of the grave except for the local Bishop of the Mormon church in nearby north Provo.

Through it all, Will had fulfilled his solemn promise to Evie that he would ultimately make it back home to his family. However, he was entirely unaware of his subsequent demise when finally returning to his homestead and seeing them there, up until the moment when Maggie tried to hug him.

For Evie, Maggie, Lucy, Ben Lockhardt, Riley and Betty Atkinson, and Otto Ollinger — all of whom were Will's closest family members and friends — it was apparent that they would never know the full details of what had happened up in the Big Cottonwood canyon. They were only left with the account of him being trapped under a massive boulder, as they assumed it was where he had met his final fate. For them, the unseen boulder seemingly represented a natural and lasting landmark for him, in which to mark the grave of a loving husband and father and a good close friend whom they all had trusted and relied upon to help with the direction and harmony of their own lives. However, it was unreachable, as this giant boulder was located way off in a distant place they could not easily access without going through the Shoshone country, where uncertainty and potential dangers were lurking. Plus, it was in such a place where the journey up to that big stone would be quite arduous, as they would also have to traverse the challenging upper elevations and rough conditions within the canyon to eventually get there. Realistically, it was not an easily accessible place to go in which to pay their final respects.

But for all of Will's stoic efforts in the aftermath of the earthquake up in the Big Cottonwood Canyon, managing to muster the inner strength to find his way out from beneath that huge boulder and survive all of the other life-threatening events that followed, only to die just a few miles from home, all seemed so anticlimactic. Plus, it would all go sadly unnoticed and unappreciated for all that he had to overcome due to the life-threatening situations he faced, in a chain reaction of events that occurred as a result of that initial tremor and rock slide.

Back within the Orem Cemetery, a notably cold breeze had picked up, suggesting that a somewhat early Fall may be in store there, as it rustled the leaves and branches of an unusually large Velvet Ash. The graves nearby had collected small amounts of the fallen leaves, including a freshly placed grave with a simple cross noticeably standing erect in the light of day, revealing its curious inscription: 'Unknown.'

In the few days following the 'sighting' that both Evie and Maggie had witnessed so painfully, Riley Atkinson had stopped by the Glover's cabin for a short visit while on his way home from town. He brought the latest copy of the Deseret News with him to share with Evie. However, with alarming suspicion, he felt he needed to bring her attention to a particular article in it. The article had referenced a man having a thick brown beard and full head of hair, in the area just east of Orem, whose body was found at the edge of the Provo River on August 28th, after having drowned there. As the article went on, it stated that the Sheriff and Undertaker of Orem had put out the word that this man did not have anything on his body in which to offer up any possible identification for him. They had little or nothing else to go on, except for the man's unusual ill-fitting attire, involving denim overalls and a white long-sleeve collared shirt. Oddly, as the article pointed out, both clothing items were remarkably short in the legs and arms, as they surmised that those were likely someone else's clothes. Plus, it pointed out that the man's head and upper torso appeared to be badly bruised, with some minor cuts being visible on his face. It went on to say that if anyone may want to respond to this description, they should contact Sheriff Ray Whitaker in Orem.

After finishing the article, Evie looked up at Riley with her mouth agape and eyes wide open, as she was taken by surprise, while realizing that the clothing's description had matched with what Will appeared to be wearing in his recent ghostly sighting, practically to the letter. If that was indeed him in Orem, it would likely cause her to wonder about the story involving the giant boulder up in the Big Cottonwood Creek country. It would indicate he had somehow miraculously escaped that otherwise inescapable situation and made it down from the mountains to get as close to home as the Little Rock Canyon road and the nearby river. The two of them were utterly dumbfounded and yet still perplexed by the article, although Evie knew at this point that she needed to go over to Orem and see Sheriff

Whitaker to try to sort all of this out and see if the body they had there might be that of her husband.

Riley told her that since he wasn't scheduled to work the next day, he would come by in the morning in his buggy and drive her over to Orem if she felt up to it. She agreed, and while dropping Maggie off with Betty for a few hours, they proceeded to follow up on this uncanny and perplexing mystery.

When relating all they knew about the decedent's description to the Sheriff, he confirmed much of it, although the reported open-toed boots that were worn had gone unnoticed by Evie. But when explaining about the visitation of her husband's apparition at home in the open doorway, the Sheriff seemed skeptical and unmoved by it. However, Evie then stated that she had reason enough to suspect the unknown man in the fresh grave within the town's cemetery was her husband, and she requested they exhume the body to make an identification. The Sheriff shrugged his shoulders with that and said, "Okay, but a one-dollar fee must be paid to the cemetery for that service. As to scheduling, I can have them make the casket available for viewing the day after tomorrow, at...say, 11 a.m."

Evie thanked the Sheriff for his cooperation and departed back to Little Rock Canyon with Riley, carrying at least some hope that if the person within the cemetery may truly be her Will, she might at least be able to piece together what might have occurred to get some needed closure.

As it was already Saturday, the 3rd of September, Riley again extended the courtesy to his good friend's prospective widow in her time of need by offering to drive her back over to Orem on Monday for the scheduled opening of the grave. So, as Monday rolled around, they once again made their way in the buggy, dropping Maggie off in Betty's care, to arrive in Orem at the prescribed time for the viewing at the cemetery.

Riley knew it wouldn't be easy for her, so he stayed by her side while the two cemetery workers pulled out the nails to remove the top covering of the simple pinewood casket. As they put the top aside to reveal the casket's contents, Evie immediately gasped when recognizing her Will, and quickly turned away, wincing and covering her mouth with a handkerchief in the initial moment of grief. In complete amazement to the two of them as they stood beside the casket, there he was, lying before them with all that was familiar to them in view except for the strange attire. However, he had been placed in a simple grave without a headstone that could provide clear recognition of who he was. Evie sobbed uncontrollably as Riley stood by and consoled her, giving her his shoulder and his reassuring empathy in her critical time of need.

As he stood there in her bereaved embrace, he couldn't help but wonder how Will had suddenly turned up in the area again after being entombed under that gigantic boulder. To him, it all seemed so incomprehensible. He also began to feel some guilt after leaving the area of the landslide at the Big Cottonwood Canyon, as he now thought things might have been different if he and Otto had stayed longer and made camp for at least another night. However, neither of them had any notion that Will would somehow emerge from beneath that giant stone and make his way back down the mountainside to come as close as a mile from home before being found at the river.

For the Sheriff, he was at least relieved that the question of the man's identity had been solved, to where he could then close the case, as it was confirmed by him and the undertaker that William Forrest Glover from the Little Rock Canyon area of north Provo had died as a result of accidental drowning. Any other possible theories or ideas regarding the circumstances that might have led to the drowning were not noted, as they didn't know anything more.

While conveying his condolences to the widow, the undertaker asked if he might have the man's full name and date of birth to establish a proper headstone for him while already designating August 28th, 1870, as his date of death. In addition to his name, dates of birth, and death being given, which would be etched into a granite headstone, along with a Christian cross at the top, she handed him twenty dollars for the headstone and his efforts while writing down exactly what she wanted it to say. With further instructions given to the Undertaker, Evie requested her husband be placed within a velvet-lined casket, while also relating to him she would bring Will's dark gray suit to be laid out in, and provide further payment to him on the following day. On the note she provided to Mr. Potts for the inscription upon the headstone, she gave her husband a most fitting summary about the person he was, in relating to all who viewed it that this was someone who was truly loved and respected.

Corporal William Forrest Glover
Union Army Veteran

Resident of North Provo and
Former Resident of Carbondale, Illinois
Devoted Husband, Father, Friend, and Promise Keeper
July 10th, 1836 – August 28th, 1870

In the buggy ride back to Little Rock Canyon, both she and Riley then came to realize that Will had miraculously made it back down from the mountains to at least get as close to home as the Little Rock Canyon road after somehow extricating himself from beneath that enormous stone that Riley and Otto had abandoned as a hopeless situation. While thinking it was all so phenomenal, to say the least, they still could never quite understand how or where he may have come by those ill-fitting farm clothes, as it also made them wonder what may have happened to the clothes he was wearing previously.

As all of that came to pass, Evie and Maggie would soon welcome Ben and Lucy's new son into the world, as his parents had sentimentally named him William Lockhardt, in honor of his deceased uncle.

After staying for another year on the Little Rock Canyon homestead, Evie sold her remaining mule, along with the wagon that brought them to Utah, to the owner of the livery stable in Provo. She then gave Violet away to Will's friend Otto in Orem, telling him that Will would have wanted him to have her, as she had always been a good little milk cow. She also donated the henhouse and her five hens to Riley, who moved it all over to his place. But she decided to keep Sunshine as an active saddle horse, intending to board her at the livery stable in town. At the same time, Evie also decided to withdraw some of the Carbondale egg farm money from the bank in Salt Lake City via the mercantile store to buy a three-bedroom Victorian-style house that Lucy told her was available right next to them, near the downtown of Provo. She thought it would be good for her and Maggie to have her sister and Ben right nearby as next-door neighbors, where she could occasionally help Lucy at her fabric shop. Plus, it would allow Maggie to walk only a short distance each weekday to Provo's version of a one-room school-house, much like Evie and Lucy had done during their years of schooling with Mrs. Johnson back in Carbondale.

With all of Will's improvements to the cabin in north Provo, it had notably given the place additional value, as Evie wound up selling the Little Rock Canyon cabin and its surrounding property for a higher amount than what she and Will had previously paid, to make up for at least half of what she paid for the house in town. However, the new buyers of the cabin would still be left to purchase a replacement cooktop stove/oven for it, as Evie had Ben and Riley man-handle her cherished stove into a wagon, carting it back to town while then carefully carrying it into her new kitchen and connecting the stove pipes. Sentimentally, it was the one familiar item from the old cabin that she wanted to keep instead of buying a new one. With it now standing within a much larger kitchen, she would continue to bake her cookies, pies, and loaves of wonderfully scented bread with the only type of stove that she felt comfortable with. However, after leaving North Provo and the Little Rock Canyon area for Provo's town proper, she would still find herself returning to the area whenever the Beard Tongues would come into bloom while also stopping by to visit with the Atkinsons.

As time went on, she would travel back to Carbondale now and then with Maggie, on the train from Salt Lake, just as Will had done, to visit with her aging parents while sharing some joy and comfort with them in their later years. But she would always return to her adopted home in Provo, Utah, to continue living there while occasionally placing Beardtongues and other blooming wildflowers upon the grave of the only man she ever loved.

In maintaining their ongoing tradition from years past, Lucy and Evie would continue hosting their year-end Christmas gatherings in Provo for family and friends, as a tribute to each of them while also honoring the memory of one special man who had become a celebrated and influential figure in each of their lives.

Author's Confession

Throughout the years, even as an author, it always seemed odd to me that while I've become quite familiar with words of the English language, their meanings, and the various ways of using them, I never managed to understand what I call the 'analysis of words,' where they are identified as nouns, verbs, and adjectives in the structural definition. Certainly, I remember from grade school when this aspect of word identification was taught, although I never truly understood or grasped it entirely to where I might be able to recognize the application of a past participle from an adverb or a pronoun, or when a consonant or a predicate nominative might come into play, accordingly. But I realize these terms and others are all about identifying words with their order and placement when structurally building sentences. However, I never really understood the analytic protocol of that process when putting words together, which might make me partly illiterate, in a sense. Instead, I've focused more on the meaning of words while somehow just naturally knowing the order and placement when forming my sentences, paragraphs, and chapters. However, when not getting things right, to begin with, I've also learned there is always editing.

ABOOKS

ALIVE Book Publishing and ALIVE Publishing Group
are imprints of Advanced Publishing LLC,
3200 A Danville Blvd., Suite 204, Alamo, California 94507

Telephone: 925.837.7303
alivebookpublishing.com

www.ingramcontent.com/pod-product-compliance
Lightning Source LLC
Chambersburg PA
CBHW030643020726
47493CB00006B/1848